THE

Q

FACTOR

I0541262

The
Q
Factor

Douglas King

E~Pride Books
Beaumont, Texas

This book is a work of fiction. Names, characters, places, and incidents are either the product of the author's imagination or are used fictitiously. Any resemblance to actual events, locales, or persons, living or dead, or coincidental.

Copyright © 2012 Douglas King

All rights reserved. No part of this book may be used or reproduced in any manner whatsoever without the written permission of the Publisher.

Printed in the United States of America. For information address E-Pride Books, 451 Yorktown Lane, Beaumont, TX 77707-1873.

ISBN 978-0-9882671-1-4

First Edition

*The whole is greater than
the sum of its parts.*

~Aristotle

CHAPTER 1

Magnus Kroft snaked his long fingers through the chaos of brown and blonde that was his hair. He shifted his lanky form, wincing at the embarrassing squeak his jeans made against the taut, tufted leather settee beneath. There was a perfection about the great hallway in which he sat that heightened his discomfort; the highly polished gleam of the intricate, parquet floor, the dust-free cherry side board that sat under some forbidding renaissance aristocrat, glaring out from the wall-sized oil painting, framed in an equally massive gilt frame. Even the air was different, cooler, more vibrant than the humid petro-chemical tainted atmosphere of the Gulf Coast Texas town he had left just four hours earlier.

Magnus took a deep breath and flexed the newly emerging musculature that was his seventeen-year-old adolescent birthright. He could sense the blood surge to his extremities, the stretch of the denim against his flexed muscles, and the cool of the conditioned air prickling the fine, blonde hairs covering his exposed arms. Magnus was more aware of his body than most. That, according to Ms. Julie, was what made him such an adept dancer. He was able to maintain his spatial orientation—that sense of up, down, left and right that others would so easily lose when spinning, leaping, flipping, or falling. It was some mystical communion with gravity, whose pull he could so deftly defy. Ms. Julie had said his *grand jeté* looked more like levitation than leaping.

He relaxed back to his former, slumped repose on the walnut-toned settee. Ms. Julie was the only person he regretted leaving behind—well, Ms. Julie and his mom. The taunting, the fighting, the isolation—high school sucked! He had been thinking about quitting anyway. He wasn't learning anything he didn't already know. Boring!

Magnus stood again to clear his head, bending at the waist, forward and back, then side to side. He threw his weight to the right leg, bent low at the knee and stretched the other leg out to the side. He felt the tendons object at first, but he ignored them. They would do what he told them to, not the other way around. This new school was a once-in-a-lifetime opportunity, or at least, that's what Ms. Julie had said.

He continued his stretches, warming the individual muscle groups and cursing the slight crick in his neck he had acquired from the stress of his first plane ride ever. Magnus worked his head in slow revolutions, isolating each muscle in his mind and willing the offending myofascial fibers to relax. He could sense the potential energy building as he brought his breathing into harmony with the cascading synaptic discharges.

This was Magnus' favorite part. The girls in his ballet class would moan and protest. They hated the stretches. That's what set Magnus apart—not his gender, but his ability to achieve such oneness with the space about him, space that he could move through like ice on ice. Space that he could move with. All that contained energy, like so much joy ready to erupt—the moment when he felt that if he pushed against the earth beneath his feet, he could soar upward, higher and higher, never to come down again.

But, his experienced awareness told Magnus that this earth, the gleaming, honey oak beneath him, was too highly polished. Its mirrored surface warned that a leap would be too risky. Magnus always heeded such warnings. He took care of his body and his body took care of him. Magnus and his body—the sum was greater than the parts. Something had to give. Don't summon the energy, Ms. Julie had warned, without releasing it. It was a spiritual law.

Magnus closed his eyes and extended his arms into the cool air that surrounded him. He let the tornado of energy welling up inside him find its own center. Then, with the left leg, he pushed the wooden floor away. Everything has a center, Ms. Julie had said. The universe swirls about its center point, the Milky Way spirals, the planets orbit, the earth spins on its axis . . . and the same with Magnus.

He lifted his weight up onto the calloused pad of sole behind his toes. At the same time his left leg formed a perfect triangle perpendicular to his body, bent at the knee with the flat of his tennis shoe resting lightly against the inside of his right thigh. His spinning barely disturbed the atmosphere. He focused his gaze on the window at the end of the hall, spotting it with every revolution, and watching it flicker past his eyes like an old movie reel—Magnus—spinning on his axis.

As the last vestige of stored energy went from potential to kinetic, Magnus felt the force of friction take over. He felt some of his energy convert to heat at the point of contact with the floor and his speed of revolution slowed. Magnus maintained his position. He hated friction, but even that powerful, cosmic leech could not defeat Magnus' sense of balance. Only after he came to a stop, did Magnus release his position and return both feet, flat on the floor. He nodded to himself with a self-satisfied smile.

"I needed that," he said into the emptiness of the hallway. The space about him echoed in agreement.

The knob of the heavy oak door by the settee rattled and the door swung inward.

"Mr. Kroft?" A white-haired woman with tightly knotted hair eyed him with aloof detachment. "The Director will see you now."

Magnus relaxed his body once more and met her gaze with equal self-possession. "Enter stage left," he murmured to himself.

The woman started to question, but he brushed past her with a haughty sniff, leaving the dimness of the cavernous hall for the bright light that streamed in from the wall of glass that silhouetted a lone figure standing behind an immaculately ordered desk.

Magnus took a deep breath. *No fear*, he told himself, and processed to the straight-backed chair in front of the desk. He stood by the chair and cocked his chin with an air of defiance, squinting into the sunlight.

"Please sit down, Mr. Kroft." The silhouette sounded like the voice of God. "I am Dr. Wesley Powell. Welcome to the Powell Institute."

The sunlight dimmed as the automatic blinds whirred

and turned, aiming the sunlight up at the ceiling. Magnus blinked as the iris of his eyes adjusted.

Dr. Powell settled into a glossy, burgundy leather chair and pulled closer to his desk. "I'm glad you chose to take advantage of our special program here," he said in a voice devoid of sincerity.

"Anything's got to be better than where I was." Magnus willed his light baritone not to crack.

Dr. Powell studied the contents of a red folder open on his desk. "I think you'll find that we are light years ahead of where you were." He scratched the streak of silver over his right ear. "Powell Institute is for special young people, extremely gifted young people." He thumbed absentminded through the folder before him. "Our mission is to nurture those gifts—help you maximize all that," he looked up for the first time, "God has gifted you with."

Magnus eyed the folder, which he assumed was his school transcript. "And what does Powell Institute get out of it?" He tried to hide his surprise at his own bold words.

Dr. Powell's eyes stared over his reading glasses at Magnus. Magnus swallowed. The gaunt, expressionless man studied Magnus for an uncomfortable two minutes before turning his attention to the red folder on his desk in which he scribbled a short note.

He looked up from his notes and narrowed his gaze at Magnus. "In exchange for providing you with the best and most progressive education that money can buy, Powell Institute is charged by our founders . . . our sponsors with studying you and your response to our . . . educational methodology."

Magnus considered his words carefully. "So I'm to be

a lab rat here," he said.

"Surely you have a higher opinion of yourself than that, Mr. Kroft." Dr. Powell folded his hands on the folder. "Lab rat is a colorful phrase, but hardly an apt analogy in your case, wouldn't you agree?"

"A rose by any other name," Magnus replied flatly. "Besides, I like colorful phrases."

Dr. Powell gave him a puzzled look. "Why is that?" he asked.

"Just because they're colorful."

"You can do better than that, Mr. Kroft." Dr. Powell sat forward in his chair. "What good is a colorful phrase if it doesn't communicate a clear picture of the facts?"

Magnus flexed his calf muscles and studied the cove molding that framed the ceiling. "I like a colorful phrase," he responded, "precisely because it communicates more than just the facts."

Dr. Powell reopened the folder and scribbled furiously. "You will start out on our University Track, Mr. Kroft." He made a series of checks in the folder. "All the subjects you study will be designed around your field of concentration. Math, science, literature, all the liberal arts will be taught as an enrichment of your main interest. You understand that this school runs year round. There are small breaks when you can . . ." Dr. Powell thumbed through the pages in the folder. "Ah," he said looking up at Magnus. "I see that going back home for visits is out of the question for you."

"My mom doesn't have a lot of money," Magnus said, looking down at the floor.

"No matter." Dr. Powell said. "You can consider the Institute your home away from home." He picked up a paper from the folder to study. "You are a dancer, Mr.

Kroft." He studied the paper more closely. "Ms. Bower gives you a glowing recommendation."

"Miss Julie," Magnus corrected. "We always call her Miss Julie." His throat tightened with emotion that he fought to suppress.

Dr. Powell noted his reaction. "I see you thought as much of Ms. . . . Miss Julie, as she thought of you," he stated flatly.

"She was a good teacher." Magnus resumed his bored facade.

"I take it you would like to continue your dance studies?" Powell asked, folding his hands in front of him.

Magnus met Dr. Powell's empty gaze. "I was told that's one of the reasons I was brought here," he said.

"Indeed." Dr. Powell made a few more check marks in the folder. "You will be taking class every morning with Madam Sonja Valenskaya."

"Madam Valenskaya!" Magnus leapt from his chair. "But she's at the Paris Opera. She is a legend!" He stared down at Dr. Powell in disbelief. "You can't be serious!"

"Oh, but—"

"How many are in the class?" Magnus was having little success hiding his excitement. "Is it a big class? Will we be studying—"

Dr. Powell held up a rigid hand to quiet Magnus' barrage. "Madam Valenskaya is taking a break from her duties at the Opera," he said, pleased with the response he had elicited from the boy. "She has agreed to be a part of our little experiment here. At present, you will be her only student."

"I'll be the only student?" Magnus flopped back in the chair, stunned.

"Count it an honor, Mr. Kroft," Dr. Powell declared,

closing the folder. "Your talents are going to get a lot of individual attention here. All your work will be rigorous and challenging. Much will be expected of you."

"I'm used to it," Magnus said, straightening defiantly.

"Your school environment will be a little less combative here, though," Dr. Powell said, removing his thin, wire-framed glasses. "I'm aware of the problems you encountered at your previous high school. You will find Powell Institute has zero tolerance for that sort of thing."

"I didn't have a problem," Magnus said. He crossed his arms defiantly. "The jocks had a problem, and I really don't care about being accepted by thick-necked, small-brained primates—there or here."

Dr. Powell's lips finally cracked into a thin smile. "There are no . . . primates here at the Institute," he said. "There are a few exceptional athletes, but," he looked down his nose condescendingly, "I doubt they will give you any trouble."

Magnus shrugged. The heavy door behind him rattled slightly.

"Come in, Samuel." Dr. Powell stood up and Magnus did the same.

The door opened and a slight, bespectacled, dark-haired boy peered around the door's edge.

"Come in, and meet our new student." Dr. Powell beckoned him into the room.

The gawky, adolescent boy sidled into the room. Despite his small, gangly physique, Magnus could see a sharp intelligence in the boy's brown eyes—an intelligence that transcended the thick, black-rimmed glasses.

Samuel stood like an inscrutable ibis beside Magnus. They eyed each other warily.

"Samuel," Dr. Powell said, resuming his seat behind the desk. "This is Magnus Kroft. He comes to us from Texas."

The boy looked singularly unimpressed.

"Take him and show him around the school," Dr. Powell continued.

"How long do you want me to take?" The boy's voice seemed on the edge of cracking. "I . . . I have a project due in the morning."

"I think you can take a little time to make a new student feel comfortable," Dr. Powell said, looking over the top of his glasses. He returned his attention to the papers on his desk. "You were new here once."

"Yes, sir." Samuel cocked his head at Magnus. He sighed and rolled his eyes. "Well, come on then."

Magnus rolled his own eyes and silently followed his escort out the door. The boy rushed ahead, his lanky arms swinging randomly in all directions. His gangly legs somehow managed to propel him forward.

"Okay, Samuel." Magnus refused to be rushed. "What's the hurry?"

"Call me Sammy," the boy said. His sudden stop caused his arms to flail about him. "Samuel is my father's name. Now keep up. I want to get back to the computer lab," he said, adjusting his eyeglasses.

"What?" Magnus walked up to him. "Are you burning copyrighted CD's or something?"

Sammy took off his glasses and wiped them on his shirt. "Don't be retarded," he said, trying to sound cool. He replaced his glasses and peered through them at Magnus. "I have an important download happening, and I want to be there when it's finished."

"How much time you got?"

"Five minutes!" Sammy looked at his oversized watch and slapped a hand to his head. "Oh, shit!"

"Well, let's get moving then." Magnus put a hand on his shoulder. "Where's the computer lab?"

Sammy looked up at him, panicked. "I can't . . . we . . . I have to show you about." His hands waved about him in a blur. "Dr. Powell will kill me if you're late—"

"Screw Dr. Powell!" Magnus gave Sammy a push start. "Show me around later."

Sammy's face lit up with gratitude. He dashed ahead in a tangle of arms and legs. "I owe you, dude!" he called over his shoulder.

Magnus took off after him. They dashed down several short corridors lined with classrooms and science labs. Magnus tried to catch a glimpse inside as he ran by, but could only see one or two kids in each room.

Sammy careened around a corner and came to an abrupt stop. "Alex!" he said, surprised.

Magnus rounded the corner to find Sammy almost holding up an older boy who was bent over and holding on to the wall. "Is he okay?" Magnus was shocked at the older boy's appearance.

"Alex, what's wrong?" Sammy asked, trying to prop his friend against the wall.

Alex's face was drawn and ashen. He was very thin—almost anorexic. "I . . . I'll be okay in a second," he said weakly. "Sometimes the stomach pain gets so bad I . . ." He caught his breath. "That's better. I'll make it now."

Sammy helped the older boy straighten. Magnus was surprised at how tall the older boy actually stood.

Alex looked up at Magnus and smiled. "Hi! You must be Magnus." His voice was weak and hoarse.

Magnus was caught off guard. "How did you know?"

He shook Alex's shaky hand.

"You'll find that the grapevine around here is very much on top of things." Alex managed a weak laugh and held his abdomen. "I'm Alex . . . Alex Ingram . . . one of the few remaining seniors around here."

Magnus returned his smile.

The older boy brushed away a tuft of brown hair that had fallen out of his thinning scalp and onto his shoulder. He noticed Magnus' surprise. "At this rate," he said lightly, "I'll be bald before graduation."

"Jesus, Alex!" Sammy kept his hold on the older boy. "You need to go to the infirmary."

"No, Dr. Powell wants me in isolation," Alex responded. "I'm too susceptible to everyone's germs." His voice grew ragged from exertion.

Sammy began to panic. "Let me go—"

"No." Alex shook his head and forced himself erect. "Dr. Powell's wants me moved into one of the rooms by the basement lab. Just roll me into the elevator and I'll take it from there."

"Okay," Sammy said, reluctantly.

"Let me help." Magnus took the boy's other arm. "Are you sure you'll be all right?"

"Yeah," Alex said, taking a deep breath. "I've made it this far." He shuffled along, obviously grateful for their help.

They backtracked to the elevator and Magnus pushed the down button. They waited in silence except for Alex's labored breathing. Magnus noted the constant tremor in the boy's hands. He looked at Sammy, concerned, but all Sammy could think to do was return his concern and shrug. Finally the elevator doors slid open and they deposited Alex in its cold, grey interior.

"Do you want me to come with you or anything?" Sammy asked, holding the door for a moment.

Alex shook his head. "I'd say pray, but you're a hardcore, freshman atheist aren't you?" He tried to laugh at his own joke but the pain in his abdomen gripped him once again.

"Damn it, Alex!" Sammy said, releasing the door and stepping back into the hall.

"Don't worry." Alex waved as the doors slid shut.

Sammy stared at the door for a moment, then turned on his heels and headed back down the hall at an urgent pace.

"Don't seem to be many students here," Magnus said, catching up to him.

Sammy punched a string of numbers into the keypad above the door handle. "We're rather exclusive," he responded and pushed against the door with a grunt. "Damn!"

"Slow down," Magnus cautioned as Sammy attacked the keypad once more without success.

Sammy took a deep breath and input his code again. This time they were rewarded with a soft click and Sammy threw the door open. The cold air rushed out.

"Christ, it's an icebox in here," Magnus said with a slight shiver.

Sammy found the light switch. "You get used to it," he called out, rushing over to one of the terminals that lined an array of long tables. He slid into a chair and attached the keyboard.

"What are you downloading?" he asked, studying the large flat screen display. He tried to identify one of the many different windows that opened in succession.

"Shit!" Sammy's fingers flew over the keys. "It's too

slow!"

"What are you talking about?" Magnus dragged a chair over from the adjacent station.

Sammy ignored him. "I need more time!" he said, his voice cracking. "I need more time!" His fingers deftly manipulated the mouse, feverishly pecking at the buttons on its top and side, while his other hand punched at the keyboard.

"I've never seen a mouse like that," Magnus said.

"Tracking detected." The flat, synthesized voice spoke calmly from the monitor speakers.

"Goddamn it!" Sammy's hands flew off the mouse and keyboard as if shocked.

"Tracking completion in five . . ." The voice droned. "Four . . . three . . ."

Sammy leapt from his chair almost knocking it over.

The voice continued its countdown. "Two . . . ," it droned.

"Shit!" Sammy's voice screeched. He rounded the end of the tables in a flurry of arms and legs. Magnus watched him wide-eyed.

"One . . . ," The disembodied voice declared.

Sammy ripped a pair of coaxial cables from the side of the server rack at the front of the room. The monitor blanked out and the speaker went silent.

The door latch clicked at the back of the room and Magnus spun around. A fat, bearded man sidled in carrying a tattered briefcase in one arm and a load of books and papers in the other.

The man looked with surprise at Magnus, then at Sammy. "Mr. Harper?" The man's high tenor voice rose.

"Good morning, Dr. Tanner," Sammy said, trying to regain his composure.

Magnus' head jerked back toward Sammy who stood smiling, still holding the cables behind his back. "This is a new student, Magnus—" Sammy pointed with his free hand.

"Kroft," Magnus finished for him.

Sammy gave him a pleading look.

Magnus stood and walked to the door with outstretched hand. "How do you do, Dr . . ." He had not quite caught the name.

"Tanner." The older man said. He started to shake Magnus' hand which caused him to drop the load of books he was carrying. Magnus dropped to his knees to help pick them up. He shot a quick glance at Sammy who quickly reattached the cables in the confusion.

"Will you be joining my class?" Dr. Tanner asked. He took the unruly stack of books and papers from Magnus.

"To be honest, sir, I'm not sure." Magnus ran his fingers through his hair. "I haven't been given a schedule yet."

"Is there a problem with the server, Mr. Harper?" Dr. Tanner's eyes squinted toward Sammy.

"No, Sir . . . I was . . . I. . . ." Sammy caught his breath.

"I've never seen a server before." Magnus said, stepping in. He flashed his most disarming smile at Dr. Tanner. "I've certainly never used a computer this fast before. It's quite amazing."

"It's my own design," Dr. Tanner stated. He puffed up proudly. He started for his desk by the server. "You won't find one any faster or more powerful," he said, dropping his load onto the desk with a thud.

"Well, we'd better get back to the grand tour," Sammy said weakly, pulling at Magnus' arm.

"It was nice meeting you, Dr. Tanner," Magnus said and followed Sammy to the door.

Dr. Tanner was busy logging onto his work station and studying the diagnostic feeds. "Yes, yes." The teacher waved a pudgy hand above the monitor. "See you in class."

Magnus and Sammy exited quickly, shutting the door behind. Sammy closed his eyes and leaned back against the door, inhaling deeply. Magnus stared at him with raised eyebrows.

Sammy fidgeted under his gaze. "What?" he asked, attempting an innocent expression.

"What?" Magnus imitated Sammy's squeaky voice.

"It's nothing you need to worry about." Sammy shrugged and adjusted his glasses.

Magnus continued to stare, his eyebrows even higher.

"It's just a project I was working on," said Sammy. He turned before Magnus could question further and started down the hall.

Magnus caught his arm. "The kind of project you don't want The Man to know about?" Magnus shot the boy a conspiratorial smile. He wondered what kind of internet porn the gawky boy had been downloading.

"I don't know what you're talking about." Sammy tried to jerk his arm free.

"I don't know much about computers, my nerdy friend," said Magnus, throwing an arm about Sammy's shoulder, "but I know a scam when I see it."

Sammy stared at his oversized feet. "This doesn't concern you, dude," he said almost squirming.

"We'll see about that." Magnus led the unwilling boy down the hall. "Inquiring minds want to know," he said. "Everything!"

CHAPTER 2

"This is Magnus." Sammy cowered back against the vending machines as if someone might strike him.

Magnus ignored him and extended a hand to a well-developed but stocky black girl with short-cropped, dyed-blonde hair who scrutinized him suspiciously. "Hi, I'm Magnus Kroft," he said, trying to sound friendly.

The girl eyed his hand for a moment before shaking it tentatively. "I'm Gail . . . Gail Doran." She pursed her lips. "You're the dancer."

"All right!" A baritone voice boomed behind her. "Disco, rave, or punk?" The tall, sandy-haired youth stood up from the table behind Gail. "And hi. I'm Tommie Carter."

"Ballet," Magnus said evenly, "and nice to meet you."

"Cool." Tommie threw a hand in the air like a circus performer acknowledging applause. "I'm the singer."

Magnus chuckled. "Country, rock, or heavy-metal?" he asked.

Tommie sniffed as if insulted. "Opera and musical theater," he said in his mocking way. "Of course!" He took a quick breath and launched into a cadenza of soprano notes ending in a high C and then dropped to a low bass F.

Magnus stood open mouthed.

"Don't be impressed," Gail said, roughly shoving the taller, stronger boy out of her way. "He's just got this weird falsetto."

"I can sing anything." Tommie faked a punch at Gail, but she just ignored him.

Gail faced Magnus. "I play the cello." She nodded at Sammy, still backed up against the soft drink machine. "He's the obligatory computer nerd."

"More like, computer whiz-kid," Tommie threw in.

"Kid?" Sammy piped up weakly. "That's not nice, Tommie."

"Oh, don't be so sensitive." Tommie grabbed the smaller boy in a bear hug.

"Quit coddling him!" Gail commanded. She gave Tommie an imperious look.

"Yes, ma'am," Tommie said with a good natured wink in Magnus' direction. "You are the alpha male around here, Ms. Doran."

Gail swung around, aware of Magnus' frown. "I'm warning you, Carter," she said, putting her face in his.

"Piss off!" Tommie gave her a dismissive wave and met her gaze head on. "You don't scare me. Remember?" He flashed her a toothy grin. "As long as you stay out of the men's showers!"

Gail put her hands on her hips. "Oh, very funny," she

said, her voice dripping with sarcasm. "Afraid you'll succumb to a little vagina-envy?"

"Hey, I'm straight," he whispered and slumped down at the table. "I'm the persecuted minority around here."

"You are so in denial." Gail tapped him on the head.

"I know what I like," Tommy said.

"You like to flame is what you like." Gail sneered at him. "You love camping about with these girls."

"Camping doesn't make you gay," Tommie shot back. He took a big swig from his bottled water. "You're just mad because most girls prefer me to you."

Now it was Gail's turn to laugh. "In your dreams, hairspray boy," she said. "You're more limp-wristed than Kieran."

"Who's Kieran?" Magnus asked, almost hating to interrupt.

"I am," said a voice behind him.

Magnus turned. He first noted the intense, violet eyes, then the perfect alabaster white skin, then the longish, jet-black hair.

The boy stood up, not quite Magnus' height. He held Magnus' gaze. "I'm Kieran Matheson." He extended a slender, pale, manicured hand. "Pleasure."

"He's the piano player." Gail sniffed.

"Pianist," Kieran corrected, still holding Magnus' gaze.

"Hi." Magnus blinked and took Kieran's hand.

"Just ignore them," Kieran said, squeezing Magnus' hand. "Gail and Tommie . . ." He gave Tommie a lazy smile. "That's Tommie with an *ie*," he added with a nod at Tommie who batted his eyelashes in mock exaggeration. "They have a bit too much testosterone between them," Kieran continued. "Always butting heads like rutting moose."

"They don't seem to be all that vicious about it," Magnus said.

"Oh, no." Kieran smoothed back his thick black hair. "They're actually good friends." Kieran walked over to Tommie and gave his sandy hair a tug. "Tommie's sort of our mascot."

"Woof!" Tommie mimicked playfully.

"He's Gail's dyke-dog and my fag-hag," Kieran added.

"Dyke-dog? Fag-hag?" Magnus blinked.

Gail laughed and threw her arms about Tommie's neck. "Good dog," She patted his head.

"See?" Tommie looked up at Magnus with a beaming smile. "Even the big lesbo wants me."

"This dog needs a bath!" Gail pulled back from him.

"You wish!" Tommie batted at her hands.

Magnus looked over his shoulder and perused the large cafeteria. He was relieved that the other students appeared oblivious to what was happening at the back corner. "Okay," Magnus said, a little sheepish. "I get the . . . dyke-dog bit, but how can *he* be a fag-hag?"

Kieran slapped at Tommie's shoulder and Tommie scooted his chair back. "Well," Kieran said, plopping down in Tommie's lap. He patted Tommie on the cheek. "He's all I've got."

"He's my little sister," Tommie said, grinning.

"I'm older than you are, straight-boy!"

"I'm bigger than you are." Tommie put his big arms about Kieran's chest and squeezed. Kieran giggled like a small child. Magnus noted what looked like jealousy in Sammy's face.

Kieran cocked his head at Magnus. "So this is most of

our little group, except for Allison and she's at practice, and . . ." Kieran looked about. "Where's Alex? Has anyone seen him?"

Magnus spoke before Sammy could. "We saw him in the hall earlier," he said. "He looked real sick."

"He is very sick," Tommie said, giving Kieran another squeeze. Kieran remained silent, his face a mask of worry.

"He was on his way to be put in isolation," Sammy interjected. "We put him on the elevator. He was going down to the basement labs on Dr. Powell's orders."

Tommie leaned into Kieran's ear. "Now don't jump to conclusions," he said, trying to be reassuring.

Kieran pushed Tommie's arms away. "I don't like this." He turned to Sammy. "Was he in much pain?"

"A lot," Magnus said from behind him. "But he was a really nice guy. I hope he's gonna be okay."

"We're all concerned." Kieran's face went blank.

"So," Gail said, crossing her arms. She studied Magnus. "What's your story?"

"Hard to say," Magnus said with a shrug. "They pulled me out of class one day and the next day I was here."

"No, no." Gail rolled her eyes. "Do you like girls, or what?"

"Wha . . . ?" Magnus stammered, taken aback.

"Straight . . . queer . . . breeder . . . flamer?" She poked a finger against his chest. "Which side of the fence are you swishing on?"

"Leave him alone, Gail!" Kieran leapt from Tommie's grasp and pulled Magnus away from Gail by the arm. "Some people may still be trying to figure things out." He stepped in front of Magnus to face Gail. "Not everyone is as sexually promiscu . . ." He paused with a sarcastic smile. "I mean . . . sexually precocious as you."

"You know as well as I do," Gail countered, squinting at Kieran, "the importance of knowing friend or foe in this place."

"Stereotypes, Gail?" Tommie called out playfully.

"Piss off!" Gail turned on Sammy. "And you!"

Sammy looked like a frightened puppy backed against the wall.

Gail bore down on him. "What are you looking so guilty about?" she asked, suspicious.

Sammy's eyes teared up.

"Damn it." She put her hands on her hips and took a deep breath. "What have you done?"

"It wasn't my fault!" Sammy shook visibly. He tried to melt into the vending machine behind him.

"Gail, quit frightening him!" Kieran stepped between them. "All right, Sammy." Kieran stood the boy up straight. "Just tell me what happened."

Sammy looked from Gail to Kieran and back again.

"I'm gonna kill him," Gail muttered audibly, cowering Sammy once again.

"All right!" Kieran commanded. His face darkened ominously. "What about *leave him alone* did you not understand?"

Gail backed away without further argument.

Magnus was impressed at Kieran's apparent command of the group. He put a hand on Kieran's shoulder. "If this is about me," he said, "it's certainly not Sammy's fault."

"What's not Sammy's fault?" Kieran looked at him without expression.

"I walked in on him while he was doing the download."

"Shit!" Gail boomed from behind Tommie.

"Download?" Kieran held up a hand that silenced her. He raised an eyebrow at Sammy. "What's he talking about, Sammy?"

"Nothing!" Sammy said, rubbing his eyes. He looked at Kieran, pleading. "He walked in while I was doing some work in the computer lab, that's all."

"Bullshit!" Magnus stepped back eyeing the group. "What are you guys up to?"

"What do you mean, Magnus?" Kieran's poker face was unchanged.

"He was up to something!" Magnus turned to Sammy. "When that computer teacher walked in, you nearly crapped your pants. If I hadn't distracted the guy when I did, you wouldn't have been able to pull the plug when you did."

Sammy covered his head as if to ward off an imaginary falling brick.

"Well," said Kieran, breaking the silence. "That explains it." He took Sammy by the arm and led him to a table away from Gail's glare. "You should be more careful, Sammy."

Sammy slumped into a chair next to Tommie, who threw a protective arm about him. Magnus could see that the smaller boy had a crush on Tommie.

"He has a hacking addiction," Kieran said to Magnus. He smiled reassuringly.

"A hacking addiction?" Magnus rolled his eyes.

"He's always snooping about the Web in places he shouldn't." Kieran gave Sammy a disappointed school teacher look.

"I see." Magnus set his jaw. "Well, I guess I should report this to Dr. Powell, being the new guy and all."

"What?" Sammy squeaked.

"Goddamn snitch!" Gail almost growled.

Kieran held up a hand and gave them all a look that demanded silence. "Well, it's your choice, of course." He offered Magnus another smile. "We'd hate to see Sammy get in trouble over this again."

"Christ!" Magnus sat down at the table across from Sammy. "She acts like she hates his guts," he said, pointing at Gail. "But *she'd* hate to see him get in trouble?" He shook his head. "She calls me a snitch?" He gave a disgusted laugh. "It would be obvious, even to someone as slow as you apparently think I am, that you are all in on, and concerned—majorly concerned about what Sammy was up to in the computer lab." He sat back in his chair. "So, you'd better fill me in, and make me a part of it all, or I'm spilling my guts and my suspicions to The Man." He glared at them all.

Kieran sat down by Sammy and smiled admiringly across the table at Magnus. "I apologize." He turned to the others. "Beauty, as well as brains," he said with a chuckle.

"I'm waiting," Magnus said, ignoring the compliment.

Kieran looked back at Gail. She shook her head vehemently. Kieran sighed. "The more the merrier." He turned his smile on Magnus. "Guess I'm just a sucker for blondes."

"Just tell me what's up," Magnus responded

"It's not that easy." Kieran leaned across the table. "Give us a little time to trust you."

Magnus started to protest.

"But," Kieran interrupted, "I will say that Sammy was attempting to access information for us from the Institute's remote database."

"What kind of information?" Magnus asked.

"I don't know what you've been told about this place." Kieran sighed and motioned for the others to join them at the table. "But you certainly can't believe that this is all a free ride."

Gail and Tommie brought their chairs over.

"Well . . ." Magnus thought a moment. "It is, as far as money is concerned. My family certainly couldn't afford a private school."

"Private school?" Gail almost spat as she sat down by Magnus.

"What Gail means," Kieran said with a laugh, "is that this is not so much a school as . . . say. . . ."

"A test tube?" Tommie rocked back in his chair.

"Good boy!" Kieran nodded.

Tommie brightened, and stood, bent over the table. "Want me to wag my tail?" he asked, wagging an imaginary tail.

The group burst into laughter.

"Nothing's free, Magnus," Kieran said, suddenly growing somber. "There's always a cost. We're just trying to find out what this one is."

Magnus considered this. "Why all the secrecy? Couldn't you just ask Dr. Powell about the studies?"

"Add naive to his list of attributes," Tommie said to Kieran.

Kieran stopped Magnus before he could respond. "Magnus, we can't explain it all to you today." He put his hand on Magnus'. "There are some things you'll have to see for yourself." He smiled at Magnus' obvious discomfort at his touch. "There's more to this place than you've been told." He gave Magnus' hand a pat and sat back in his chair. "Something evil."

"These bastards," Gail said, interrupting, "are using us for some sort of experimentation—and I'm not talking about psychological testing—I'm talking needles, knives, injections!"

"No one said anything about that." Magnus said. His features dropped.

"Duh!" Tommie laughed.

"We don't have any hard facts just yet." Kieran said. "But we're working on it." He nodded to Sammy and checked his watch. "Right now, we have classes to get to." He stood and the others stood with him. Magnus looked up at them.

"Don't quite know what to think, do you?" Kieran asked, laughing.

"For all I know you're just pulling my leg," Magnus said, getting up from the table.

"True." Kieran motioned the others to the door. "The question is, are you going to wait and see, or are you going to turn us in?"

"Good question." Magnus pursed his lips.

Gail slammed the table again. "Goddamn it!"

"Shut up, Gail!" Kieran said evenly. He walked around the table to Magnus. He smiled up at Magnus, inches away. "So, you're a tease, too."

Magnus fought the urge to step back. "I don't know what you're talking about," he said.

"Bull!" Kieran stepped back for him. "Well?"

It was Magnus' turn to smile. "I'll keep quiet . . ."

"If?" Kieran fixed his gaze.

"If I stay informed." Magnus looked away from Kieran, relieved that no one else was eavesdropping on their conversation. "If something's going on around here like you say, then I want to know."

Kieran took Magnus by the arm. "But are you also willing to help?" he asked.

"Like I said, I don't know much about computers," Magnus said, stealing a glimpse of Kieran's striking profile. He let himself be lead to the door.

"Fair enough." Kieran felt his stare and looked up suddenly, catching Magnus off guard. "But, you've already proven that you can make one hell of a distraction." He winked.

Magnus could not stop his face from blushing.

CHAPTER 3

Magnus shoved his empty duffle bag to the back of the small closet. The room reminded him of the motel room he and his mom had occupied for the week after she left his father. But at least this room was his. He picked up the thumbtacks and rolled up paper from his bed and studied the walls. The nondescript floral prints and landscape prints that were strategically framed on the walls brought a sneer of contempt to his face.

He unrolled his American Ballet Theater poster and tacked it to the door. It had been a gift from his former teacher. His eyes misted over again as he studied the perfectly proportioned, muscular figure frozen in a perfect *grand jeté* over the rest of the dance company pictured. That was the goal, he reminded himself. Even this place wasn't going to interfere. A knock at the door interrupted his daydream. He opened the door tentatively.

"Hey, gorgeous!" Kieran swept into the room. He

stood looking about. "Sort of the eighties, mobile home look. We'll have to help you make it your own." He sat down on the bed with an exhausted sigh. "I thought that class would never end. What use does a concert pianist have for goddamn algebra?"

Magnus stood holding the door. "Come in," he said, with some amusement.

"Hello?" Kieran tested the mattress bounce. "I'm already in!" He snapped his fingers in the air. "Let's keep up. I'm on a schedule." His smile lit up the room.

"Don't let me interrupt."

"Nonsense!" Kieran patted the bed at his side. "Have a seat and tell me about yourself."

"Can't," Magnus said, glancing at his poster behind the door. "I really need to get to the studio and get some practice in."

Kieran bounced off the bed to see what Magnus had looked at. "On second thought," Kieran said, staring at the poster with overt interest. "Tell me about him, instead." He stepped back admiring the masculine form. "Is this Adonis someone you are personally acquainted with?" He grabbed Magnus' arm with mock concern. "Should I be jealous?"

Magnus was determined to keep his cool. He glanced back at the poster. "Probably," he said with a shrug.

"Bitch!" Kieran gave him a good-natured push.

"I'm sorry," Magnus said, trying to disguise the disappointment he felt. "But I've got to do my bar exercises or I'll stiffen up." Kieran started to retort but Magnus put a hand over the boy's mouth. "Don't even go there," he said.

"Whatever are you talking about?" Kieran batted his eyelashes and plopped back down on the bed. "Do you even know where the dance studio is?"

Magnus scratched his temple.

"Thought so," Kieran said. "I'll take you. I have a break this hour, and I'd love to see your moves."

"Look, Kieran . . ." Magnus put an exasperated hand to his head.

"Don't worry," Kieran interrupted. "It's no trouble. Happy to help."

Part of Magnus wanted to stay and talk with Kieran. The other . . . "I appreciate your showing me where the studio is, Kieran." He looked for the right words. "But I'm not used to someone watching me while I practice."

"Humor me." Kieran gave him the once over. "Don't you have to change into tights or something?"

"You're gonna wear those things out if you're not careful." Magnus said, pointing at Keiran's fluttering dark lashes. "And yes, I have to change." He gestured for the door. "So, if you'll excuse me?"

"Well, you're not going to change with the door wide open, are you?" Kieran jumped up, threw the door shut with a slam, and then pounced back on the bed.

Magnus stood abashed. He looked at Kieran who pretended to ignore him.

"Right," Magnus said, finally. With a flash of inspiration, he went to his small closet and opened the door. "Only be a minute," he said, stepping inside.

Kieran frowned as the closet door pulled shut. He lay back on the bed with a smirk. "Well?" he called out impatiently. "Are you ever going to come out of the closet?"

The closet door opened slightly, and Magnus stuck his head out. "Ha, ha, very funny." He pulled the door shut again.

Kieran giggled. He slid off the bed. "That's long

enough." He jerked the closet door open.

Magnus stood, fully costumed in gray sweat shirt and black tights. "I'm ready," he said, pushing his sleeves up to just below the elbows.

Now it was Kieran's turn at disappointment. Magnus reached for his gym bag with an amused smile.

"I could never wear tights," Kieran said with a shrug. "Don't have the legs for it."

Magnus stepped out of the cramped closet.

"But *you* certainly can." Kieran admired the view.

"Stop staring," Magnus said, rolling his eyes.

"I'm appreciating." Kieran gestured dramatically. "Get used to it, sweetheart. You're a dancer."

"I am used to it . . . on the stage," he said, shouldering his gym bag. He refused to meet Kieran's steady gaze. "But, you're hardly appreciating my art."

"The hell I'm not!" Kieran followed Magnus to the door. "I'm going to be your biggest fan."

"I wonder how hard it is to get a restraining order." Magnus sighed audibly and gave Kieran a sidelong smirk.

"Let's not jump the gun," Kieran said, taking Magnus' free arm. "First there's marriage, then divorce, then restraining orders."

Magnus laughed in spite of himself. "All I want to do right now is my bar exercise," he said, trying to pull away.

"And then?" Kieran's lashes fluttered over his electric blue eyes.

Magnus had unconsciously froze, enthralled by the slighter youth's striking appearance.

"Now you're staring," Kieran whispered, leaning into Magnus' ear.

"I was just thinking . . ." Magnus blushed.

"Do tell," Kieran said, slowing their walk.

"I was just thinking," Magnus continued with recovered composure, "that you could benefit from a little exercise at the bar." He gave Kieran's shoulder a test squeeze. "And maybe a little more protein."

"I get all the exercise I need at the Steinway," Kieran said with a dismissive wave.

"Just a suggestion," Magnus said.

"Your concern is duly noted." Kieran pulled him down another hallway to the right. "There!" He pointed. "The double doors at the end."

"This is weird." Magnus looked about at the other empty classrooms. "The place is almost deserted. Where is everyone?"

"In class, or on a break—off doing their own thing." Kieran pulled at the two doors.

They stepped into the spacious studio lined with mirrors.

"I expected to see more of us milling about." Magnus dropped his bag on a bench beside the doors.

"There were more of us," Kieran said, surveying the room. "But our numbers keep dwindling." His voice trailed off.

Magnus sensed a deep sadness in Kieran's voice. "What's wrong?" he asked.

"Enough chit-chat." Kieran brightened instantly. "Show off for me!" He sat on the bench and waved Magnus out onto the highly polished floor. "Good God, all the mirrors. I hear dancers need a mirror over the bed in order to perform properly."

"I have no intention of showing off for you," Magnus said with a groan. He started his stretches. "If you want entertainment, I know there must be a TV somewhere you can go watch." He sat on the floor, grabbed his right foot with both hands, and slowly bent his forehead to his knee.

"That looks painful." Kieran watched with wide-eyed interest.

"It is." Magnus smiled at the floor. He switched to the other foot. "But only until the muscles get warmed up."

"Same thing at the piano. No pain, no gain!" Kieran watched every lithe, muscular move with growing fascination. "Scales, finger stretches . . . same thing."

Magnus moved to the bar and began the familiar, rhythmic exercises. He was fully aware of Kieran's watchful stare. "Don't you ever blink?" he asked, reversing his position at the bar. "It's hard to concentrate."

Kieran's smile seemed to engulf the room. "Sorry," he said and sat back on the bench with his legs crossed. "You seem to be doing just fine."

"Wish I had brought my MP3 player." Magnus paused in his routine. "A little music always helps my focus."

Kieran bounced from the bench. Without a word he darted across the dance floor to the baby grand sitting against the back wall. He pulled it out a little and opened the lid. "I have just the thing." Kieran stretched his fingers dramatically. His hands levitated over the keys for a moment and then he let them fall lightly.

Magnus stood quietly listening to the opening roulades of a Scarlatti sonata. Kieran's fingers flew over the keys, shaping the phrases in an almost effortless economy of movement.

"All right!" Magnus returned to the bar with renewed vigor. He took a deep breath and let the air and music fill him. In an explosion of rhythmic motion, he gradually added to the intricacy of his exercise.

"Faster!" Magnus called out.

"You asked for it!"

The melody accelerated measure by measure. Kieran looked up from the keys at intervals to see if Magnus was keeping up. Magnus let out an occasional whoop as he would spin from position to position. The final notes poured out of the piano and Kieran fell forward onto the keys with exhausted laughter.

Magnus stood, hands on hips, sweating and panting. "Most excellent!" He crossed the dance floor with fluid grace.

Kieran watched him with undisguised admiration.

Magnus sat on the bench beside Kieran and tried to catch his breath. "I wish I could do that," he managed to say.

"Well, you know." Kieran pulled a handkerchief from his back pocket and daubed at Magnus' forehead. "It just takes practice."

Magnus closed his eyes and let Kieran continue his ministrations. "Oh, I think it takes a pretty phenomenal gift of talent as well," he said.

Kieran smiled at the compliment. "Horowitz always said . . ." He noted Magnus's blank look. "That was a famous pianist. Anyway . . . Horowitz always said that there were people running around in the streets with more talent in their little finger than he had in his whole body." Kieran brushed a wet lock of hair out of Magnus' face. "The difference, he said, between those people and him, was pure and simple discipline and hard work."

They held each other's gaze.

"Play something else for me," Magnus said, leaping to

his feet.

"What do I look like, a jukebox?" Kieran closed the keyboard with mock insult.

"Oh, please?" Magnus moved out onto the dance floor with a flourish. "Before, I was working on a piece with my teacher that was set to a piece of piano music."

"Classical or pop?" Kieran asked.

"Classical," Magnus responded, trying to think of the name.

"Major or minor?" Kieran opened the keyboard with renewed interest.

Magnus' brow wrinkled. "I'm not really sure." He hummed a few notes. "Something like that."

"Ah." Kieran studied the keyboard. "Polymodal chromaticism." He laughed at the return of Magnus' blank expression as his right hand began the romantic melody.

"Yes!" Magnus went into a grand arabesque and slowly began to collapse his form into a deep knee bend, following the shifting rubato of the rhythm. "That's beautiful," he said, slowly spinning on the ball of his right foot. "What is it?"

"Strauss." Kieran looked up to watch Magnus' fluid, muscular movements. "Richard," he added, stressing the hard German *ch*. "Not Johann." His fingers negotiated a delicate arpeggio with ease.

"I'm not familiar with him." Magnus rotated in a perfect arabesque line. "I could dance to this forever."

Kieran sighed, letting the last few resolving chords linger.

"Over so soon?" Magnus stood in the center of the dance floor, hands on hips.

"Nothing lasts forever," Kieran said, shutting the

keyboard. He spun on the bench to face Magnus.

"Sure it does," Magnus replied, stretching.

"Sorry to disappoint you." Kieran laughed. "But every piece that has a beginning, has an end."

Magnus skated across the polished floor. "I'm not talking about length, doofus!" He spun Kieran back around on the bench and pushed in beside him. "I'm talking about longevity."

"That's an awfully big word for a dancer." Kieran elbowed him playfully.

"That's an awfully bony elbow for a pianist." Magnus opened the keyboard back up. "What was that piece called anyway?"

"*Im Abendrot.*" Kieran could feel the heat radiating off Magnus. He inhaled the sweet, musky smell of the dancer's exertion. "From Strauss' *Four Last Songs.*"

"What does it mean?"

"The music or the title?" Kieran said, playfully.

Magnus gave Kieran a sidelong glance. "Have you ever been lifted over a dancer's head?" he said, flexing his biceps.

"Literally, it means *At Twilight.*" Kieran said, smiling down at the keyboard. "It's really a tone poem with a beautiful text by a German poet whose name I can't remember. I love the theme." He played the arching melody of the repeating theme.

"That's a dancer's piece of music. I've got to choreograph it." Magnus took Kieran's hands and put them back on the keys. "Play it again."

Kieran could feel himself begin to blush and draped his arms over his head in mock boredom. "I have a CD with Elizabeth Schwarzkopf singing the whole song cycle." He regained his composure. "I'll loan it to you."

"Thanks." Magnus smiled down at Kieran. "Elizabeth who?"

Kieran giggled despite himself. "I don't see why you think you need to do any further choreography," he said, ignoring the question. He met Magnus' gaze, startled to find his face mere inches from the flushed dancer's. "I thought what you were doing with the piece was very nice."

"Nice?" Magnus' eyes danced.

Kieran studied the gold flecks in Magnus' large green eyes. "I said *very* nice."

The studio door swung open with a whoosh of new air.

"What are you boys doing in here?"

Magnus jumped from the bench to face the broom-wielding man in brown overalls. Magnus looked at Kieran with concern. "Pardon?" Magnus said, turning to the man.

"Why aren't you in class?" The man shook his broom at the two boys.

"Goddamn it, Wheeler!" Kieran stood slowly to face the man. "This is the last time!" His eyes flashed with anger. "I have told you time and time again not to interrupt me when I'm practicing!"

"Mr. Matheson!" The older man straightened with recognition.

"I am tired of this!" Kieran stepped from behind the piano bench. "I have spoken to Dr. Powell about this once already and you were warned not to bother me." Kieran moved between Wheeler and Magnus. "You've annoyed me for the last time!" Kieran's voice rose in anger. "Get out!"

"I didn't see it was you, Mr. Matheson." Wheeler

backed out the door. "You usually practice in the recital hall. I thought . . ."

"Think? You?" Kieran's voice grew more strident. "I said get out!"

The door slammed shut.

"Crap!" Magnus put his hands on top of his head. "Who was that?"

Kieran giggled unexpectedly. "Nobody." His face betrayed none of the previous anger. "Just the janitor who, for some reason, has gotten it into his empty head that he's also a guard dog."

"He seemed to be afraid of you." Magnus reached out to give Kieran's slight biceps a squeeze. "Maybe you've got some muscles I don't know about."

"You'd be surprised." Kieran checked his watch. "Damn! "English Lit!"

"That means I've got dance class." Magnus grabbed up his backpack.

"Listen." Kieran shut the piano. "Meet me in the lunchroom at twelve. The tribe has some important things to discuss."

"The tribe?"

"That's our moniker," Kieran called back, heading for the door.

Magnus shouldered his bag. "Are you the chief?" he asked with a light touch of sarcasm.

"Me?" Kieran turned and leaned against the door. "Oh, no. I'm more what you would call a shaman."

"Spooky!" Magnus laughed.

"At twelve, then?"

"Kieran?" Magnus called after the boy.

Kieran paused and looked back, his face framed in a crown of curly black hair.

"Can we do this again?" Magnus asked.

Kieran smiled slowly. He cocked his head at Magnus. "I would love to." With that, he darted out the door.

Magnus stood for a moment, hands on head, staring at the door. "Good," he said aloud, and headed for the door.

CHAPTER 4

Magnus shook the residual water from his hair as he rushed down yet another unmarked hall looking for the lunchroom. There had been no time after dance and a quick shower to blow dry his hair, and make his appointment with Kieran on time.

Finally, he spotted a familiar head peering out of one of the doors. "Sammy," he called with a wave. "Where's the lunchroom?"

"We're in here." Sammy waved him in.

Magnus braked with a skid and stopped at the door. "This is the lunchroom?" he asked.

Sammy grinned and nodded. "Don't they believe in signs around here?" Magnus adjusted his backpack.

"They . . ." Sammy's voice cracked for emphasis, ". . . believe in letting the rats find their own way through the maze." He pushed the door open to let Magnus pass.

"Where's the cheese?" Magnus slid past him.

"Cheddar or Brie?" Kieran was sitting at a corner table with Gail, Sammy, and a petite, auburn-haired girl with perfect, mocha-colored skin, he didn't recognize.

"Sorry." Magnus dropped his backpack into an empty chair. "I couldn't find the place."

"I guess it's true what they say about dancers." Gail dug into a bag of potato chips. "Not the brightest people on the planet."

"Well," Magnus said with a frozen smile. He raised an eyebrow at her. "We certainly don't have the scent tracking capabilities of a lesbian in heat."

Kieran screamed with delight. "That's calling a bitch a bitch!" He reached across the table to pat Gail's arm.

"Screw you!" she said, and shot him the bird.

"I'm not your type, honey." Kieran dismissed her with a wave.

"That's 'cause he really wants me," Tommie said, smiling through a mouthful of chicken.

"I'm not your type either, little boy." Kieran batted his lashes at Tommie. "And don't talk with your mouth full."

The pretty girl beside Tommie giggled.

"Oh!" Kieran put a hand on Magnus' shoulder. "You haven't met Allison." He gestured to the beaming girl. "Allison, this," he nodded at Magnus, "is Magnus Kroft. Magnus, Allison Ryan."

"Hi, Allison." Magnus smiled broadly and reached out a hand.

"Hi, Magnus," she said, taking his hand shyly. "We've heard so much about you."

"Wha . . . ?" Magnus stuttered.

"It was all good," said Kieran, interrupting. He leaned into Magnus' ear and whispered. "Allison and Tommie are an item."

"Keep your voice down!" Tommie dropped his chicken breast into the white cardboard box in front of him.

"No one heard," Kieran responded. "Everyone else is too far away."

"That doesn't mean no one else is listening," Tommie said. He warily eyed the other diners scattered about the room.

"Don't be overly paranoid, Tommie." Kieran took Magnus' arm. "Sit here by me, Magnus. I've already gotten you a lunch box." Kieran slid the small, white box over in front of Magnus.

"Yum!" Magnus sat obediently. "What's for dessert?"

"Well . . ." Kieran said, casting Magnus a side-long glance.

"Never mind." Magnus opened his lunch box hurriedly, shaking his head.

"You have to watch yourself around Kieran," Allison said. She gave Magnus a knowing look.

Tommie shoved his lunch box and its demolished contents to the center of the table. "Conversations with Kieran," he said, "tend to be one long running double entèndre."

"You should work on your French." Kieran stuck out his tongue at Tommie.

"See what I mean?" Tommie said, sitting back into his chair.

"Shut up, you silly twit!" Kieran swatted at him.

"God, this boy wants me!" Tommie said, ducking.

"I want you dead!" Kieran jumped up from his chair. He leapt behind Tommie and wrapped his arms about the larger boy's neck. "You're such an asshole!"

Magnus paused mid-bite. The others at the table, including Tommie, were laughing loudly while Kieran jerked Tommie's head back and forth.

Allison noticed Magnus' confusion. "They do this all the time," she explained.

"Gotcha!" Tommie suddenly broke the strangle hold and spun Kieran around onto his lap. He held the struggling Kieran tightly. "Now settle down there, missy?" he said through the laughter.

"Let go of me, you Cretan!" Kieran struggled to break free.

Magnus could not help laughing.

Kieran ceased his struggle. "I just hate you!" he said, giving Tommie the evil eye.

"Show me how much." Tommie turned a cheek to him.

Kieran sighed and planted a quick kiss on Tommie's cheek. "Now let me go," Kieran said, "before I pee on you!"

"Have I told you, he's the little sister I never had," he said to Magnus, releasing his grip on his prey.

Kieran stood up before Tommie could change his mind. "Eat shit and die!" He quickly regained his composure. "Okay. That's enough playing to the cameras."

"They may have cameras in the classrooms, but I doubt they've bugged the lunchroom." Magnus fell into his chair chuckling.

"You would be wrong." Sammy slid his small, lanky frame into a chair at the end of the table.

"Really," Magnus said with a smirk.

"Really." Sammy looked up above their heads.

Magnus followed his gaze. "Good God!" he said, surprised. The small video camera was perched high in the corner and was aimed out into the cafeteria.

"Don't worry," Kieran said. "It can't see into this corner of the room. That's why we sit here."

The group sat silently, eating.

"Come on, people," Magnus said, looking about the table. "You're acting spooky!"

Kieran gave Magnus a benevolent smile. He looked at Sammy. "Well?" he asked.

Sammy shrugged and nodded.

"Sammy." Kieran pointed to Sammy's briefcase.

Sammy grabbed up his hard-side briefcase and released the clasps with a flourish. The top popped open and Sammy removed a small black box.

"What's that?" Magnus took a tentative bite from his chicken breast.

Sammy threw a concerned look at Kieran.

Kieran waved at the box.

"Haven't you ever seen a radio before?" He opened Magnus' bag of potato chips for him. "Dancers need their carbohydrates."

Sammy set the black box down on the table and adjusted a few small dials.

Magnus grimaced at the sudden release of very loud punk rock music. "Is that necessary?" he asked, putting his hands to his ears.

"What's the matter," asked Tommie. "Don't you like a little rock 'n roll?"

"Whatever!" Magnus rolled his eyes.

Sammy adjusted a few more small dials on the box. Magnus could hear a high-pitched whine rise up behind the blaring music. The small group watched Sammy as he continued his adjustments. The volume of the punk rock gradually went down until there was a balance with the annoying whine. Finally, Sammy nodded to the group.

"Good." Kieran tapped the table. "Now we can talk."

"We could talk better if we turned that noise off all together," Magnus said, wincing against the irritating hiss of the electronics.

"Yeah." Tommie gave Magnus a blank look. "But then they could hear us."

"They?" Magnus shook his head.

The group seemed to lean into the table in unison.

"There's something you need to understand about this place." Kieran looked into Magnus' eyes. "We are being listened to." He leaned in closer. "Every word we say, wherever we are, anytime of day."

"Are you serious?" Magnus started to laugh.

Kieran nodded to Sammy. Sammy reached into his briefcase and pulled out another odd device that looked like a large spoon attached to a small transistor radio. He climbed atop the table clumsily, almost knocking Magnus' sandwich on the floor.

"Hey!" Magnus grabbed the sandwich from the edge of the table.

"Sorry." Sammy turned a dial on the device, which then emitted a low-pitched humming noise. As he raised the spoon end towards the overhead light fixture, its low hum shot up to a high-pitched squeal. As he lowered it from the light, the squeal returned to a low hum.

Magnus shrugged, not understanding.

"It's a radio frequency detector," Sammy said, matter-of-factly.

"A what?" Magnus looked at Kieran.

"A device that detects electronic listening devices," Kieran responded.

"Bugs!" said Tommie, almost spitting.

"You can't be—" Magnus sat up.

"I am absolutely serious." Kieran put a hand on Magnus' arm. "There's a microphone above every table in here."

Magnus sat mouth agape.

"And a surveillance camera," Tommie added in a conspiratorial tone.

Before Magnus could speak, Kieran gave his arm a squeeze. "Look over at the serving window," he said.

Magnus obeyed as if in shock.

Kieran patted his arm reassuringly. "Just above the window." Kieran nodded to the front of the cafeteria line. "The small square of tinted glass."

Magnus looked and saw the small blank square of tile where Kieran indicated.

"They can't see us clearly over here," Kieran said. "Except for mine and Sammy's backs. We're just outside the angle of vision. That's why we always sit here. Sammy's made some very careful measurements and calculations to ensure we can't be seen. He's also rigged an interference pattern behind the music to keep us from being heard."

Magnus nodded at the small black box sitting beside Sammy's briefcase. Kieran nodded back. "I don't understand." Magnus closed his eyes.

"We don't have much time," Kieran said with some urgency. "Accept the fact. We . . ." He gestured to the whole group. "Each and every one of us is under constant surveillance, everyday."

"Why?" Magnus looked from one to the other. "What for?"

"We're not really sure," Kieran said unconvincingly.

"Yes we are," Tommie interrupted. "You might as

well tell him the truth."

"We don't know for sure," Kieran said, taking a deep breath. He gave Tommie a hard look. "But we do have some ideas."

"I'd say we have a pretty good idea," Tommie mumbled.

"Sammy has confirmed the presence of bugs and cameras in almost every room in the building," Kieran said, ignoring Tommie's statement.

"Including the showers!" Sammy interjected.

"The showers?" Magnus ran his fingers through his still-wet hair in horror.

"Filthy perverts!" Gail cracked her knuckles to emphasize her disgust.

"I don't understand." Magnus pushed his food away, shaking his head. "What possible reason could anyone have for—"

"Reason?" Gail threw her hands up. "Probably some internet porn—"

"Gail!" Kieran stopped her with a look.

"Why not just sabotage the system?" Magnus asked, still not believing. "Cut the wires."

"Can't." Sammy looked up from his gadgets. They're on an encrypted, wireless system. I haven't been able to break the encryption yet or I'd be able to jam the reception."

"This doesn't make any sense!" Magnus refused to show any concern.

Kieran leaned into Magnus. "Why do you think you were brought here?" he asked.

Magnus shrugged. "Dr. Powell's doing a study of gifted kids." He surveyed their visible skepticism with growing unease. "In exchange for our superior training and education, he gets to study our performance and progress."

"Shit!" Gail rolled her eyes.

"Think about it," Tommie said. "What do cameras and bugs everywhere have to do with progress and performance?"

"Oh it probably has a lot to do with performance!" said Gail, again interrupting.

Sammy giggled.

"Gail!" Kieran glared across the table at her. "Why don't you let that bone go for a minute?"

Sammy giggled again. Gail glared him into silence.

"This isn't about sexual voyeurism," Kieran continued, "or pornography, or anything like that."

"Besides." Sammy giggled yet again. "If there were any pornography involved, Tommie would be the first to know."

"Damn straight!" Tommie threw his fists into the air in a sign of victory.

"You are such a pervert!" Gail groaned.

"Tommie is the resident expert on internet porn." Kieran smiled at Magnus.

"I prefer the term *connoisseur*," Tommie said with a sniff.

The quiet girl next to him suddenly stirred. "Tommie, you promised." Allison pushed his arms from her shoulders. "You said you weren't doing that anymore."

Tommie grimaced and gave her a pleading look. "That was all before I met you, Allison." He put his arm back around her shoulder. "I was just joking around."

Gail snickered.

Magnus waved their arguing aside and turned to Kieran. "This is all making me very tired," he said sharply.

"Obviously you have something you want to tell me and I would appreciate hearing it straight out . . . without all the preamble."

"I'm sorry," Kieran said, lowering his eyes. His voice betrayed his hurt. "The preamble, as you call it, was necessary. You have certain preconceptions about why you are here, and I needed you to question those before I throw out something as fantastic as the truth about what this place really is about."

Everyone sat quietly for a moment. Magnus could not look at Kieran, regretting his previous sharp words. Finally, he took a deep breath. "Sorry I sounded so short," he said, looking at his hands. "I'm not upset at all of you." He turned to look at Kieran. "I'm upset at this . . . this absurd situation."

"Don't give it another thought." Kieran smiled warmly. "We all understand your frustration."

"I say show him the Q File." Sammy closed his briefcase with a snap.

"Shut up, Sammy!" Tommie pointed at the smaller boy as if aiming a gun.

"The what?" Magnus raised an eyebrow.

"Sammy's right," Allison said, giving Tommie a stern look. "The only way he'll believe is if he knows what we know."

"We don't know if we can trust him yet," Tommie said, shaking his head.

"I agree." Gail glared at Magnus. "That file is all we have. For all we know this guy could be another Powell spy."

"Take a paranoia pill, Gail!" Kieran's eyes closed.

Magnus started at the hard edge to Kieran's voice. He was surprised to see Gail back down.

"We have enough real problems to deal with without imagining others," Kieran said, taking a deep breath. He waited for anyone to contradict him. "Magnus is not a spy."

"Thanks." Magnus tried to sound nonchalant.

"Besides," Kieran continued with a shrug. "Sammy checked his background out thoroughly."

"What?" Magnus swallowed air.

"The Net is a fountain of info," said Kieran, smiling at him.

"Where you lived," Sammy said, "how long, school records, your mom's credit report . . ."

Magnus stood up sharply. "You had no right—"

"Calm down!" Kieran took Magnus' hand and pulled him back to his chair. "We needed to know, Magnus. We needed to know if we could trust you. There wasn't time to waste on niceties."

"We're in deep shit," Tommie said, coming to Kieran's defense. "And we have to know who we can count on."

Magnus repressed his anger and slowly sat back down. "Just tell me what's going on," he said. "If I can help, I will." He put his hands palms-up on the table. "What kind of trouble are you in?"

"Make that *we*, fancy pants," Gail said with a smirk. "What makes you think you're so special?"

"All right." Magnus rubbed his temples. "What kind of trouble are we in?"

"Are we all agreed, then?" Kieran asked the group. "Shall we bring Magnus into our circle?"

Sammy nodded and Allison followed. Gail shrugged noncommittally.

"He seems okay to me," Tommie said. He winked at

Kieran. "Wouldn't want to deprive you of the company."

"Shut up, Tommie." Kieran smiled and dismissed him with a wave.

Tommie laughed and ignored him. "I mean, damn," he said to Gail. "I haven't seen him this love sick since Bart."

"He was insufferable then," Gail said, rolling her eyes but agreeing.

"Shut up!" This time Kieran did not smile. His face was crimson.

Magnus wasn't sure if it was anger, embarrassment, or both. "Who's Bart?" he asked.

"We're getting off the subject!" Kieran stuttered. He face was flushed. He looked about the room anxiously. "Where the hell is Alex? Has anyone seen him?"

The group looked at each other questioningly.

Sammy put down his sandwich. "Not since Magnus and I put him on the elevator," he said quietly.

"Damn it!" Kieran's brow furrowed. "This is all too familiar." His eyes looked like they might tear up.

"Shit," Tommie muttered, getting out of his chair and coming around to Kieran.

"What a drama queen," Gail said, putting her head on the table.

Tommie stood behind Kieran and put a comforting hand on his friend's shoulder. He looked at Magnus apologetically.

Magnus was speechless.

"Calm down, little girl," said Tommie, putting his arms about Kieran. "I'm sure Alex is all right."

Kieran stiffened and forced the tears back. He gave Magnus an embarrassed look. "Don't pay any attention to me," he said.

"Are you okay," Magnus asked with concern.

"In time." Kieran took a deep breath and tried to smile. "Just a combination of too little sleep and too much of this ... asshole!" He twisted roughly in Tommie's embrace. "Get off me!"

"He still loves me." Tommie smiled broadly at Magnus.

"Piss off!" Kieran broke free.

"We're a family again," said Tommie, heading back to his chair.

Kieran stretched his arms out onto the table with an exasperated groan. He eyed Magnus' confused expression. "Sorry," he said.

"I hope I don't offend anyone by saying that this is a very dysfunctional family," Magnus said.

Gail almost choked with laughter. "Are we really that normal?" she boomed.

The laughter was infectious and diffused the momentary tension.

"Okay." Kieran tapped the table with his fingertips. "Back to the troubles at hand."

The door to the lunchroom opened abruptly, followed by the noisy entrance of three boys, pushing, shoving, and yelling.

"Look, dudes!" The oldest pointed to the small group sitting around the table in the corner. "It's the fag fraternity!" He laughed loudly.

Tommie jerked his arm from around Allison and looked at Kieran.

"Well," Kieran said with a bored sigh. "If it isn't the bubba squad. Hello, Marcus," he said to the oldest of the three ruffians at the door. "You're looking especially ape-like today."

"Go screw yourself, Matheson," Marcus brushed the oily strands of brown hair from his eyes and adjusted his heavy glasses.

"But, Markie." Kieran held out his arms. "You know I'd much rather screw you."

"Fag!" Yelled out the overweight, pimple-faced boy just inside the door.

Kieran stood up and flashed his teeth. "Better a fag than a closet-case, chronic masturbator like yourself, James, dear," he said. "You might want to switch hands, though. That right arm's looking a bit worn out."

"Give him a break, Kieran." Gail laughed raucously. "That's about the only exercise he gets."

"Kick her dyke ass, Marcus," said the taller, skinny boy behind Marcus.

Gail jumped from her chair. "Yeah? Why don't you come try it yourself, Marcus Downs?" She turned to Magnus. "That's Downs as in Down's Syndrome."

Magnus couldn't help laughing.

"They're like the math club around here." Sammy grinned at Magnus. "Talented at doing calculus and even more talented at doing themselves." He dissolved into a fit of giggling at his own joke.

Marcus took a menacing step forward. "Shut up, pencil dick," he said, jabbing a finger at the smaller boy's chest.

Kieran stepped between them and caught some of the boy's jabs. "Go back to your hole, Marcus." He flinched at the hard jab from the angry boy's finger.

There was a crash. Everyone's attention went to the back of the table where Tommie's chair had bounced off the wall.

Tommie stood, red-faced with anger, fists clenched.

"Did I just see you touch him, you piece of shit!" Tommie circled the table menacingly toward Marcus who stepped back instinctively. Tommie bore down on him. "I hope you don't need that goddamn finger," he said through clenched teeth. "Cause I'm gonna break it off and shove it up your ass!"

The three offending youths backed into each other retreating for the door.

"He got in my way," Marcus protested from the safety of the door.

"Not my problem!" Tommie moved in front of Kieran, pointing at Marcus. "Your ass is mine, dip-shit!"

"Oh, those trips to the gym are paying off," Kieran said, giving Tommie's bicep a squeeze.

Marcus marshaled his forces and the three boys lined up in front of the door. "You'd better rethink your butch routine, Carter," Marcus said with renewed confidence. "There are three of us against your sorry one."

"I thought you said these guys were math whizzes," Magnus said standing. He stepped up beside Tommie. "I count two of us."

The boys at the door squirmed slightly.

"Oh, hell!" Gail joined her two friends. "You two sit down and rest," she said giving her knuckles another good crack. She glared at Marcus. "I'm gonna hang your puny balls from the flagpole."

"Okay," Tommie said, suppressing a laugh. "Let's do it."

He lunged violently for the three boys who scrambled out the door, slamming it behind them. The three defenders stood listening to the retreating calls of "fag," "queer," and the like beyond the closed door.

"Damn, boyfriend," Tommie said, turning to Gail,

laughing. "Are you sure you're not already packing a pair of balls down there?" He made a grab for her crotch.

Gail slapped his hand away laughing. "Damn right!" She gave his arm a punch. "And a bigger pair than you've got."

Everyone fell back into their chairs laughing.

"What is their problem, anyway?" Magnus asked, stretching.

"A thing called denial," Kieran said, giving him a wink.

"Methinks they doth protest too much," Tommie said with Shakespearian flair.

"Okay," Kieran said, rapping on the table. "Meeting back to order."

"I've got to go to my music history seminar." Tommie looked up from his watch.

Gail grabbed his watch arm for a look. "I've got algebra," she said rising quickly.

"We've all got to get to class." Kieran gave Magnus an apologetic look. "Sorry, love." He waved at the group. "We'll all meet in Magnus' room at mid-afternoon break." He threw his hands in the air. "And can someone find out what's going on with Alex?"

They all nodded and got up to leave.

"Oh!" Kieran stopped. "Sammy, bring the file." He looked back at Magnus. "All will be revealed then." He batted his lashes at Magnus.

"Okay." Magnus grabbed up his backpack. "Anyone know where I can find music history?'

"You'll be in my class, then," Tommie said, getting up from his chair.

"Good," Magnus said, relieved. "At least I'll know someone in the class."

"Okay," Tommie replied. "You can sit by me." He yawned. "But I snore."

"Just show me how to get there," Magnus said with a laugh.

"No sweat." Tommie bent over to give Allison a peck on the cheek. "Later, babe."

"Tommie!" Kieran squinted his eyes at Tommie.

"Don't worry, little sister," Tommie said, giving Kieran a pat on the head and nodding toward Magnus. "I won't tell your boyfriend anything too embarrassing about you."

CHAPTER 5

"What's up?" Tommie trotted down the hall towards Magnus.

"Oh, my God." Magnus propped himself up against the wall. "I have never been so bored in my whole life!"

"You've got to be kidding." Tommie adjusted his backpack. "That was the first time Dr. Schwartz actually had something interesting to say."

"Then it's worse than I thought." Magnus yawned. He fell into step with Tommie. "I found all that crap about castrati both boring and painful!" He grabbed his crotch in feigned agony.

"I think castrati rock, dude!" Tommie slapped Magnus on the back. He tried to look serious and intense. "What artists will give up for their art," he intoned in his velvety bass voice.

"Certainly not my testicles!"

"You have no soul."

"Yeah," Magnus responded, regaining his balance. "But I have my testicles."

Tommie sucked in his breath, tossed his head back, and sang. The soprano high C reverberated down the hall like a siren.

Magnus stopped and stared at him, mouth agape. "How did you do that?" he asked, unable to believe what he had just heard.

"I have a bizarrely extended falsetto," Tommie said with a shrug. He sang a four octave arpeggio from the bottom of the bass cleft to way above the treble with no perceptible break in the registers. "Just call me Queen of the Night," he said with a self-satisfied smile.

"You're a hard one to figure out." Magnus shook his head.

"You're the only one who thinks so. Kieran says I'm pathetically uncomplicated."

"How long have you known Kieran?"

"Ah!" Tommie nodded as if understanding. "Fishing are we?"

"No, just making small talk."

"Hmmm." Tommie gave him a sidelong glance. "Okay. I've known that girl since first grade. We've been best friends like forever."

"And after all this time you're still confused about his gender?"

Tommie clapped his hands together with delight. "Let's not confuse gender with sexual orientation," he said.

"*Touché.*" Magnus stopped at the door to his room. "Looks like we're early."

"The best thing about Schwartz is that he always lets class out early," Tommie said, stopping in front of the door to Magnus' dorm room.

"Probably prevents a lot of suicides that way," Magnus said, opening the door.

They went in laughing. Magnus deposited his backpack on his desk. He turned to find Tommie stretched out on his bed.

"Dude, wake me when the tribe gets here." Tommie yawned.

"Shoes!" Magnus plopped down on his desk chair pointing at Tommie's feet.

"Damn!" Tommie kicked off his sneakers. "You and Kieran are certainly birds of a feather."

"You don't know me." Magnus kicked at one of Tommie's stray sneakers.

"Magnus," Tommie said, pretending to ignore Magnus' discomfort. "That's a cool name. Means *big* doesn't it?"

"Tommie with an *ie*," Magnus countered. "That's really a girl's name, isn't it?"

"You're quick." Tommie winked at him. "We're gonna get along nicely, I hope."

"Hope?"

"Like I said." Tommie stretched himself out comfortably. "Kieran's my best friend. I'm closer to him than my own family." He paused. "Or what's left of them. Kieran doesn't hurt easily, but we've all got ... self-esteem issues." He laughed. "I know that's hard to believe having met Kieran, but ... he feels things very deeply." Tommie turned on his side to face Magnus. "I don't like it when he hurts ... and I don't like people who hurt him."

Magnus studied him for a moment. "Kieran's very lucky to have you for a friend," he said. "But, despite what he says, you're proving to be somewhat enigmatic."

"How so?"

"I was given the impression you and Allison have something going." Magnus said.

"We do indeed," responded Tommie, turning on his back, stretching with hands behind his head.

Magnus gave him a questioning look, but Tommie just laughed. "I love Kieran, but I'm not in love with him," he said.

Magnus cocked his head to one side.

"Are you relieved?" Tommie asked. "He's not my type," he continued, smiling up at the ceiling tile. "I like tits. Kieran likes ass. I like pu—"

"Okay, okay!" Magnus threw up his hands. "I get the point."

"You didn't let me get to the best part."

"I was way ahead of you." Magnus relaxed. "So you think I'm gonna hurt Kieran?"

"I didn't say that." Tommie looked straight at him. "But you could."

"Well. I hope not," Magnus said with a shrug. "I won't do it on purpose, anyway."

"Deal!" Tommie thrust out a hand.

Magnus shook it tentatively.

"And," Tommie added, squeezing hard. "I wish you the best of luck." He nodded at Magnus, impressed that he hadn't flinched. "Knowing Kieran, you'll need it."

"Kieran and I are just friends, Tommie."

"Well yes." Tommie giggled like a girl. "I can see that."

A loud knocking shook the door.

"That's a lesbo knock if ever I've heard one." Tommie made no move to get up.

Magnus shook his head and reached to open the door.

"Don't get dressed on my account." said Gail, bursting in sporting her usual scowl. She looked down at Tommie, sprawled out on Magnus' bed. "I always said you were a big bottom."

"Oh, baby, talk dirty to me!" Tommie rolled over onto his stomach. "Come on, big girl, strap one on and get to it!"

"I bet Allison says the same thing to you," she retorted, slapping him on the rear and trying not to break a smile.

"Says what?" Allison stepped into the room.

Tommie sat up quickly on the edge of the bed. "Come sit here," he said, making room for her.

Gail plopped down next to him instead with a self-satisfied smirk.

"Here, baby." Tommie took Allison's hand and patted his knee with the other. "Sit on my lap."

"Did Mr. Schwartz give you any homework?" Allison settled in Tommie's lap and looped her arms around his neck.

"Nah." Tommie nibbled at her neck making her giggle. "Just more reading."

"Don't they make you sick," Gail said in mock disgust. "Baby this, sweetie that. Another Hallmark insulin moment."

"Greetings." Kieran stuck his head in the door. "Good. Everyone's here." He pulled Sammy into the room. "We don't have much time, Sammy, so get it going."

Sammy fumbled in his briefcase and pulled out his laptop. "Can I borrow your desk?" he asked Magnus.

"Be my guest." Magnus gestured to the small desk at the foot of the bed.

Kieran sidled over to Magnus, smiling up at him.

"Don't tell me." Magnus smiled back at him. "Sam's making a satellite link and we'll be able to control Pentagon tracking satellites, and . . ."

"Don't be such a drama queen," Kieran said, putting a finger to Magnus' mouth. "Who needs the Pentagon?"

"We have our own surveillance system," Sammy said, maneuvering about the mouse pad.

Magnus' eyes widened.

"Sammy has rigged a network of Bluetooth motion sensors throughout all the halls in the building," Kieran said, patting Sammy affectionately on the head.

"In all the overhead light fixtures," Sammy said proudly.

"Right next to their own spy cameras." Tommie laughed. "Sweet!"

"Ah the irony." Kieran sighed. He purposefully backed up against Magnus. "You see, we're not allowed to be in each other's rooms for any length of time."

"And eventually," Gail broke in. "They'll come and check us out when they don't see us all leave anytime soon."

"Okay?" Kieran nudged Sammy's shoulder.

"All clear," Sammy replied. He pulled a sheaf of paper out of the briefcase and passed them on to Kieran. Kieran passed them out to each one in the group.

"What's this?" Magnus studied the two-sided document.

"Our alibi." Kieran waved the paper in the air. "Just hold on to it. You'll know what to do when it's time." He turned to Sammy. "Okay, open up Magnus' file."

"My file?" Magnus looked even more confused.

"The school," Kieran said, shushing him, "if that's what you want to call this place . . . has a medical file on each of us." He looked up into Magnus' gleaming hazel eyes. "In your school orientation, you had a plethora of blood, urine, hair, and other samples taken at that time, right?"

"Plethora?" said Magnus, playing it dumb.

"You also had a brain scan, EEG, full body MRI?"

"I guess that's what all that was." Magnus' brow wrinkled.

Kieran stroked Magnus' cheek with his fingers. "Did you ever stop to ask yourself why? What does a school need with all that medical data?"

"Well," said Magnus, pulling away from Kieran's touch. He thought about what he had just been told. "I guess I just figured they were being thorough and all because I'm a dancer. You know, mapping possible injuries . . ."

"Bullshit!" Tommie almost spat.

"Bullshit, indeed!" Kieran did not take his eyes from Magnus'. "Sammy here is a whiz with a computer keyboard. But, I think about all he's prone to is Carpal Tunnel Syndrome."

"You think?" asked Sammy. I studied his wrists.

"Not to worry, Sammy." Kieran put a hand on the younger boy's shoulder. He pointed to the laptop. "Keep monitoring."

Sammy smiled up at Kieran. Magnus was struck by the younger boy's almost worshipful respect for his older classmate. With a nod from Kieran, Sammy quickly turned back to his laptop.

"Are we still clear?" Kieran asked Sammy.

"Clear." Sammy's voice broke slightly.

"Okay." Kieran moved beside Sammy and motioned for Magnus to join him. "Split the screen, Sammy." Kieran pointed to the right of the screen as Sammy complied. "Now scroll it down to the summary."

Magnus watched as Sammy pulled the scroll bar almost to the bottom.

"Read," Kieran commanded. "Quickly!"

"What am I looking at?" asked Magnus, squinting at the screen.

"A summary of all the tests being run on you," Kieran almost whispered.

Magnus read down the full page of test orders, trying to make sense of the almost incomprehensible technical language.

"It sure is a lot," he stammered.

"NASA astronauts don't have this much testing done," Tommie said, poking his big toe into Magnus' calf.

Magnus' face clouded as Sammy scrolled down another page, and then another. "I know what a few of these things are," he said. "But most of it's Greek to me."

"Stop here." Kieran pointed to a section in the list of tests and Sammy immediately stopped the scroll. "Now look at these."

"What's a Hap . . . Haplotype?" Magnus asked.

"Ah ha!" Kieran folded his arms. "That's a group of DNA genetic marker tests. That—"

"Genetic marker!" Magnus' voice rose.

"Yeah," Gail interjected. "They're mapping your entire DNA sequence."

"I don't understand." Magnus closed his eyes, shaking his head. "Why—"

"Why, indeed." Kieran shook a finger at him. "Now

will you at least admit, at this point anyway, that something's going on around here you haven't been told about? Something secret? Something behind your back?"

Magnus was silent for a moment. Finally he took a deep breath. "I take it you all have an idea what is going on," he said.

"All these medical tests, gene mapping, surveillance." Kieran pointed at the computer screen. "Open his psych file, Sammy." He put a hand on Magnus' shoulder.

"We have to hurry," Sammy said nervously, changing screens. "They'll know we're in the system in another few minutes if I don't back out soon."

Magnus watched the report come up. His name. His Social Security number. He read quickly. The information was private. Very private. He felt his face grow hot.

"Who all has read this?" He looked hard at Kieran.

Kieran could not meet his gaze and he stared at the floor. "I glanced over it," he said tentatively.

"Oh, great!"

"But just me!" Kieran grew frantic. "Okay, the other's have glanced over it. We had to. We had to know if you were one of us!"

Magnus turned away, humiliated.

"There's nothing in your file any different than mine, or any of the others," Kieran said, putting a hand on Magnus' back.

Magnus pulled away, but Kieran stood his ground.

"Magnus, there's nothing in there that you have to be ashamed of!" Kieran said. "Nothing any of us have to be ashamed of." His voice was soft and gentle. "If I didn't show you then you wouldn't believe us!" He tried to appear angry. "I could have not told you at all!"

"Give him a moment," Tommie said. He slid out

from under Allison and went over to Kieran. "Let him have a moment to get a handle on things."

"Has anyone . . ." Kieran's exasperation was close to becoming tears. "Has anyone seen Alex?"

"It's all right, Kieran," Tommie said unconvincingly, embracing him.

Allison got off the bed and went over to them. She stretched her arms about them both. Gail remained on the bed. She watched Magnus. "We're unwilling lab rats, Magnus," she said. "We're part of some sort of experiment or study or something and it has something to do with gayness."

Magnus could not look at them.

"It's time, Magnus," Tommie said, kissing Kieran on top of the head.

"You're not gay!" Magnus finally turned to face Tommie. "You and Allison . . ."

"No, I'm not." Tommie grinned at him. "But I can pass."

"Pass? What . . ."

"If I don't, I'd be kicked out of the school," Tommie said. "So Kieran and I pretend to carry on together."

"Vomit!" Kieran slapped Tommie's chest.

"And Allison and I do the same," Gail interjected. "She's a tennis player so, naturally—"

"I'm supposed to be the next Martina," Allison said, giggling.

"I'm the only *real* lesbian around here." Gail sat forward, resting her elbows on her knees. "What she sees in him, I'll never know." She smiled at Allison.

"How about a real man!" Tommie flexed a bicep.

"Shit!" Gail almost gagged. "Real man, yeah. You're what . . . the next Swedish Nightingale?"

"From your bitchy mouth to God's ear." Tommie nipped Kieran's ear lightly. "Come on, Kieran. Smile. Magnus isn't mad anymore."

"In coming!" Sammy hammered a finger on the laptop's power switch and killed it.

"You're on, Kieran!" Tommie flopped back onto Magnus' bed.

Sammy threw the laptop into his briefcase and snapped it shut.

"Papers up, people!" Gail shook the wrinkles out of hers and held it up like a sheaf of scripture. Allison quickly sat down next to her and Tommie followed.

"Magnus," Tommie said in a stage whisper. "Sit here. He motioned to the floor in front of him.

Magnus was still obviously shaken, but he obeyed silently and sat on the floor between Tommy's legs.

"So," Kieran said, recovering his usual even composure. "If you'll look at Roman numeral III under the Romantic Period." He bit his upper lip and forced himself into character. "We'll want to discuss the transition from Liszt to Debussy, and from there . . ."

The door opened as if on cue.

CHAPTER 6

"That wasn't even a close one." Tommie dragged Magnus down the sidewalk by the hand.

"Where are we going?" Magnus' frown deepened. "I've got practicing to do."

"Keep your tutu on," Tommie said. He pointed across the expanse of school yard toward a large pond surrounded by cascading oak tree branches. "We can talk over there." Tommie jerked Magnus' forward. "There's no surveillance."

"What do we need to talk about?" Magnus asked, reluctantly following.

"Try being a little sociable." Tommie plopped down on the embankment, pulling Magnus down with him.

"Can I have my hand back?" he asked, annoyed, glaring down at the hand that Tommie was still gripping.

"Nope." Tommie chuckled. "We're being watched from the roof."

Magnus turned his head.

"No!" Tommie grabbed at Magnus' chin with his other hand. "Don't be so obvious, for God's sake!"

"I don't see anything . . ." Magnus tried to focus his peripheral vision upward.

"They're there." Tommie clasped Magnus' hand with both of his own.

"What the hell are you doing?" Magnus twisted uncomfortably.

"Adding credence to the fire that is our uncontrollable passion for each other."

Magnus' jaw dropped much to Tommie's amusement. "Who—"

"Chill!" Tommie stretched his legs out, but didn't release Magnus' hand. "We'll make them think you're coming between me and Kieran."

"Oh, for God's sake!" Magnus groaned.

"Seriously." Tommie kissed Magnus' hand. "We like to keep 'em guessing."

"Okay." Magnus stretched his legs over the bank as well. "But let me assure you, we're *all* guessing about you."

Tommie chuckled. They sat in silence, watching the small gaggle of ducks swimming about, diving for tadpoles. Magnus looked back and forth from the ducks to Tommie. But, except for holding Magnus' hand, Tommie merely stared out across the water, humming softly.

Finally Magnus' impatience was too much to contain. "I have practice to get to." He tried in vain to jerk his hand away from Tommie. "Let go, Tommie! I've got work to do."

Tommie sighed, pulling Magnus back onto the grass

bank beside him. "You gays just don't know how to relax, do you?"

"I don't have time to waste!"

"Then find some." Tommie glanced up to the school rooftop and at the same time, put his arm around Magnus' shoulder. "We need to talk."

Magnus winced and tried to draw away. "I'm not in the mood to play your games," he said, pulling at Tommie's hand.

"I'm in the mood for love . . . ," Tommie sang to the ducks. He smiled at Magnus' darkening glare. "Okay, okay." He shifted closer to Magnus. "We need to talk about Kieran."

Magnus rolled over on the ground sharply to face Tommie squarely. "What is it with all this pretense?" he asked. "Why are you doing this? If there's something bad going on around here why don't you just leave the school? You don't have to be here!" Magnus caught his breath.

"Calm down!" Tommie sat looking at Magnus, as if through a microscope. "First of all," he began, "I do have to be here."

"You're straight!"

"Damn straight!" Tommie flashed his white-toothed grin. "But Kieran's not . . . and whatever affects Kieran affects me."

"That's your choice!" Magnus interjected.

"That's my choice," Tommie said emphatically. "I have no family but Kieran."

"What do you mean?" Magnus blinked.

"Dancers!" Tommie rolled his eyes. "I mean that I have no one in the world who gives a damn about me but Kieran." He smiled. "And Allison."

"You mean . . ." Magnus swallowed hard.

"Oh, I'm not an orphan . . . not completely anyway." Tommie paused, frowning. "We all have our little secrets."

"Okay." Magnus nodded. "But you know mine."

"Okay." Tommie looked down at the grass. "Mine is a father in prison," he said. The skin about his ears reddened.

Magnus tried not to betray his surprise.

"For murdering my mother," Tommie continued.

They both sat in silence.

"He wasn't crazy or anything like that." Tommie tried to laugh. "I mean, I didn't inherit the loony gene or anything like that."

"Well, not a bad loony gene, anyway," Magnus said, trying to lighten the conversation.

"No." Tommie lay back into the grass, releasing Magnus' hand and clasping his own behind his head. "But my dad had a tendency . . . no . . . My dad *was* a raging drunk. So, I've at least probably inherited the drunk gene."

"So," Magnus asked, lying back in the grass as well. "How did you and Kieran come to be friends?"

"We've been friends forever . . . well, at least since first grade when I got picked to go to a special school for the gifted that Kieran was also a part of." Tommie smiled up at the sky. "I don't know. We just gravitated together due to a shared interest in music . . . and being different."

"You're different, all right." Magnus gave Tommie a playful punch in the arm. "But you said the two of you have been friends since the first grade?"

"Ain't ya never met no child prodigy before?" Tommie sounded like a cartoon dog. "Even a school for the gifted has assholes in it. I looked after Kieran. He looked after me."

"Right." Magnus chuckled. "Puberty must have been a lot of fun for the two of you?"

"Oh, boy!" Tommie sat up, almost choking on laughter. "You have no idea. Kieran's pretty much just tolerated me since then."

"Tolerated?"

"Well." Tommie shrugged. "Our other differences became more apparent with the passage of time."

"I don't think for one minute that Kieran just tolerates you," Magnus said, shaking his head. "It's obvious that he gives you a hard time and vice versa, but I can also tell that he harbors a great deal of admiration and caring about you."

"Admiration is a gross overstatement." Tommie laughed, but Magnus could see a glimpse of satisfaction on Tommie's face.

"I don't think so."

"Okay. We'll just say that Kieran and I have a love/hate relationship."

Magnus smiled nervously looking for the right words. "Was . . . ," he stammered. Was your relationship ever . . . What I mean is . . . were you and Kieran . . . was Kieran . . ."

"In love with me?"

"Well . . . yes."

"Let's just say that there was a time . . ." Tommie thought for a moment. "Sixth or seventh grade . . . when we were both a little confused."

"Understandable." Magnus kept his eyes on the sky.

"But only in our minds . . . not anything physical." Tommie smiled up at the clouds. "Well, not much anyway. Just some awkward experimentation. "He turned over on his side to face Magnus. "Worried?"

"About what?" Magnus started to face Tommie, but jerked his head back to the sky.

"You can't even look me in the eye!" Tommie returned Magnus' punch to the arm. "Come out, come out, wherever you are!"

"You are so full of crap!" Magnus repressed the smile forming on his lips.

"You like him, you like him," Tommie sang.

"Kiss my ass!" Magnus couldn't help the nervous grin and turned away.

"I knew it!" Tommie lay back on his hands with a satisfied grunt.

"Shut up!" Magnus could feel the heat enveloping his flushing face.

Tommie scooted over closer and leaned into Magnus' ear. "You think Kieran's hot, don't you!" He said smugly. "You'd like to—"

"Okay, okay!" Magnus interrupted. "Just shut up!"

Tommie dropped back onto the grass, humming softly. After a few minutes, Magnus felt more in control. Either that or he was sick of Tommie's self-satisfied humming—he wasn't sure which.

"All right," Magnus said, taking a deep breath. He sat back up. "I admit I like Kieran." He looked for a way to confuse the issue. "But I also like you." He waited for a reaction but none came. "As a friend."

"Oh." Tommie turned back to Magnus, looking up at him with fluttering eyelashes. "How sweet," he said, somewhat sarcastically.

Magnus ignored him.

"I'm happy to be your friend, okay?" Tommie said,

sitting up on his elbow. He leaned into Magnus. "But why can't you just admit the truth. What is so bad about being a little intrigued . . . a little interested in Kieran . . . as something a bit more than . . . a friend."

Magnus could feel his face blushing again. Try as he might, the smile came anyway.

"Aha!" Tommie flopped back into the grass. "I knew it. I thought I was gonna have to dynamite that closet door you've been holding onto."

Magnus covered his face. "Jeez," he said through his fingers. "You're awfully melodramatic for a straight boy."

"And you're awfully reserved for a gay boy."

"I save it for the dance floor."

"Allison's saving it for marriage," Tommie said with a long, audible sigh.

They both laughed.

"There's one thing I don't understand." Magnus pulled a piece of stray grass out of his mouth.

"Shoot!"

"If something's going on that's so bad around here . . . I still don't understand. Why don't you just leave . . . go back home?"

"I don't have a home to go back to." Tommy shrugged. "I couldn't afford the education I'm getting, either. Besides . . ."

"I don't mean to be so nosey," Magnus interrupted.

"Don't worry about it." Tommie smiled at him. "Kieran is my family. He's pretty much responsible for the clothes on my back." He laughed. "In case you haven't figured it out yet, he's a spoiled little rich boy."

"No!" Magnus feigned surprise.

"Kieran tends to take care of everybody in one way or another." He gave Magnus a knowing look. "If you're not careful, he'll try to take care of you, too, if you know what I mean."

"Whatever," Magnus said, rolling his verdant eyes. He seized the opportunity. "Tell me about Bart ... and Alex."

"Ahhh." Tommie scratched his belly. "Curiosity killed the cat!"

"I'm not a cat."

"No?" Tommie chuckled.

Magnus looked at him silently.

"Okay, okay." Tommie shielded his face as if Magnus was going to punch him. "Let's see ... Bart and Alex."

"Boys!" The gruff, threatening voice bellowed from behind them.

Magnus and Tommie sat up quickly.

"You boys shouldn't be out here alone." The man stood in the dark of the sun's glare.

"We had a break between second and third periods," Tommie said evenly, shielding his eyes against the sun. "We thought we'd get a little sun for a change."

"You need to get back inside ... now!" The bulky man sneered at them.

Neither Magnus nor Tommie moved.

Magnus whispered to Tommie, "Who the hell is he?"

"School security," Tommie said, standing. "One of Dr. Powell's goons." He smiled his most disarming smile at the man. "Hardcastle." He looked the man over. "When are you going to get that uniform cleaned?"

"Tommie!" Magnus almost choked.

The guard looked as if he could break a telephone pole with his bare hands.

"Well, I mean, look." Tommie gestured at the hulking figure. "I think it reflects badly on all of us."

"Shut your trap, Carter," said the guard bristling, "or you'll spend some time in the playroom!"

"Play . . ." Magnus stood.

"Later!" Tommie interrupted. "Let's go before Neanderthal man gets more upset!"

"Just a minute!" The guard stopped them. He pointed at Magnus. "You're the new kid, right?"

Magnus nodded.

"Kroft, isn't it?"

Magnus nodded again.

"I thought so." The man sneered at him. "You need to report to the Infirmary."

"The Infirmary?" Magnus shook his head. "I'm not sick."

"The Infirmary," the man growled. "Now!"

"Come on." Tommie grabbed Magnus' hand and pulled him along.

The guard shook his finger at them as they headed up the hill toward the school.

"Don't think you're fooling me," he called after them. "I know what you were up to."

Tommie looked back over his shoulder with a toothy grin.

"I just bet you do!" he yelled at the guard.

"I'm gonna be watchin' both of you!" The man spat into the grass.

Tommie linked his arm with Magnus'. "Walk slowly," he instructed. "I don't have much time before we're back under surveillance."

"What's going on?" Magnus allowed himself to be guided up the hill.

"Now listen." Tommie kept his gaze straight ahead. "They're gonna put you through some more medical rigmarole and then try to tell you you've got a virus, or a vitamin deficiency, or something . . ."

"Why—"

"Just listen." Tommie squeezed Magnus' arm. "They'll give you some pills." He stopped at the door and jerked Magnus around to face him. "Whatever you do, don't take them!"

"What are they . . . the pills I mean?"

"We'll talk later," Tommie said. "They're watching. Just don't take any of the pills!" Tommie pulled the door open.

They stepped back into one of the school's many brightly lit hallways. Magnus started to speak, but Tommie put a finger to his lips. He gave Magnus a long hard look. "See you in the break room." He turned to go, but stopped quickly and spun back around. "Oh, yeah."

"What now?" Magnus threw up his hands.

"One for the cameras!" Tommie pulled Magnus to him and gave him a noisy kiss on the cheek.

Magnus jerked away uttering something unintelligible, while Tommie dashed off laughing. Magnus brushed the palm of his hand over his cheek, staring down the hallway.

"Nothing worse than a messy kisser," he said to himself, smiling. He took a moment to get his bearings. "Infirmary," he muttered, heading down the hall in the opposite direction from Tommie.

He turned the corner quickly only to be met by a shadow bearing down in his direction. "Watch it!" he cried, hugging the wall to avoid being run over by another uniformed giant.

The guard stopped before slamming into Magnus. "You Kroft?"

Magnus looked up at the towering hulk. "Yeah," he nodded, wondering why he hadn't noticed any of these guards before.

"You're wanted in the infirmary." The guard pointed down the hall.

"Yeah," Magnus said with undisguised insolence. "That's where I was going before you almost creamed me." He straightened his sleeves. "One of your buddies already gave me the message."

"Down and to the left," the guard gestured. "I'll take you."

"I know where it is!"

"I'll take you anyway." The guard looked down at Magnus menacingly.

"Suit yourself," Magnus said, lowering his head, annoyed.

He squeezed around the guard and dashed off down the hall. The guard moved quickly to keep up with him. The steel door to the infirmary was painted a matte, ominous grey—quite different from all the other highly polished, walnut doors throughout the school.

Magnus turned the knob. "It's locked," he said.

The guard came up behind him, eclipsing even the overhead fluorescent lighting. He reached over Magnus' head and rapped loudly on the metal door.

Magnus looked up at the guard's impassive face. "Maybe no one's there," he said.

The guard ignored him and knocked again with even more vigor. Magnus heard the latch snap and the door opened expelling a whoosh of air.

"Good morning, Magnus."

"Dr. Powell!" Magnus stood frozen.

"Come in." Dr. Powell held the door open and smiled

disarmingly.

"I wasn't expecting . . ." Magnus recovered and entered the cold, sterile room. "I mean . . . I didn't know you . . ."

"Were a medical doctor?" Dr. Powell laughed. "Many people make that mistake. They expect a school superintendent to be a PhD and not an MD. I have both" He guided Magnus into one of the small exam rooms.

"I'm not sure why I'm here," Magnus said, stumbling up onto the exam table. "I thought every test in the book had been run during my intake physical."

"That's true." Dr. Powell donned his stethoscope. "But the liability insurers of the school insist that students at risk for injury as much as you, be thoroughly checked out." He gestured to Magnus' shirt.

"That makes sense," Magus said, obediently unbuttoning his shirt. "I take it that I checked out okay."

Dr. Powell made a noncommittal noise in this throat, already pecking about Magnus' chest with the business end of the stethoscope.

Magnus decided to take a chance. "So, Dr. Powell, what's a Haplotype?" he asked.

"What's that?" The doctor's hand froze. He straightened and his face grew strangely taut.

"A Haplotype," Magnus continued. "I think that's how you say it. What is it?"

Dr. Powell tapped the end of his stethoscope on the middle button of his white lab coat. "Where did you hear that word?"

Magnus buttoned his shirt back before answering. "I think one of the lab guys mentioned it when I was having blood drawn last week." He looked up innocently. "Is it some kind of disease or something? I hope I don't have anything like that."

"You don't have anything to worry about." The doctor relaxed a little.

"That's good news."

Dr. Powell sat down at the small desk beside the exam table. "You're in excellent shape, young man," he commented and began writing in the chart.

"And I feel fine," Magnus said. He watched the doctor scribbling into his chart.

"I am a little concerned about one or two of your lab results, however," Dr. Powell, said, adjusting his eyeglasses.

"Really?" Magnus tried to sound concerned and not suspicious.

"Nothing serious," Dr. Powell said, waving a dismisssive hand. He stood and reached up into one of the white laminate cabinets lining the wall of the exam room above the desk. "But you put your body through an inordinate amount of physical stress. Dancing is very demanding."

"I don't feel like anything's wrong, though."

"Of course not." Dr. Powell extracted a small prescription bottle from the cabinet. "But we need to increase your supplements to be sure your body has the resources it needs to maintain and prevent injury." He thrust the small, amber container into Magnus' hand.

"What's this?" Magnus turned the bottle over in his hand."

"It's a special nutritional supplement I've developed for our more physically active students."

"Supplement?"

"Oh, a concoction of various vitamins, minerals, amino acids, etc." Dr. Powell smiled his reassuring smile. "I'm surprised you're not already on such a regimen."

"No one's ever said I needed it before," Magnus said, opening the bottle and studying the contents.

"At this school, Magnus," Dr. Powell said, patting Magnus on the shoulder, "you can rest assured that we are going to do everything possible, above and beyond the call, to ensure your health and well-being. Keeping you in tip top physical condition is at the top of the list."

"Okay." Magnus recapped the bottle and scooted off the exam table.

"I want you to take one now and then repeat at every evening before supper." Dr. Powell pointed at the bottle. "Let's get you some water."

"Now?" Magnus asked giving the bottle a shake.

"No time like the present." Dr. Powell led Magnus over to a water cooler by the exit.

"Shouldn't I wait until supper then?" Magnus thought quickly.

Dr. Powell pulled a cup from the dispenser and filling it with water. "The sooner we get you started," he said, "the sooner we can make optimum improvements in your physical performance."

Magnus opened the small vial of pills and extracted one of the pale, yellow tablets. He turned it over in his fingers.

Dr. Powell thrust the paper cup of water into Magnus' other hand. "There you go," he said cheerfully. "Bottoms up."

Magnus could hear Tommie's words of warning ringing in his ears. He smiled up at Dr. Powell and popped the tablet into his mouth, followed by a quick sip of water. "All gone," he said, opening his mouth for inspection like a small child.

Dr. Powell gave Magnus another congratulatory pat

on the shoulder. He beckoned for the pill bottle and Magnus placed it into his hands. "Good man!" Dr. Powell said. "Remember, one every evening before supper. Just pop round here to the infirmary and someone will dispense you a dose."

Magnus nodded and tossed the cup into the small waste can.

Dr. Powell looked pleased. "I'll want to see you back in about two weeks to repeat some tests," Dr. Powell said.

"More tests?" Magnus frowned.

"I want to see that the pills are doing their job," Dr. Powell said, opening the door for Magnus. "One of the staff will let you know." He shut the door leaving Magnus alone in the hall.

Magnus dug the bitter tasting pill from under his tongue before its coating had time to dissolve. He stuffed the sticky pill into a used gum wrapper and shoved it into his pants pocket.

"Vitamins, my ass!" He began to retrace his steps back to the cafeteria.

CHAPTER 7

Magnus stood in front of the cafeteria door. He yawned noisily, a residual effect of the short power nap he took after his visit with Dr. Powell. Third period had let out five minutes before and Magnus knew that everyone would be in the cafeteria. He took a deep breath and pulled open the door. As anticipated, the group was huddled at the back in their usual surveillance-free zone.

"Magnus," Kieran jumped up from the table.

"What's up?" Magnus pretended not to notice that they were all looking at him as if he had just returned from the dead. "What's on the menu today?"

"Did you take the pill?" Tommie sat back from the table.

"Are you okay?" Kieran's eyes were red.

Magnus grabbed a chair opposite of Tommie. "Take a chill pill everyone." He sat down and took a French fry off Allison's tray. "The answer is yes and no."

"What does that mean?" Gail said through a mouthful of macaroni and cheese.

"Yes, I'm okay," Magnus laughed. "And no, I didn't take the pill."

Tommie didn't look convinced.

"I put it under my tongue," Magnus assured him, "and pretended to swallow it."

"Say no to drugs," Gail said with a satisfied nod.

"This isn't funny!" Kieran slammed the table with his fist. His reaction seemed to take everyone by surprise. "They're already trying to start him on the therapy." His face contorted in anguish. "You know what that means!" Kieran's composure broke. "First Bart ... then Alex! Jesus Christ!" He turned on the group. "Have any of you seen Alex?"

They all looked at each other.

"Goddamn it!" Kieran stormed out of the room close to tears.

"More drama." Gail dropped her head to the table.

"Hush, Gail!" Allison gave her a hard look. "I'd feel the same way if I were in Kieran's shoes." She rested her head on Tommie's shoulder and looked up at him. "If they had picked you, I would have died!"

"I wasn't the one who was picked," Tommie said. He straightened suddenly. "Wait a minute! You said you didn't swallow it. You have one of the pills?"

Magnus reached into his pocket and pulled out the wrinkled gum wrapper. He sat it down on the table in front of Tommie. Tommie snatched it up instantly and began to unravel the wrapper. Gail slipped over behind Tommie and everyone peered down at the small, jaundiced pill.

"What is it?" Magnus asked. "It's supposed to be a

vitamin and mineral supplement of some—"

"Bullshit!" Gail bent over Tommie's shoulder for a closer look. "Supplements like that are usually the size of horse pills."

"Some of the writing is still visible." Tommy folded the tablet back into its wrapper and stuffed it into his jeans. "I'll get Sammy to try and identify it."

"Where is he?" Magnus asked.

"Probably in the computer lab." Tommie gave Allison a peck on the forehead. "Sorry, love. Gotta go."

"I'm going with you." Magnus started to rise.

"What about Kieran?" Allison pointed at Magnus sternly. "Someone needs to see about him."

"He's a big girl," Gail said. "He'll be okay."

"That's not good enough." Allison turned back to Magnus. "You should check on him."

"But . . ." Magnus raised his hands pleading.

"She's right." Tommie headed for the door. "He'll probably be in his practice room."

"But he's mad at me," Magnus pleaded, confused. "I don't think he wants anything to do with me right now."

"What an idiot!" Gail muttered. "For a gay, you're not very sensitive."

Allison laughed and went around the table to Magnus' side. "Of course Kieran wants to see you," Allison said. She went around the table and put an arm around his shoulder.

Magnus stood in silent desperation.

Allison spun him around and took his face into her hands. "Love can be very confusing," she said knowingly.

"Love?" Magnus sputtered.

"Boy you're dense." Tommie rapped his knuckles on the side of Magnus' head.

"Kieran is in love with you." Allison took Magnus' hands in hers.

"That's silly." Magnus tried to pull away. "We just met and anyway . . ."

Allison put her hand over his mouth. "And, if you'd stop trying to act like a tight-assed, over compensating, closet case . . ."

"You go, lady!" Gail played the table like a drum.

"Then you'd admit that the feelings between you and Kieran are mutual." Allison stepped back, hands on her hips. "Now. You go find Kieran." She gave him a gentle shove. "And you make sure he's all right!"

Magnus sighed in resignation. "Yes, ma'am." He gave her a mock salute and started for the door.

Gail started to speak but Allison held up a hand to her. "Shut up, Gail!"

"Oooo," Gail said, laughing with delight. "I just love it when you act butch!" She looked up at Tommie. "You should try it sometime."

Tommie shot her the finger as he guided Allison out the door.

Magnus stood, shaking his head. "None of this makes any sense."

He made his way down the halls, now fully aware of the video monitors. He was only now becoming able to recognize the small cameras perched at each corner of the hallway pointing down the middle. He turned into the long hallway that lead to the music practice rooms. He could hear the loud, percussive sounds of a piano being played with a punishing attack. Magnus stood still beside the door, nodding in recognition of the anger, anguish, and desperation of the sounds. How many times had he felt that same inner agony and hashed some sense of form or order out of it through his dance.

He peaked through the small rectangular window in the middle of the door. Kieran was hunched over the piano keys, pounding way with an uncommon strength and agility. He was still making magnificent music, but there was an agitated, almost manic quality to the playing. Magnus opened the door slightly. Kieran was oblivious to his surroundings, encapsulated in his own private world. Magnus slipped into the room, shutting the door quietly behind him. He moved over to a small sofa that faced the side of the piano, and eased himself into its cushions. He sat silent as Kieran completed the final cadenza, fingers moving with a rapidity that defied what Magnus thought human hands were capable of.

The final chord hung in the air like an electrical charge. Magnus sat, mesmerized. Kieran sank down against the piano rail, all his energy spent. His breathing was labored. After a moment Magnus stirred on the sofa. Kieran's eyes darted in his direction and fixated on Magnus' face. They looked into each other's eyes, waiting.

"Hi," Magnus said, finally. He forced a smile.

Kieran didn't answer, but his eyes conveyed an emotion that was unfamiliar to Magnus.

"Kieran," Magnus pleaded. "Talk to me."

Kieran's arms embraced himself as if the air were too cold.

"Kieran." Magnus started to get up.

Kieran held up a hand to stop him. Magnus sank back onto the sofa. Kieran stood, exhaling deeply. He shuffled over to the sofa and sat down beside Magnus, burying his face in his hands.

"Kieran," Magnus said softly. "I didn't mean to make you so upset."

"You . . ." Kieran looked up. "You didn't upset me." He sighed heavily. "I'm upset about what's going on . . . what's happening to you."

"I'm all right."

Kieran looked up into his face. Magnus was shaken by the anguish in Kieran's expression.

"I'm all right!"

"Right now you are." Kieran took Magnus' hand and held it in both of his. "It's later down the road that worries me."

Magnus looked down at his hand gently cradled in Kieran's, thinking about the strength . . . the hidden power in those hands. He smiled down at Kieran.

"What?" Kieran blushed and tried to return Magnus' smile.

"Aren't you worried about the cameras?" Magnus said trying to lighten the mood. He scanned the crown molding for any sign of a camera.

"There aren't any in here," Kieran said softly. "My teacher won't allow it." He brought Magnus' hand up and brushed his lips against it. "I'm supposed to be able to express myself unencumbered by someone watching over my shoulder."

Magnus chuckled and squeezed Kieran's hands. "I don't know that this is the kind of self-expression they were referring to," he said, sheepishly.

"Oh, they know we're in here together," Kieran said, batting his eyelashes flirtatiously. "They'll be rushing down here in about 5 minutes to . . ." He flashed Magnus a mischievous grin. "Break us up."

Magnus put his other hand over Kieran's. "I don't want you to be so upset." He looked directly into Kieran's fathomless, amethyst eyes.

"I can't help it." Kieran shrugged. "I'm so afraid for you. I . . ." He stopped and swallowed hard. "I don't want you to go away . . . to disappear out of my life."

"Kieran." Magnus poked him in the ribs, playfully. "Nothing's going to happen to me. I'm not going anywhere."

"I wish I could make you see how serious this is . . ." Kieran said, reclining his head on Magnus' shoulder. "How out of our control the entire situation is."

"Talk to me about it." Magnus put his arm around Kieran. "Tell me why you're so worried . . . so afraid."

"There were other boys before you." Kieran pillowed his head against Magnus' chest.

"Should I be jealous?"

"Absolutely!"

"Slut!" Magnus gave Kieran a playful slap on the top of his head.

"I wish," Kieran said, snuggling closer to Magnus. He was silent a moment. "It was the first of the semester last year. Alex. You met him. He was . . . is a swimmer." The sorrow in Kieran's voice was palpable. "And there was Bart . . . a senior . . . and set to be class valedictorian. He was a gymnast."

"What happened to him?" Magnus said softly, reassuringly.

"Bart was started on Dr. Powell's so-called vitamin therapy. It made him sick."

"How?" Magnus remembered the bitter, yellow pill and wondered if Tommie and Sammy had managed to identify it.

Kieran began to tremble and pressed himself harder against Magnus. "Well, it didn't really make him sick," he said. "I guess, what I meant to say was Bart just began to catch every cold and virus that was around. He was constantly sick. Two bouts with pneumonia . . . and the stomach pains . . . it was horrible."

"Then what?" Magnus tightened his arm about Kieran.

"Then he was gone," Kieran said quietly. "Dr. Powell told all of us that Bart was a runaway." Kieran shuddered. "That was a lie. Bart had no reason. That and the fact that he was too sick to run away."

"Go on."

"I had a little crush on Bart, but he and Alex were very close." Kieran smiled up at Magnus. "Sort of like us."

"Whatever." Magnus laughed. "What really happened to Bart?"

"The pills, the sickness . . ." Kieran's smile left as quickly as it had appeared. "He withdrew, and then . . ." Kieran's voice broke.

"Go on," Magnus encouraged.

"Toward the end of last semester," he continued, motionless against Magnus' chest. "Tommie found Bart hiding in the gym. He was terrified."

"What about?"

"Bart said he had seen another missing student, Michael Peters . . . dead . . . in one of the basement labs."

"Dead!" Magnus shook his head. "That's insane!"

"That's what he said." Kieran looked at Magnus in earnest. "It sent him over the edge. He wasn't the same after that."

"He must have dreamed it or something," Magnus said. "It doesn't make sense."

Magnus could feel Kieran's hot breath against his chest. He was aware of his own heart pounding in his chest. The intimacy of their embrace was so new, and Magnus realized he was afraid of betraying just how unsure and uncomfortable such intimacy was for him.

"Bart went missing within three weeks of that," Kieran said, breaking the silence.

"How did the school explain that?"

"Runaway," Kieran said with disgust. "We always run away it seems."

"It would be understandable," Magnus said, trying to make sense of it all.

"Bart never ran from anything," Kieran said, shaking his head. "He was confrontational . . . in your face. He had an abusive father and a useless, passive, worthless mother . . . and he didn't run away from that." Kieran's voice rose in desperation. "He wouldn't fall apart like that for anything! He wouldn't lose all hope because of a bad dream . . . no matter how nightmarish!" The anger rose in him. "And now Alex!"

Kieran buried his face in Magnus' chest. Magnus pulled him even closer. They sat quietly for a moment, their breathing synchronous.

Magnus took Kieran's chin in his hand and turned his face to his own. "Alex." Magnus said quietly. "What was his take on all this?"

"He was devastated," Kieran said, shuddering. "He pulled away from the group for a time and just kept to himself. He's not been the same since Bart disappeared."

"When did he start getting sick?"

"Toward the end of last semester," Kieran said, his voice trembling. "Vitamins!" he spat, and looked hard into Magnus' eyes.

"So," Magnus cocked his head to one side. "What do we do about all this? Is there a plan?"

"Tommie suggests that we throw a wrench into the process at every opportunity."

"How?"

"We have to screw up the medication schedule."

"Again, how?"

"It's pretty simple, really." Kieran sat up to face Magnus. "Availability. This weekend's one of the family visitation periods. Families have the choice of coming here to visit or bringing us home." He shifted excitedly. "You need to get out of here then. The only way they can give you the medication is to send it with you."

"I can't go." Magnus looked down at his feet. "My mom doesn't have the money to fly me back to Texas."

"Good!" Kieran giggled. "I don't mean it the way it sounds," he said, seeing Magnus' expression. "This means you'll just have to go home with me!"

"What?"

"Now don't argue!" Kieran grabbed up Magnus' hands again. "My father is in no position to object to my bringing a friend home. Besides, he's probably holding court in the Manhattan townhouse."

"Your Dad's certainly liberal if he'll let you do that," Magnus said lightly.

Kieran rolled his eyes. "My father doesn't have a clue."

"Are you serious?" Magnus laughed.

"What's that supposed to mean?" Kieran feigned insult.

Now it was Magnus' turn to roll his eyes. "Your father and I need to have a talk."

"I'm sure I have no idea what you're talking about." Kieran said, slapping at Magnus playfully. "Anyway. When I go home my father will probably find a need to run off to New York or somewhere else with a good lineup of bars." He smirked. "For some reason I make him nervous."

"I know the feeling." Magnus hoped that the sound he had made sounded like a laugh.

"Quick!" Kieran jumped up suddenly. "Look like your dancing!" He dashed over to the piano.

"What?" Magnus stood, confused.

"We're about to have our first fight," Kieran said, throwing open the keyboard lid. He flashed a smile at Magnus. "Make believe, of course. Now dance! The plays afoot." Kieran began playing something fast that Magnus wasn't familiar with. Magnus' eyes darted to the door as the knob turned. He kicked off his tennis shoes and began a pirouette.

"Now say something mean to me," Kieran whispered above the music.

The door opened slowly and a set of eyes peered through the crack.

Magnus turned out of his spin and clapped his hands loudly. "Damn it, Kieran!" said Magnus, now understanding the role he was supposed to play. "If we're gonna do this you have to keep a steady tempo!"

Kieran took his cue and slammed his hands onto the piano keys. "I have to have some room for expression!" He jumped up to face Magnus, eyes blazing. "It's rubato! Got it? Rubato!"

Magnus couldn't help but admire Kieran's acting ability. "There's a difference between rubato and emoting!" he yelled back. He clapped his hands together again just as he remembered his teacher doing. "Rein it in!"

"Kiss my ass!" Kieran was really into it now. "And

while we're on the subject . . ." He jerked his head in the direction of the slightly opened door. "What the hell do you want?" He yelled at the intruder.

The door opened all the way and a security guard stepped in. "What's going on here?" The guard stammered.

"We're working, you idiot!" Kieran exploded. "That does it!" He turned to Magnus. "We're obviously not going to get any useful work done this afternoon." He slammed the piano shut.

"I agree." Magnus grabbed his shoes and started for the door. "This way you can get your metronome out and work on those tempos." He slid out the door. "Shut it! Quick!" He yelled to the guard.

The security man pulled the door shut just as one of Kieran's shoes slammed against it. The guard grinned at Magnus. "Whew! That was close," he said.

Magnus shrugged and started down the hall. "There's a difference between artistic temperament and being a spoiled brat!" he said over his shoulder.

The security guard gave him a thumbs up.

Alex slowly made his way out the door of the small basement room where Dr. Powell had put him. He inched down the corridor leading to the basement lab, holding onto the wall and stopping every five or ten feet to allow a spasm of pain to subside. He knew where he was going; remembering the story Bart had told him. He gripped his abdomen, waiting for it to pass, and tried to laugh at the irony of it all. But it was too hard. Somehow he knew he would end up down here . . . like Bart. That memory burrowed into his pain, amplifying it, massaging it. This is how Bart had felt was his one recurring thought.

"Bart . . . Bart . . ." Alex leaned back against the wall, sobbing, repeating the name over and over again.

Finally the pain abated enough that he could move a few more feet toward his destination—the locked, reinforced steel door at the end of the hall. A small red warning light above the door blinked incessantly . . . ominously . . . mockingly . . .   calling Alex closer and closer . . . one moment fighting . . . the next moment . . . relenting. That's where Bart had found Michael. Alone. Cold. Dead. Where Alex had searched for Bart . . . but to no avail.

Alex moaned and pulled himself along the wall. Not long now. For a moment he was once again overcome with the need to fight it, run, and find help from someone. But his body would betray him. The unrelenting pain sapped his will of everything except the inexorable drive toward that damned, blinking light.

Alex comforted himself. Thinking about Bart made the difficult journey seem shorter. Finally, he found himself in front of the long, narrow one-way mirror at the center of the door. He looked at his reflection and grimaced. Pain was so ugly. He reached for the call button and pressed hard. Another agonizing moment passed before the door opened.

"Come in, Alex." The voice was void of emotion.

Alex struggled into the lab without speaking. He squinted against its brightly lit interior. Dr. Powell closed the door behind him and Alex could hear the latch click securely. No one would bother them now. Dr. Powell motioned to two white-coated assistants to come; each one taking a hold of Alex under the arm.

"Have you been taking your medicine?" Dr. Powell asked, heading over to a bank of monitors while the two assistants helped Alex over to the exam table. One was older and grey-headed, and seemed to look at Alex like the boy was an injured bird.

"The vitamins?" Alex asked between clenched teeth.

Dr. Powell ignored him, flipping switches and adjusting knobs on the monitors. Yes, the . . . vitamins."

"Yes." Alex tried to settle himself into a comfortable position on the hardness of the steel table, but it was useless. "I've been taking them. They're not helping."

Dr. Powell again ignored him. "Take off his shirt and lay him down," he ordered. "Get those monitors hooked up."

The two assistants worked together getting Alex's shirt off. It was difficult for Alex to lay back. The pain made his body revert naturally to a fetal position. The grey-haired man busied himself hooking various monitor wires up to Alex's chest, abdomen, and scalp. The other had disappeared somewhere behind Alex.

"Can you give me something to ease this pain?" Alex pleaded between clenched teeth.

Dr. Powell took no note of him. The doctor was gloved and the grey-haired man left Alex to help the doctor don a teal green surgical gown. Finally, the other assistant—Alex didn't think he was much older than himself—returned into view, drawing up a dark blue solution into a hypodermic needle.

Dr. Powell moved over to the exam table, his eyes glued onto the monitors. "Goddamn it!" he muttered under his breath. He nodded to the grey-haired assistant. "Look at the burst-suppression waves!"

The grey-haired man bit his lower lip and nodded.

"The new genetic material is being rejected!" The doctor glared down at Alex. "Rejection! I thought you said you were taking your supplements."

Alex winced as the younger man inserted the long needle into a vein in the inside of Alex's arm.

"I took the damn things," Alex managed to say. "I did just what you told me to do."

Dr. Powell looked unconvinced, but his expression soon returned to inscrutable. "Well," he said, assuming the persona of the kindly country doctor. "Let's see what we can do about that pain."

Alex sighed with anticipation. He felt a burning sensation where the needle went in, and he waited for some effect from the blue medicine. He didn't have to wait long. All sensation in his body began to fade. It seemed to begin in his feet and slowly work its way up.

"Thank God!" Alex moaned as the relief traveled faster. It became difficult to breathe. At the same time his body began to relax and abandon its fetal habitus.

"Prep him and draw the specimens," Dr. Powell said, stripping his gloves off his hands and throwing them across the room in disgust. "I want the autopsy results before noon tomorrow."

Alex felt more than mere relief. It was almost bliss. His eyes released a stream of tears, but he could not feel them. "Bart," he whispered. He exhaled the contents of his lungs and surrendered to a dark, comforting, overwhelming nothingness.

CHAPTER 8

Magnus did not sleep well that night. Try as he might, he could not shake the feeling of dread he had begun to fight since his conversation with Kieran. He tried to focus on the positive of having finally had the courage to be physically expressive to another person . . . another boy. But the tale Kieran had spun about Bart and Alex was too disturbing, and Kieran's anguish too real. He dressed hurriedly and headed off for the cafeteria. If only the little yellow pill *was* a vitamin/mineral supplement. That, at least, would give him some reason to dismiss the growing paranoia he was beginning to share with the group.

The cafeteria was packed. Magnus was seeing many of the kids for the first time. He realized how insular and guarded he had been since arriving at the Powell Institute. He stood at the door for a moment, watching his own clique of friends in their familiar corner. Magnus shook his head. They really didn't trust anyone outside the group.

"Out of the way, fairy!"

Magnus recognized the voice of the boy named Marcus. He was aware of every eye in the cafeteria watching.

"You're blocking the door." Marcus almost snarled at Magnus.

"Piss off, Marcus!" He glared at the nerdish man-boy. "I'll move when I'm ready."

Marcus bristled. "No dancing queen's gonna . . ."

Magnus lunged at Marcus before he could finish the insult. Magnus was the boy's equal in height but far superior in strength. He slammed Marcus up against the wall, his arm shoved into the gurgling boy's throat, holding him up on his tiptoes. Satisfied, Magnus released his hold and Marcus dropped back onto the balls of his feet, stunned.

"This dancing queen can bench press two-fifty." Magnus stood his ground and got in his opponent's face. "And if you want to dis' me you'd better damn well be prepared to back it up, 'cause I will stomp your sorry ass in the ground!"

"You'll regret this!" Marcus stuttered, shaking visibly. "My father will have you thrown out!" He sidled past Magnus to the door, his posse in tow, nodding and mumbling in agreement. They all left in a huff.

The room broke out in spontaneous applause. Magnus smiled shyly and started for the familiar corner. His way was blocked by a tall, thin boy with wildly spiked, apple-red hair . . . Magnus stared . . . and tinges of blue on the ends.

"Hi," the boy said, giving Magnus the once over. He

was almost nose to nose with Magnus.

Magnus stepped back. "Hi," he responded, unable to take his eyes off the spectacle of the boy's hair.

"Back off, Conner!" Kieran said, appearing suddenly out of nowhere. He grabbed Magnus' arm and pulled him around Conner and behind himself. "This is private property!"

"What?" Magnus stuttered.

"Possessive little bitch, aren't you?" Conner tossed an arrogant smirk at Kieran.

The whole room groaned in unison.

"Wait for it!" Tommie whispered from the corner. Magnus decided to keep his mouth shut.

"Why, Conner," Kieran turned, hand on hips. "I haven't seen you in a while." His lips curled up, more in a snarl than a smile. "What happened to that little freshman you've been chatting up since the first of the semester? Did he outgrow you too?"

Again the assembled spectators groaned in unison.

Conner sniffed and looked down his nose. "Why, Kieran, I had no idea my conquests were adding to your feelings of inferiority."

"Uh oh," Tommie whispered as the room groaned even louder.

"Oh, Conner, dear," Kieran replied, unfazed. He made a production of caressing Magnus' muscular arm. "Don't give it a second thought. Unlike you, I'm only interested in men. Not these little boys you keep trying to usher into puberty."

"Slam dunk!" Tommie almost shouted.

Before Conner could reply, Kieran pointed at the boy's head, wiggling his index finger.

"Oh, and love the hair." He spun Magnus around and

pushed him toward the table in the corner. "It almost looks real."

Tommie whooped and led the table in a stadium wave. Conner spat some unintelligible expletive and stormed back to his group on the other side of the cafeteria. Magnus grinned broadly and sat down obediently at the table. Kieran pulled out a chair beside him.

"In case you're wondering, Magnus," Tommie said, shoving a hand full of potato chips into his mouth. "You just got pulled into . . . The Feud."

"Feud?" Magnus asked.

"Not feud . . . *The* Feud. The two of them have been trading insults ever since they met." He gestured to Kieran. "Sure you can handle this she-devil?"

"I'll go get us something to eat," Kieran said, patting Magnus on the arm.

"I'll go with you." Magnus started to get up.

"Absolutely not!" Kieran pushed him back into his chair. He stroked the back of Magnus' straw-colored hair. "It's my job to wait on you." He dashed over to the sandwich counter.

"Damn!" Tommie gave Magnus an admiring look. "You've conquered the beast!"

Magnus smiled and shrugged.

"What's *that* say?" Gail leaned across the table, staring at Magnus' forehead.

"What?" Magnus asked nervously.

"Wait, what's that say?" Gail squinted. "That big red stamp on your forehead . . . oh, yeah." She sat back down. "Kieran Matheson's bitch."

Sammy choked, spewing soda out of his nose. Everyone laughed.

"Don't listen to them, Magnus," Allison said. She reached over and pinched Tommie's arm.

"Ouch!" Tommie cried out in mock pain.

"She tries to say the same thing about you and me," Allison said, taking Tommie's hand under the table.

"And what do you say?" Tommie asked in mock horror.

"I am my beloved's, and my beloved is mine."

"I love it when you quote scripture to me." Tommie leaned over and gave her earlobe a nibble. "It makes me soooo—"

"Horney!" Gail interjected.

Allison pushed Tommie away, laughing.

Kieran returned with a tray of sandwiches and chips. "I got you a roast beef and a turkey."

"He's fattening you up for the kill," Tommie teased.

"Don't be an ass!" Kieran gave him a dismissive wave. He squeezed Magnus' bicep with his other hand. "This requires a great deal of nutrition to maintain." He slipped his arm into Magnus'. "He can bench press two-fifty, you know."

"That might have been a slight exaggeration," Magnus said sheepishly. "In the heat of the moment."

"Aha!" Tommie picked some chips off Allison's tray. "Probably more like a hundred."

Magnus looked up at the ceiling. "Probably more like two hundred."

"Liar!"

"Have *you* ever lifted a binge-eating ballerina over *your* head?" Magnus asked.

Kieran stuck his tongue out at Tommie who responded by giving his best body builder's pose.

"We have some information," Kieran said, again

ignoring Tommie. "Tell him, Sammy."

"You identified the pill?" Magnus looked up from his sandwich.

"Well, yes and no." Sammy responded, adjusting his eyeglasses nervously. "We know its name and what class of drug it is, but we don't know what its exact chemical makeup is."

"You said *drug*." Magnus looked at Kieran and then back at Sammy. "So you're saying it isn't a vitamin/mineral supplement?"

"Oh, please!" Tommie tipped his chair back onto two legs. "Tell us, Sammy."

"It's not a vitamin by any means," Sammy said, proud of his discovery. "It's one of a class of anti-rejection drugs—"

"Anti-rejection?" Magnus' voice almost cracked. "Rejection of what?"

"Tissue or organ transplant," Sammy said, annoyed at having his presentation interrupted. "The drug is designed to suppress the body's immune system so that it will not reject a donor organ, tissue, or cells."

"You've lost me." Magnus' appetite was gone. "Why would I be given such a drug? It doesn't make sense."

"It does explain why Alex and Andrew were so sick all the time," Kieran said, putting his hand on Magnus' shoulder and resting his chin on it.

"Without an effective immune system, they were sitting ducks for every opportunistic infection they came in contact with."

"But why?" Magnus persisted.

"That's what we need to find out," Kieran replied.

"Clearly, however," Sammy continued, raising his voice slightly. "If he's been put on anti-rejection therapy, the plan here must be to put something into Magnus that they don't want his body to reject."

Everyone sat silent, trying to digest this revelation.

"What could it be?" Magnus asked, looking from one to the other.

"Whatever it is," Tommie said softly, "it killed Bart . . . and it's made Alex deathly ill." His words settled over the group like a dark cloud.

Sammy shook his head.   "Well, not technically. Actually—"

"Shut up, Sammy," Gail barked. Her tone hit the small adolescent boy like a slap in the face. He shut his eyes and began to shake uncontrollably.

"Damn it, Gail!" Allison threw her arms around Sammy. "It's okay, honey. You didn't do anything wrong." She stroked his hair. "Gail, I told you to stop yelling at him!" Gail started to respond, but Allison cut her off. "What about that did you not understand?"

"Well, gee, Allison." Gail tried to look contrite. "It pisses me off when he starts correcting everyone . . ."

"Get over it!" Allison's eyes flashed. "He's just being Sammy. We expect him to do that. Who are you, of all people, to tell him not to be true to his own nature?" Allison patted the boy's face and he tried to smile. "That's better, she said, soothing. "You know you don't have to be afraid with us."

Sammy nodded.

"Christ!" Gail threw her hands up in the air. "The only place you can find a little testosterone around here is to sit at a table full of girls!"

"I got your testosterone right here, dude!" Tommie stood up and grabbed his crotch.

Gail blew a raspberry at him. "The only place you've

got testosterone is up your ass!"

The mood at the table lightened.

"Sammy, you need to get on to class," Allison said, patting the boy's leg.

He stood up without a word . . . obviously still upset. Tommie beckoned the boy over. He took Sammy by the shoulder and looked the boy in the face until slowly, Sammy looked up and managed a tentative grin.

"That's more like it," Tommie said, giving the boy a bear hug.

Sammy shyly put his arms around Tommie's neck. Magnus caught Kieran's eye who mouthed the words "puppy love".

"Now," Tommie said, releasing Sammy. "You'd better make a hundred on that history test today."

"I will," Sammy said, his confidence returning.

"You don't," Tommie said, giving the boy a slap on the rear end, "and I'll turn you over my knee."

"Wheee!" Sammy giggled and almost skipped out of the room.

"Now that's super-sensitive," Magnus said, shaking his head.

"There's a reason for that," Kieran said.

Magnus gave him a questioning look.

"Abused." Tommie sat back down and took Allison's hand.

"Physically?" Magnus asked. "Or . . ." His soft voice drifted off.

"Brutally," Allison said. "It was pretty bad."

"His parents?" Magnus was beginning to understand.

"Both!" Allison glared down at the table. "Pentecostals. Apparently Sammy's caring parents thought you could beat gayness out of a child." She shuddered. "When mommy got tired, Daddy took over."

"WWJD!" Kieran almost spat the words.

Magnus looked puzzled.

"What Would Jesus Do, dear?" Kieran tapped Magnus on the forehead. "Where have you been?"

"Yeah." Tommie put Allison's hand to his mouth and kissed it. "And this one . . . she'll let Sammy come in her room at night and sleep with her, but I don't get those same privileges."

"He's just a baby gay, you ass!" Allison said, rolling her eyes.

"Not so much a baby that he wouldn't rather sleep with you, Tommie," Kieran said, laughing.

Tommie did his body builder's pose again. "That boy couldn't handle all of this!" He changed poses.

"Oh, God!" Allison moaned.

Tommie's face shrank to a child-like pout. "My parents beat me, too," he cooed, trying to snuggle up to Allison.

Allison gave him a mock slap in the face. "You're not sleeping in my room," she said.

"Your parents didn't beat you enough," Gail said, throwing her bread crust at Tommie. She stopped suddenly, recognizing her gaff. "Oh, crap!" she moaned.

"Don't sweat it, Butch," Tommie said, throwing the piece of bread back at her. "I'm not Mr. Sensitive."

"Okay, okay!" Kieran signaled for quiet. "Enough macho bonding. We have more important things to discuss, and we don't have much time before class."

The table grew quiet.

"Right." Kieran leaned in. "The first wrench in this death machine. Magnus won't be here for Dr. Powell's vitamins over the weekend. That'll give us some time . . ."

"He's going home over the weekend?" Gail asked.

"Not exactly," Kieran replied, trying to ignore her.

"Then what . . . exactly?" Gail persisted.

"Suffice it to say . . ." Kieran refrained from looking at Gail. "Magnus will be leaving the school for parent's weekend. Now . . ."

"Where's he going?" Gail persisted.

"Yeah," Tommie chimed in. "Gee, Magnus, no offense, but I didn't think your mom had the resources to fly you back home."

Magnus only shrugged and smiled.

"That's not important." Kieran drummed his fingers on the table. "Now we're getting off track."

"Kieran," Allison said, thinking she had caught on. "That's so sweet. You got Magnus a plane ticket, didn't you?"

"It's not important!" Kieran almost screamed.

Tommie narrowed his eyes at Magnus. Magnus merely stared at the ceiling.

"Aha!" Tommie shouted.

"I give up!" Kieran slammed the table. He pulled at Magnus' shirt collar. "Come on. We have to get to class."

Tommie laughed victoriously.

"What?" Allison and Gail asked at the same time.

"Kieran's gonna have a house guest this weekend," Tommie said, pointing from Kieran to Magnus.

"Oh." Allison blinked.

"Shackin' up!" Tommie chanted.

"Shut up!" Kieran pulled Magnus up in a huff. "You ignorant Cretan." He pulled at Magnus. "Let's go!"

"Yes, master." Magnus stood obediently.

"Don't be silly." Kieran hooked his arm with Magnus' and pulled him along to the door.

"Watch out, Magnus!" Tommie called after them. "He's got you on his hook!"

Magnus waved at them over his shoulder.

"Of course," Tommie continued, "once he gets you in the boat, I'm not so sure the Virgin Kieran will know what to do with you."

Everyone laughed. Kieran was not amused. He turned ominously.

"Uh oh," Tommie said. "Here it comes."

"Well," Kieran said, putting his hands on his hips. "I was gonna say look who's calling who a virgin, but . . ." He gave Allison a knowing look. "I guess I can't really say that to your boyfriend." He turned on his heels and led Magnus out the door. He slammed it shut to the sound of Tommie singing, "Love Is a Many Splendored Thing."

"Excuse me?" Allison tapped Tommie on the arm.

"Yes, my sweet?" Tommie sat back down, laughing.

Allison gave him an enigmatic look. "Exactly what did Kieran mean by that?" she asked.

Tommie's laughter ended abruptly. "What?"

"You heard me." The hurt in her voice was evident. "What did Kieran mean when he said he couldn't call you a virgin?"

"Wha . . ." Tommie hesitated. "I don't think that's what he said." He gave Gail a pleading look. "Was it?"

Gail sat back in her chair and clasped her hands behind her head. "I heard what Allison heard, dude," she said, looking away.

Tommie looked stricken. "But—"

"What . . . did . . . he . . . mean by that?" Allison's face grew as steely as her tone.

Tommie took a deep breath and dropped his head into his hands. "Shit!"

CHAPTER 9

Magnus lugged his over-stuffed backpack off his bed and dumped it on his desk chair. He took a moment to smooth the bedspread back to its pristine state and glanced about to see if there was anything he might have forgotten. The door opened.

"Hi!" Kieran popped his head in. "Ready?"

"I've got to start locking that door," Magnus said, sighing dramatically.

Kieran ignored him and pulled his large rolling suitcase into the room. "God, that's heavy," he said, plopping back on Magnus' bed.

"Kieran, I just made the bed," Magnus said, only half-joking.

"And a good job you did." Kieran yawned. "There'll be no demerits from the anal retention police today."

"Whatever," Magnus eyed Kieran's impressive luggage. "I'm only taking a few pairs of shorts and tshirts. Is that okay?"

"Stunning!" Kieran said, frowning at the backpack. "You got it all in there?"

"How much are you taking?" Magnus adjusted the position of his backpack self-consciously.

"I'm only kidding," Kieran said, giving Magnus a playful kick. "We're going to the beach house in the Hamptons. It's not like I need to take *all* my hat boxes and ball gowns."

"Good," Magnus said, laughing. "Mine are all at the cleaners."

"Okay." Kieran sat up on the bed. "The car will be here in about thirty minutes."

"You wanna go say bye to everyone?" Magnus asked. "You know we should have asked Tommie to come with us."

"Tommie will be just fine. Allison's staying at the school too. Tommie will have a lot to occupy his time."

Magnus sat down beside Kieran and slapped him on the thigh. "That was mean."

"He deserved it!" said Kieran in self-defense.

"He was just joking around with you and you went too far."

"Why are you defending him? He was being just as mean to me."

"You know that's not true." Magnus turned to face him. "You don't screw around with other people's relationships. Allison means a lot to Tommie."

"Aren't I important to you?"

"Christ!" Magnus sighed. He took Kieran's hand. "Yes, you are." Kieran brightened and started to speak but Magnus interrupted. "But I don't like the way you're treating Tommie. He loves you too. You're his family."

Kieran sulked in silence.

Magnus turned Kieran's face to his and put his forehead against Kieran's. "When we get back you need to make this right."

"Or what?" Kieran bit his lower lip.

Magnus narrowed his gaze in mock disapproval. "Or I'll have to give you the spanking you deserve."

Kieran broke into a salacious smile and put his arms about Magnus' neck. "Do you want to borrow my belt?"

"You're sick!" Magnus groaned. He pushed Kieran back onto the bed, laughing. They lay next to each other for a few minutes in silence. Magnus looked at the ceiling. "So you'll talk to him when we get back?"

"Okay, okay." Kieran sighed heavily. "God, what I won't do for you!"

"Good." Magnus sat up quickly. "Footsteps!"

"Damn Nazis!" Kieran jumped to his feet, pulling Magnus with him. "Come on. We'll leave our bags here. I've got an errand for us to run."

Magnus followed Kieran out the door. Sure enough, a security guard was just bearing down on them.

"Take a chill-pill, Mr. Rent-A-Cop," Kieran said, waving. "The 'mos are moving on." He pulled a giggling Magnus past the guard. "The sex was great! Sorry you missed it!"

Kieran wiggled his fingers in a good-bye gesture at the guard. He and Magnus sprinted down the hall. Together, they burst through the stairwell door and raced down to the first floor taking two steps at a time, laughing the whole way. Once at the bottom, they both fell against the wall and caught their breath. Kieran was panting heavily, but Magnus was barely winded.

"You're going to get us in so much trouble," Magnus

said, still laughing. He pulled Kieran over to him in a hurried embrace.

Kieran allowed Magnus to hold him up, grateful for the support while he caught his breath. "I'll just . . ." he said, trying to pull in enough air. ". . . tell them you seduced me."

"Not just a slut," Magnus said. "But a lying slut!" He playfully pushed Kieran away from him.

"That's *lying queer slut* to you, mister!" Kieran said, finally catching his breath. He combed a few stray black curls out of his face.

"I stand corrected." Magnus reached out to tussle Kieran's hair. "Maybe, *lying queer vain slut* would be more accurate."

"Ha, ha!" Kieran said with a smile. "Count yourself lucky."

"I do," Magnus replied and leaned back against the wall.

Kieran beamed and made a beeline for Magnus, who held him at arm's length.

"You've done enough damage to my reputation for one day." Magnus flicked Kieran on the end of his nose. "What's this errand we need to do?"

"See?" Kieran slapped himself on the side of the head. "You've distracted me. Come on."

Magus followed Kieran around several corridors until Kieran stopped in front of the familiar elevator doors where Alex was last seen.

"What are we doing here?" Magnus hoped Kieran wasn't going to say what seemed inevitable.

Kieran pressed the down button. "Before I leave this place, I want to know how Alex is."

"We're not supposed to go down to the basement."

Magnus took hold of Kieran's shoulder. "You know that."

Kieran shrugged. "We're not put on this earth to do whatever someone else says."

"Crap!" Magnus covered his face with his hands. "We're screwed."

The elevator door opened and Kieran pushed a reluctant Magnus into the elevator. "Don't worry. This shouldn't take long," Kieran said.

"We're gonna be late for the car." Magnus slumped against the back wall of the elevator.

"Nonsense." Kieran checked his watch. "We've got about fifteen minutes at least before the car gets here."

The doors opened, again revealing a dimly lit hall.

"What about cameras?" Magnus asked before they exited.

"We'll find out!"

"Again, crap!"

Kieran laughed and grabbed Magnus by the arm. "Come on!"

They stepped into the hall which was lit by a single fluorescent fixture. The one working bulb flickered tentatively resulting in something like a strobe effect in the hall.

"See?" Kieran pointed. "No cameras."

Magnus perused the walls, ceiling, and corners for any sign of a camera. There was none.

"As I thought," Kieran said, heading off to the left. "We're not supposed to be down here, so . . . no cameras. I'll have to remember that," he said, throwing a smile over his shoulder to Magnus.

Kieran moved from one to the other of the two doors on the left side of the hall and then to the two on the right. He peered into the small window above the knob of each door. "Empty," he said. "It doesn't look like anyone's been in them." He paused to think. "Damn it! Powell's secretary said that Alex was down here in quarantine for some sort of virus. More bullshit!" He turned his attention to the other end of the hall. "Let's try down here."

The small, blinking red light over the door made Magnus even more uneasy. "Wait!" He tried to pull Kieran back. "That definitely looks like a place we shouldn't be snooping around."

"I'm not leaving until I find Alex." Kieran's look was pleading. "I can't leave without knowing that he's all right."

"All right, all right," Magnus said, relenting. "But let's make it quick . . . in and out . . . zip, zip!" Kieran nodded.

They approached the grey, steel door with caution.

Kieran pressed his nose against the glass of the small rectangular, framed-out window just above the doorknob. "I thought that was another window," he said, tapping on the glass. "But it's only a mirror."

"They obviously don't want anyone looking inside," Magnus reasoned.

"All the more reason why we should." Kieran tried the door knob, but it was locked. "Figures," Kieran said in disgust.

"We ought to go," Magnus said. "There's no way we can get in there now."

"Don't be so sure." Kieran replied, pulling a small set of keys out of his pocket. He bobbed his eyebrows with conspiratorial glee.

"Oh . . . my . . . God!" Magnus stared at the keys, mouth agape. "Where did you . . ." He stopped, shaking his head. "On second thought, I don't want to know."

"We got hold of the night custodian's keys." Kieran chucked. "He likes to nap sometimes." He manipulated one of the keys between his thumb and fingers. "Tommie and I went over the wall and had copies made . . ."

"Over the wall?" Magnus questioned.

"Just an expression, dear," Kieran said, patting Magnus' cheek. "Anyway, we've found what all the keys unlock except for these on the end." He slipped one of the keys into the lock. "I've been wanting to settle this matter." He turned the key, but to no avail. He went to the next key and tried it. Nothing.

"Hurry!" Magnus said urgently.

"Keep your pants on!" Kieran tried the next key. There was a click as the deadbolt retreated. "Bingo!" Kieran almost shouted.

"Crap!" Magnus resigned himself to the fact that they were going in. "Let's get this over with."

Kieran opened the door slowly. They both peered into the unlit room. Magnus pushed Kieran through the door quickly and slipped into the room behind him.

"Shut the door," Magnus said. "Just in case."

Kieran shut the door and then hugged close to Magnus. "We need to turn on a light," he whispered.

"Why are you whispering?"

Kieran gave him an un-amused look. "Just find the switch."

Magnus felt along the wall beside the door until his fingers found a bank of four light switches. He flipped the first one and a line of fluorescent lights blinked on, casting a cold glow across the floor along the wall with the door. Magnus and Kieran squinted against the sudden bright light. They stood unmoving, clinging to each other, taking in the lay of the room.

"It's a lab, all right," Kieran said, not letting go of Magnus.

"I don't see anyone here, especially Alex," Magnus said. "Can we go now?"

"Just a minute." Kieran walked to the middle of the room, studying his surroundings. "What the hell is this place?" He stood by a long and shiny steel table that had a half-inch raised lip all the way around, making it more of a tray than a table.

"Kieran?"

Kieran ignored Magnus' plea. He opened a few of the brushed steel cabinets above the polished steel countertops that spanned the back of the lab.

"Kieran?" Magnus called out again. "We're gonna get major screwed if we stay much longer." He caught his breath at a sudden realization. "Kieran! They would've seen us going into the elevators!"

"We're not hurting anything," Kieran said without concern. "We are justifiably worried about Alex and we came down to check on him. And besides ..." He winked at Magnus. "The door was opened."

Magnus groaned and rolled his eyes. "I hope your dad can pay my bail."

Kieran only laughed. "What's that?" He pointed to a bank of small, square doors, one on top of the other, that covered the wall on the narrow end of the room, still in partial darkness. "Turn on another light," he called out to Magnus as he walked tentatively across the gleaming white linoleum floor toward the object of his curiosity."

"Damn it to hell," Magnus muttered, flipping another switch.

The light went on over Kieran's head. He studied the

double bank of doors. "They look like little refrigerator doors," he said, moving in for a closer look.

"We're gonna die!" Magnus almost wailed, rushing over to Kieran's side. "Kieran, we've got to go!"

"Okay, okay!" Kieran grabbed for one of the door handles. "Just let me check this out real quick. It might be useful later." He pulled the handle and the small door popped open. A waft of fog-like condensation poured out. Kieran and Magnus peered into the frigid interior.

"It's empty," Magnus said, relieved.

"What the hell?" Kieran pulled on the end of the steel tray inside and it slid out, clattering over its rollers. "This is like those refrigerator units they keep bodies in!"

"What?" Magnus looked down at the empty tray.

"You know." Kieran slid the tray back into its icy niche. "Like in morgues." He looked at Magnus excitedly. "Don't you ever watch horror shows or police dramas?"

"Whatever." Magnus took hold of Kieran's shoulders. "Let's go!" He tugged at Kieran. "Please!"

"One more." Kieran refused to budge. He reached for the next door's handle. "What could they be using these things for?"

He yanked at the door and it opened with a loud pop as well, as if an interior vacuum was released. The tray mechanism slid out automatically this time and almost knocked Kieran off his feet. Magnus caught Kieran as he fell back.

"Holy shi . . . !" Magnus gasped.

Kieran's jaw went slack and an unintelligible sound escaped his lips. The mists of the cold condensation parted. This tray was not empty.

"Alex!" Kieran's hand went to his mouth. His throat seemed to close off and he couldn't speak.

"Shit! Shit! Shit!" Magnus shouted in a repeated litany.

They both fell back away from the cold, bluish corpse before them.

"Alex!" Kieran managed to squeak out again. His eyes released a floodgate of tears. "Alex!" he cried out again, his voice stronger.

The body had been laid out on the sliding steel tray head first, partially covered by a clean, white sheet. Magnus and Kieran stared down at the sightless eyes. It was Alex. Magnus recognized the boy's features despite the lax facial skin. They could see the top of a loosely-sutured, two-pronged incision that began on both sides of the body's upper chest and disappeared under the starched sheet.

"Alex!" Kieran sobbed.

Magnus recovered enough to act. He struck out with his foot and kicked the tray back into its refrigeration unit. The door clicked shut automatically as the tray slammed into its grotto.

"Come on, Kieran!" Magnus said desperately, but Kieran was as frozen as the corpse they had just witnessed. "Now!" Magnus pulled Kieran to him and almost carried him to the door.

"Oh God, Magnus!" Kieran tried to respond to Magnus' urging, but the shock still held him paralyzed and helpless. "Oh, God," was all he could manage.

Magnus pulled him from the room, hitting the light switches with his free hand. He paused out in the hall to steady Kieran on his feet. "Kieran?" He shook the boy roughly. "Kieran, listen to me!"

Kieran struggled to open his eyes. He turned his anguished face up to Magnus.

Magnus took the boy's face in his hands. "Kieran, we

need to get out of here. Quickly!" He wiped Kieran's tears away with his thumbs. "I'll carry you if I have to."

Kieran swallowed hard through clenched teeth. Magnus' strength gave him the impetus to respond. He nodded, and together they ran for the elevator.

"Wait!" Magnus cried out as they reached the elevator doors. "They'll probably be waiting for us."

"The stairwell," Kieran said gasping, trying not to hyperventilate.

"But it's locked!" Magnus almost shouted. He had not released his embrace of Kieran.

"The key," Kieran stammered, his voice strangled.

Magnus pulled him to the door at the end of the hall. He grabbed the keys out of Kieran's pants pocket and tried one in the door lock without success.

"Let me." Kieran was pulling himself together at last.

Through tears, he manipulated the right key forward and handed it to Magnus. Magnus thrust it into the door lock and it turned easily. He pulled the door open and pushed Kieran through. Magnus paused. He recognized the sound of the elevator's mechanism engaging.

"Oh, shit!" he cried out, leaping into the stairwell behind Kieran.

They bounded to the top of the stairs. Magnus pushed Kieran ahead of him. By the time they reached the first floor landing, Kieran was gasping for air. Magnus wrapped an arm about Kieran's waist as if, by physically touching him, he could transfer some of his own physical strength to Kieran. Kieran grabbed Magnus' arm gratefully, and nodded to the stairwell door. Magnus nodded back and carefully turned the door knob pushing the door open a crack. He peered out into the hall.

Satisfied, he opened the door enough to poke his

head out. "Clear," he said flatly.

Attached at the waist, they moved quickly down the hall for Magnus' room. They reached the dorms without incident and grabbed up their luggage. Quickly, they headed for the side porte-cochere. No words passed between them until they were safely in the waiting limousine and on the way out of the Institute gates.

The wide-eyed look on Kieran's face worried Magnus that he might still be in shock. He threw an arm around Kieran's shoulder. "Come here," he said softly, and pulled Kieran close.

Kieran laid his head against Magnus' chest. His breathing was erratic, but the tears had stopped. Magnus could feel the pulsating tension in Kieran's body.

Finally Kieran spoke, his voice low and full of anger. "They're not going to get away with this." He pressed hard against Magnus. "Somehow, they'll pay."

"Kieran, we have to tell somebody."

"What good would it do?" Kieran asked, pulling away slightly. "We've already been through this once." He laid his head back on Magnus' chest. "With Bart."

For a minute, Magnus thought Kieran might start crying again, but there were no sobs and there were no tears. He let Kieran do the talking.

"When Alex found Bart's body, no one would believe him." Kieran pounded his fist on his thigh. "I didn't believe him!"

Magnus strengthened his embrace and put his other hand to Kieran's face and held it tightly to his chest.

"I'm not going to cry anymore," Kieran whispered.

"If you need to cry ... cry," Magnus said softly, brushing Kieran's forehead with his lips.

"No more." Kieran shook his head. "I have to think."

"Were the police notified when Alex . . . found Bart?"

"Everyone and their grandmother were notified." Kieran closed his eyes. "Alex called everyone he could until his phone was taken away. He was in such a state, even his guardian . . . his own uncle wouldn't believe him. The police came and made a cursory search, but found nothing. Dr. Powell obviously had time to clear away all the evidence. Bart became nothing but a runaway."

"And Alex?" Magnus wanted to keep Kieran talking.

"He was changed . . . heartbreakingly changed. He lost his will to participate in anything and began to keep pretty much to himself. He didn't even complain when he got sick . . . as if he didn't care. I should've . . ." Kieran's voice broke.

"No!" Magnus turned Kieran's face to his own. "Don't you do that! This is not your fault."

"I just didn't know what to do." Kieran covered his face in anguish.

"How could any of us know how to handle a situation like this?" Magnus hugged him again. "Alex would be grateful . . ." Magnus searched for the right words. "He would be grateful that you searched for him . . . that you found him . . . that someone knows the truth!"

Kieran forced back the tears. He wiped his face with his hands.

"Kieran." Magnus leaned close to Kieran's ear. "Somehow . . . some way, we're going to find a way to expose this . . . this god-awful ugliness."

"We will," Kieran said, steeling himself. The tears had stopped. "Somehow."

"Maybe your dad could help?"

"My father?" Kieran laughed bitterly. "You can't count on him for anything."

CHAPTER 10

The plane ride had passed uneventfully. Kieran had slept the whole way, his head on Magnus' shoulder and with Magnus' arm about him. Magnus was finding it easier and easier to ignore the curious or disappointing glances from the other passengers, or the amused looks from the stewardess. Now, in another limousine headed for Kieran's family beach house in the Hamptons, he was also aware of the driver's eyes in the rear view mirror, observing.

They had no more gotten in the car than Kieran had grabbed Magnus' arm and looped it over his shoulder. Magnus didn't object and, in fact, was beginning to enjoy Kieran's closeness.

"That driver sure is curious," Magnus whispered in Kieran's ear.

"Good help is so hard to find," Kieran whispered back. They both giggled.

"God, you'd think we were making out or something," Magnus whispered again.

Kieran shifted in the seat, snuggling closer to Magnus. "Well, if he's gonna watch," he said loudly, "we should give him something worth watching?" The driver's eyes went back to the road.

"Kieran!" Magnus laughed, pulling away. "Give me a break!"

"What?" Kieran's face dissolved into a pout. "You're embarrassed to be with me, aren't you?"

Magnus settled back into the seat and put his arm back over Kieran's shoulders. "This is hard ..." He shifted uncomfortably. "This is new for me. I don't know what to do, when to do it, or even if I should do it. So ..." He bumped up against Kieran playfully. "I've gotta ... walk before I can run."

"You are so damn cute," Kieran said, batting his lashes.

"Cute?" Magnus shook his head. "Cute is for babies."

"But you are a baby ... my baby." Kieran nuzzled under Magnus' chin. "We'll grow up together."

"I think I've got some catching up to do."

Kieran kissed Magnus lightly on the cheek. "You're doing just fine," he chuckled at Magnus' blush. "I like where we are ... together."

They sat quietly for the rest of the ride. Magnus was relieved that Kieran was coping well enough to joke around some more. Magnus enjoyed the views from the beach road. However, the size of the houses started to make him a little uncomfortable. So did the silence. He could sense Kieran's thoughts had returned to their earlier discovery.

"This is a really nice place," Magnus said, stretching

his neck to catch a large sailboat in the distance. "Makes our Gulf Coast beach communities look like a trailer park."

"It's the Hamptons, baby!" Kieran said with a dramatic gesture. "As Tommie would say, this is the way to live." His expression darkened suddenly.

"What is it?" Magnus asked with alarm.

"The moment we get to the house," Kieran said, "we need to send an email to Sammy to let everyone know what's happened."

"What about Alex's family? Shouldn't we tell them something?"

Kieran shook his head. "You'll note that most all of us are from family situations where, either there is no family, or the family we have was glad to get rid of us in the first place."

"That's not my situation," Magnus said.

"The rest," Kieran continued, "are from families with little or no social standing to make much trouble for the Institute."

"Now that would be me, I guess," Magnus said. The realization of how devastating his own disappearance would be for his mom . . . how helpless she would feel. "Sons of bitches!" He almost spat.

"Gay kids are almost always running away from something," Kieran said sadly. "It's about the only form of control kids have. I think that the Institute is just using that accepted fact as a convenient cover for killing us."

"I've never run away from anything," Magnus insisted.

"Magnus." Kieran smiled up at him. "The very fact that we're in this school in the first place, means we've run away from something."

"But . . ." Magnus stopped, realizing that the only reason he had been interested in leaving his school back in Texas and coming to the Institute was to get away from all the crap he had been taking from other students. "Damn!" he said with disgust. "I guess you're right."

The car pulled off the road into a long circular drive.

"We're here," Kieran said with a sigh. "At last!"

Magnus stared out the car window. His eyes widened. "I thought you said we're going to your beach house," he said with wonder.

"Yeah, and?" Kieran responded.

"This is a hotel or something," Magnus said, pointing out the window.

"Welcome to the world of conspicuous consumption."

"Your world?"

"My world." Kieran threw open the car door. "Come on! You're about to see first hand how money can't buy happiness."

"Nobody really believes that old line, you know," Magnus said, climbing out of the car behind Kieran. He stared up at the shingled façade of the hulking, two-story home.

"Well, they have never been to the Matheson house before." Kieran took Magnus' arm.

"We'd better get our bags," Magnus said, looking back at the sleek, black limousine.

"I should've called ahead," Kieran said, throwing up his hands, "and had our driver come get us rather than the airport limousine service."

"You too good to tote your own bags?" Magnus backtracked to grab their two bags that the driver had set out of the trunk.

"Ha, ha." Kieran pulled a ten dollar bill out of his pocket and offered it to the driver. He slapped Magnus' hand and made him put the bag down, before pulling him up the walk to the home's heavy, teak doorway flanked by beveled panes of etched glass.

"Gee," Magnus said, half-joking. "If I'd known you were such a good tipper, I'd have carried your bag for you, Mr. Matheson."

Kieran turned on his heels. "Shut up, or I'll French you right in front of the butler."

"Butler?" Magnus jaw dropped. "At a beach house."

"Come on, little boy," Kieran said, rolling his eyes.

"You *are* a spoiled, little rich bitch, aren't you," Magnus said. He pulled Kieran over to him in a bear hug. "Just like Tommie said."

"And don't you forget it," Kieran said, reaching up to press the doorbell.

"Don't you have a key?" Magnus asked.

"Somewhere," Kieran said, pushing the doorbell again. "But I've decided it's best if we're just a complete surprise to all concerned."

After a moment, the door was swung open by a short, stocky, bald man in coat and tie. His initial, bored expression quickly changed. "Mr. Kieran," the man stammered in surprise. "We weren't expecting you."

"It's good to see you too, Henry," Kieran said with a disarming smile. He brushed past the butler, pulling Magnus with him into a grand foyer. He turned to Henry. "This is Mr. Kroft. He will be joining me for the weekend."

"Mr. Kroft." Henry noted and went to retrieve their bags from the doorway. "Will Mr. Tommie not be joining us as well?"

"No," Kieran replied. "Mr. Tommie will *not* be joining us as well. And do stop with the Mr. Tommie and Mr. Kieran, Henry. You make us all sound like hairdressers."

Henry bobbed his head without comment and started up the sweeping staircase with the bags.

"I'll help with that, Henry," Magnus said, starting after him.

The offended look Magnus got in return surprised him.

"Henry can handle it, Magnus," Kieran called after him. "Come on!"

Magnus retreated back to Kieran's side with a shrug.

"Henry." Kieran waved behind him. "We'll be in the music room ... and we're both famished. Would you have Mavis throw something together to last us until supper?"

"Very good, sir," Henry responded, starting back up the stairs with his load.

"Mavis?" Magnus asked.

"The cook," Kieran replied. "Henry's wife."

"Of course," was all Magnus could say.

Kieran led Magnus through a set of double doors into a cavernous room with very high ceilings. Magnus tried not to look like a yokel as he glanced about the room. Kieran headed for the large, black Bösendorfer concert grand that commanded the rear center of the room. He flipped open the keyboard and ran a short scale.

"Needs tuning," Kieran said with a sigh. "Damn climate." He looked back to find Magnus staring up at the sparkling chandelier overhead. "It is a little big, isn't it?" He sidled up to Magnus and linked arms with him.

"It's as big as a Volkswagen," Magnus said. "Of

course, the room is as big as my house."

"We owe it all to my grandfather's greed," Kieran said with a shrug. "Well, that and various third world countries he raped for their resources."

"I take it grandpa is no longer with us?"

"Alas," Kieran declaimed. "He died shortly after I was born. My father was at the New York office when it happened. My mother on the other hand . . ." He smiled cherubically. "Rumor was that she was the one who poisoned him . . . others say he was *overdosed* on some of his medications."

Magnus tried to read Kieran's expression. He spoke carefully. "These things . . . happen."

"Don't they, though?" Kieran guided Magnus over to a mammoth, ornate desk. "My mother hopped a plane for Europe before the funeral." He plopped down in the desk chair. "And she never returned." He pulled out the computer keyboard drawer.

"Wow, Kieran!" Magnus stood stunned.

Kieran merely laughed and manipulated the mouse next to the keyboard. "Don't look so horrified," he said. "You don't miss what you've never known."

"That's a good line," he said, standing behind Kieran. "Wish I believed it." He put his hands on Kieran's shoulders.

"The story of my life." Kieran sucked at his bottom lip in a child-like pout. "Poor little rich boy."

"Better than poor little poor boy, like me!"

"This'll take a few minutes," Kieran said, pulling up his email. His fingers flew across the keys.

"Not at that typing speed," Magnus said. He proceeded to read some of the titles in the floor to ceiling bookcases.

"I have to link this up to our internet cloud and into Sammy's encryption software," Kieran said, typing furiously. "We don't want any of this intercepted by Powell."

"I haven't read any of these." Magnus craned his neck to identify some of the books on the upper shelves. "Of course, the only leather-bound book I've ever had was my Bible I had to take to Sunday School as a child . . . and it was probably faux-leather."

"I doubt if anyone's ever read these particular volumes." Kieran clicked the mouse to send his email. "My father collects them. It makes him feel . . . educated . . . if not useful." He jumped up from the chair. "There. That'll give the guys most of the facts . . . just enough to scare the shit out of them!"

"No sense us being terrorized alone."

The doors opened and Henry paraded in carrying a tray. "Your lunch, sirs," he said, unloading the tray onto a small table by one of the arched windows. "Will there be anything else?"

"No." Kieran took Magnus hand and pulled him over to the table. "That'll do for now." He sat down quickly. "Oh, my favorite lentil soup. Bless that Mavis!"

"Lentil?" Magnus joined him at the table.

"It's the best," Kieran chirped happily. He saw Magnus' reluctance. "Try it. You'll see."

"Okay, if you say so," Magnus said, unsure.

"By the way, sir." Henry cleared his throat. "Your father is in residence."

"What?" Kieran stopped before the spoonful of soup touched his lips.

"Mr. Matheson, your father."

"I know who he is." Kieran turned sharply in his

chair. "He's here?" The spoon dropped back into the bowl of soup.

"He went for lunch at the Eversols." Henry cleared his throat again. "But I expect him back before dinner."

"Great!" Kieran let out an exasperated groan. "If I'd known that I would have gone to the New York apartment."

"Well, sir, if you had called . . ." Henry fidgeted with his tray.

"That'll be all, Henry," Kieran said, cutting him short.

"Yes, sir." Henry retreated from the room.

"Damn it!" Kieran sat back from the table. "That spoiled my appetite."

"The soup really is pretty good." Magnus smiled sheepishly.

"I hope you enjoy it."

"Come on, Kieran. Eat." Magnus held Kieran's spoon up to him. "Don't you think it's a good thing your father's here? Maybe he could help?"

"My father has made a career out of denial." Kieran took a reluctant spoonful of soup. "Well, that and dinner parties."

Magnus decided a change of subject was in order. "Don't suppose we'll have lobster and caviar for dinner, huh?"

"Caviar's nasty," Kieran said with a grimace.

They both laughed.

"I can't imagine what it would be like to grow up like this . . . with everything," Magnus said.

"Well, not everything." Kieran's smile became sardonic.

"I'm speaking materialistically." Magnus kicked Kieran lightly under the table.

"So." Kieran kicked him back. "You want to be a material girl?"

"You tell me."

"You haven't even seen my room yet," Kieran said, bobbing his eyebrows.

"Will it make me feel even poorer?"

"Probably." Kieran picked up his bowl and slurped down the remainder of his soup.

"Very chic," Magnus groaned.

Kieran ran an embroidered napkin over his lips. "Come on!" He jumped up from the table. "I'll take you to my boudoir."

"I should've known it wouldn't be just a bedroom like the rest of us," Magnus said, standing.

"Now don't hate the rich." Kieran took his arm. "It's not fashionable any more. Come with me."

"Lead on," Magnus said. He walked beside Kieran to the door. "When are you going to show me the ballroom?"

"Ballroom!" Kieran howled. "This is the beach, darlin', not the Ritz."

"What?" Magnus pushed Kieran out the door into the foyer ahead of him. "No ballroom? Down South we think all you rich Jew-boys have ballrooms. Now I'm disappointed."

"And you're an anti-Semitic gay-boy!" Kieran shook a fist in the air playfully. "I'm sorry you're dis . . ." He stopped short on the stair landing and spun around to Magnus. "How do you know I'm Jewish?" He grabbed for his crotch in mock horror. "Have you been peeking?"

"You wish!" Magnus made a playful grab for Kieran's protective hand.

"Sounds more like *you* wish," Kieran responded,

batting Magnus' hand away. "Now I know your game. You came here to steal the family jewels!"

Magnus straightened, shaded his brow with his hand, and began to look about down the dark hallways. "Yeah. They must be around here someplace."

Kieran laughed and swung an open hand at Magnus' face, barely missing. "Pig!"

"Princess!" Magnus retorted.

Kieran struck a pose. "You say that like it's a bad thing."

Magnus grabbed Kieran and pulled him into a tight embrace. "My sincere apologies." He beamed down at Kieran. "I'm only worried about how high a dowry this princess commands."

"Maybe more than you've got," Kieran said, teasing.

"Huh!" Magnus shook Kieran lightly. "Now you'll never know if I love you for you or . . ." He gestured widely. "Your money."

"I don't care why, I just . . ." Kieran paused. His expression changed to stunned bliss. He pressed into Magnus and he held the confused boy's gaze. "You just said you love me."

"Well, I . . . I . . ." Magnus stammered. His jaw dropped.

"Don't deny it!" Kieran threw his arms about Magnus' neck. "You said you love me and you can't take it back." His gaze melted into Magnus'.

"So?" Magnus shrugged. Try as he might, he could not turn his eyes. "Where did a nice Jewish boy like you get those astonishing Liz Taylor eyes anyway?"

"Do you use that line on all the boys?"

Magnus drew Kieran closer. "I don't think I've ever had occasion to use a line before."

"Good." Kieran raised his chin. "So ... are you prepared for what comes next?"

Magnus felt the tension in his body build. "No," he said, telling the truth.

"Tough!" Kieran pulled Magnus' head down to his own. "Take it like a man."

Magnus caught his breath. His lips met Kieran's in a tentative first kiss. He closed his eyes to stop the room from spinning.

After a moment, Kieran pulled back. "Okay," he said, taking Magnus' face in his hands. "Enough practice." He pulled Magnus face to his, roughly.

Their mouths melted together, lips parted. Their tongues intertwined in the first blush of passion. They broke their embrace slowly. Magnus put a hand to his burning cheeks. His heart was pounding, his legs paralyzed. Kieran stepped back a few inches. He looked up into Magnus face. Liking what he saw, he hugged Magnus tightly, pressing his cheek against Magnus' cheek.

"Wow!" was all Magnus could manage, still reeling from an unfamiliar, but powerful emotion.

"I ... I've never been kissed like that before," Kieran said sighing.

"Ditto." Magnus couldn't stop grinning. "Actually, I've never kissed anyone ... except my mom." He chuckled. "And certainly not like that!"

"Are you okay with it?" Kieran straightened, his face inches from Magnus'.

Magnus put a hand to his mouth since the stupid grin would not go away on its own. "I'm not sure," he said, again being completely honest.

"Good." Kieran kissed the tip of Magnus' chin. "I'd like to think I have a powerful effect on you."

Magnus threw his head back, trying to clear his thoughts, but no clear thought would crystallize. He could only *feel*. An overpowering desire for the scent of Kieran's hair, a need for Kieran's closeness, and something more. It suddenly frightened him. Magnus broke the embrace. He stood, eyes wide, panting like a man on the edge of a cliff.

"What's wrong?" Kieran's face fell. He started to panic. "You didn't like . . . I'm sorry . . . I . . ."

"No, no!" Magnus tried to reassure him. "I . . ." He sighed. "I guess I can't even finish my sentences now." He wanted to, but could not bring himself to close the narrow distance between them. He dropped his head. "I wanted to kiss you." He looked back up at Kieran, his eyes pleading. "It was a great kiss . . . but . . ."

"But what?" Kieran put a hand on Magnus' chest. "Are we okay?"

Magnus put his hands on top of his head. He tried to break the spell by laughing. "We're better than okay." He took a deep breath. "I'm not used to being so . . . off balance."

"So I do have a powerful effect on you," Kieran said, relieved.

"Oh, yeah!" Magnus tried to shake the swirling from his head. "It was a knockout punch. I'm not sure where I am or . . . what I'm doing."

"Good." Kieran reached out for Magnus' hand. "I'll give you a little time to collect yourself." He tugged Magnus close to him, again inches from Magnus' face. "But in a little while . . ." He brought his lips close to Magnus'. "Watch out!" He broke away and pulled Magnus into a long hallway. "Now you have to see my room."

Magnus resisted. He began to laugh uncontrollably.

Kieran threw Magnus' hand away and stood, hands on hips. "What's so funny?"

But Magnus couldn't stop laughing. He bent over and grabbed his knees, shaking his head. "I don't know," he managed. Finally he held his breath as if he were trying to cure the hiccups.

Kieran stood watching, unsure what to do.

"Okay, okay!" Magnus gasped in a deep breath. "I'm sorry." He was still chuckling. "You have totally screwed me up."

Kieran grinned at him.

Magnus slapped his own cheek. "I feel like an idiot." He raised his open palms in a plea. "I need professional help!"

"Yes, you do." Kieran grabbed Magnus' hand back up. "And you're in luck." He pulled Magnus up close again. "The doctor is in."

"Again, oh, crap!" Magnus spun Kieran around and pushed him down the hall. "Show me your room. I'll consult with the doctor later."

Kieran resisted Magnus' prodding, batting at the boy's hands all the way down the hall. He grabbed at one of the door knobs. "Here!" He shouted with near hysterical laughter of his own. "Stop tickling!"

"Aha!" Magnus stood back. "Now I've found your weakness."

"That's not fighting fair." Kieran brushed his hair back and tried to recover his composure.

"All's fair in love and war," Magnus said, feigning a few grabs at Kieran.

Kieran slapped at Magnus' hands. "Stop! My God! I've never known anyone so determined to get me in the bedroom!"

"You have such a one-track mind," Magnus said, rolling his eyes.

"Are you saying you're not on the same track?" Kieran put his hands on Magnus' waist.

Magnus encircled Kieran's waist with his hands. He grinned at Kieran. "Oh, I think we're on the same track." He pulled Kieran to him and kissed him on the forehead. "I just think your car's traveling a bit faster than mine."

Kieran raised his eyes to Magnus'. Once again he took Magnus' face in his hands. "You are so beautiful!"

"So are you," he said in turn, blushing.

They embraced for a moment.

Finally Kieran pulled away. "Okay," he said. "Slower. I can do that." He smiled seductively. "We'll just enjoy the scenery for a while."

"And the journey."

Kieran smiled and nodded, reaching for the door knob behind him. "Come into my parlor said the spider to the fly." He pulled the door open.

"I'd better stay by the door in case I have to make a run for it," Magnus said, pushing Kieran into the room.

"So unfair!" Kieran donned his pouty face.

Without warning, he grabbed Magnus' hand and jerked him hard into the room. Magnus stumbled across the carpet, falling in a heap on top of a canopied, oak bed. He quickly recovered and rolled over so he could see what Kieran was up to. Kieran slammed the door shut.

He turned back to Magnus, batting his eyelashes suggestively. "Wow . . . right to the bed. I'm impressed."

"Very funny." Magnus climbed off the high, four-poster bed. "Have I mentioned your bed is as big as my bedroom?"

"Remember, love." Kieran snapped in the air. "It's not how big it is. It's what you do with it that counts."

"That's another line nobody believes," Magnus said with a smirk. "And certainly not you." He headed for a heavy, mahogany dresser covered with framed pictures. "And I use my bed for sleeping."

"Oh well." Kieran sighed. "Can't blame a guy for trying."

"I'm not complaining." Magnus smiled and picked up one of the pictures. "I assume this would be your . . ."

"My mother," Kieran stated flatly, sitting on the edge of the bed.

"She's very beautiful." Magnus held the picture up for Kieran's view. "It's a fairly recent picture from the look of things."

"She sends me one from time to time," Kieran said with a nonchalance that was unconvincing. "So I don't forget what she looks like."

"Kieran!" Magnus said, somewhat taken aback by Kieran's bitter tone.

"I'm just being honest." Kieran looked down at the floor, kicking his legs back and forth. "She's not someone I can make any further emotional investment in. I'll only end up more hurt and more screwed up."

"I don't think you're screwed up." Magnus sat the picture back atop the bureau.

"Thanks." Kieran flopped back onto the bed. "It must be love. We're already lying to each other."

"I'm not lying." Magnus made a dash for the bed and dove onto it perpendicular to Kieran, causing them both to bounce in a trampoline effect.

"Careful, Tarzan!" Kieran grabbed the bed clothes to steady himself.

Magnus leaned over Kieran's face and looked down at him. "I don't think you're screwed up."

Kieran stuck his tongue out at him.

"I don't." Magnus bumped his forehead against Kieran's. "Well . . . no more than me, anyway."

"Good." Kieran smiled up at him. "If you're not lying to me then that means we're still on our honeymoon." He reached for Magnus.

"Whoa there, my little Jewish princess!" Magnus batted Kieran's hands away playfully. "I think we've got a ways to go before the honeymoon phase."

"Phase?" Kieran pursed his lips. "What, are you working off some sort of relationship grid or something?"

"Sure. Don't you watch Oprah?"

"O.M.G!" Kieran poked at Magnus' ribs. "What's a guy got to do to finally arrive at one of these relationship milestones you keep spouting off?"

Magnus looked down into Kieran's purple eyes. He felt his resolve, or was it fear, begin to melt. "I'm sure you'll think of something," he said, trying to stay in control. He flipped over onto his back, making them bounce about again.

"That does it!" Kieran pounced, pinning Magnus to the bed.

They wrestled playfully, one pinning the other. Magnus applied his secret weapon.

"No tickling!" Kieran shrieked, surrendering.

"You'd better behave." Magnus climbed off the bed, smiling broadly.

"That's not in my nature." Kieran laid back, hands behind his head. "Love me, love my nature."

"Blah, blah." Magnus said, sticking out his tongue. He returned to the bureau.

Kieran watched Magnus perusing the various photos littering his dresser. "You never answered my question," he said.

"What question?" Magnus picked up another picture. "Is this you? You were so cute."

"Don't change the subject, and yes I was, and I still am." Kieran crossed his legs. "How did you know I was Jewish?"

Magnus tried to bat his eyelashes like he had seen Kieran do. "Well, maybe it was the Mezuzah hanging by the front door, you think?"

"Hell's bells." Kieran snorted. "I forgot all about that old thing. My father's search for an identity. How do you know about Mezuzah's?"

"I've got a question for you." Magnus returned the picture.

"Shoot!"

Magnus leaned back against the bureau. "How come there are no pictures of your father?"

"Oh, him."

"Yes, him." Magnus crossed his arms. "Your father's not an absentee parent. Why no pics?"

"Well, there's absence and then there's absence," Kieran said, looking up at the ceiling.

"What's that supposed to mean?"

"My father would be happy if I weren't anywhere around him. You'll see. There's no resemblance whatsoever between us. I know he thinks I'm not really his, but he hasn't got the balls to demand paternity testing."

"I can't believe—"

"You don't know my mother."

Magnus looked at Kieran, mouth ajar.

"And why all these questions?" Kieran sat up and smiled. "What's your game mister? What's your interest in the Matheson clan?"

"In order to get closer, don't you think we should get to know each other a little better?"

"Well, there's get to know," Kieran smiled seductively, "and then there's *get to know* . . . you know?"

"You are so sex-obsessed!"

"I think that's perfectly normal for sixteen going on seventeen."

"Crap!" Magnus laughed. "If you're gonna sing the score from *Sound of Music*, I'm leaving. And besides, you're seventeen going on eighteen."

"Such an asshole!" Kieran threw one of the bed pillows at Magnus. "I did have a thing for that little blonde number, Rolf." He threw Magnus a suggestive wink. "I likes my blondes."

"Rolf was a Nazi," Magnus responded, shaking his finger at Kieran. "A Jewish princess has no business lusting after a Nazi . . . blonde or otherwise."

"Kinky, huh?" Kieran cocked his head to one side.

"I give up!" Magnus laughed. "Do we need to dress for dinner?"

"We're at the beach. Remember?"

"Just checking. I know how you rich people like to play dress-up." Magnus sniffed. "When do I get to see this beach?"

"Oh, let's take a walk before dinner," said Kieran, brightening. "I love to walk on the beach at dusk."

"I'd better change into my grungy jeans, then," Magnus said, looking himself over. "I don't want to get sand all over these."

"I'll change too," Kieran said, jumping off the bed.

Magnus started for the door. "It's a plan. Show me where my . . ." He stopped. "Kieran?"

"Yes, love?"

"Why are my bags in your room?" Magnus pointed to a corner by the door.

"Well, I thought . . . I just . . ." Kieran sighed dramatically. "Okay, okay!" He started for the door. "I'll show you to *your* room."

"Thank you. You're too kind," Magnus said, his eyes twinkling.

"Schlep your own bags!"

Kieran brushed past him and pulled the bedroom door open.

Magnus retrieved his luggage and pulled it out into the hall. "Schlep?"

"This way," Kieran said, ignoring him. He strutted down the long hallway.

Magnus followed, struggling with his luggage.

Kieran stopped at the last door and opened it with a flourish. "Your room," he said as Magnus stumbled up with his luggage. "Far, far away from my room."

Magnus just grinned at him.

"So you can feel safe at night," Kieran added. He stepped aside to give Magnus free access. "I think the door locks too."

Magnus shoved his luggage through the door. "Now no need to get all huffy," he said, suppressing a chuckle.

"I am not huffy!" Kieran crossed his arms.

"Remember, we're enjoying the journey."

"Oh, I intend to," Kieran said, eyeing Magnus up and down.

"Well." Magnus stepped in the doorway, holding the door. "See you downstairs."

Kieran narrowed his eyes at Magnus. "I'll get you, my pretty," he said, starting down the wide hallway. "And your little dog too!"

"I don't have a . . ." Magnus caught the innuendo. "Wicked Witch of the West!"

"Hick!"

"Sissy!"

Kieran turned, hands on hips. He raised his eyebrows.

"Virgin!"

"You don't know me!" Magnus pretended to glare at him.

Kieran spun on his heels and headed on down the hallway. He waved behind him. "You love me!"

Magnus watched Kieran sashay down the hall. He smiled to himself, shutting the bedroom door slowly.

CHAPTER 11

Magnus sat on the edge of his bed and untied his tennis shoes. He suppressed a yawn and lay back on the plush mattress. Both he and Kieran had underestimated how tired they both were after their walk, which really consisted more of chasing and running from the incoming surf, in between holding hands and lively banter.

Magnus smiled to himself, enjoying the memory of the past couple of hours. He had not really counted a relationship into his future plans. His previous school had been a lonely place for a boy like him. He had concentrated on his dancing every waking moment. But now? It would be impossible to sleep. His mind was racing with a million unconnected thoughts. So much had happened over the past few days. It was no use. He sat back up on the bed. All he could really focus on was Kieran. Every random thought went back to Kieran.

Every surging emotion or feeling went back to Kieran.

Still, there were important decisions to make, serious plans to formulate before they returned to the Institute. But all he really wanted to think about was Kieran—Kieran's touch, Kieran's smell, Kieran's eyes.

"Goddamn it!" He dropped to the floor and pumped out several sets of pushups. He sat back on his heels, panting. No good. He wanted to be with Kieran. Maybe he *was* in love!

He stood slowly, stretching backwards. He arched his back and threw his head back. What was stopping him? He straightened and looked at himself in the mirror, glaring. "You stupid, dumb-ass!" Magnus closed his eyes and slapped the sides of his head with his hands. "You sorry little faggot!" He shot himself the finger in the mirror.

Magnus darted to the door, a decision made. He padded down the hall in his stocking feet, shaking his head and muttering expletives at himself. It was the same ritual he had carried out every time before he had a performance—before stepping out onto a stage. Triumph or Tragedy? It all depended on how he handled the fear.

By the time he reached Kieran's door, he was ready for anything. He rapped lightly and waited, but there was no response. He turned the knob and cracked the door open. Kieran was stretched out in his underwear on his stomach atop the bed covers, arms wrapped about a pillow. Magnus stepped into the room quietly and tiptoed over to the bed.

"Tighty-whities," he said to himself, chuckling quietly. He sat gingerly on the edge of the bed, watching Kieran sleep.

Kieran reacted to the movement by turning onto his

other side, still sleeping. Magnus reached out to touch Kieran's hair. He let his hand run down Kieran's shoulder and arm. Kieran stirred and opened his eyes.

"Hi." Magnus caressed Kieran's lips with his forefinger.

"Hi," Kieran replied. He sat up on his elbows with a yawn. He became fully aware of Magnus' gentle stare. Kieran smiled up at him. "Couldn't sleep?"

"I haven't been able to do anything ..." Magnus clasped his hands in his lap. "Except think about you."

Kieran's lips parted. He rolled over onto his back. "What were you thinking about me?"

"Well ..."

"Well?"

"Let's just say ... they were very unclean thoughts."

Kieran beamed and stretched back onto the pillow, hands behind his head. "My favorite kind." He nudged Magnus with his hip. "And how did those ... thoughts bring you down to my room. I'm not exactly dressed for entertaining."

Magnus laughed. He let his fingers tussle the small patch of hair' at Kieran's breastbone. "Well, Ma'am. I think that dress is ..." He donned his Southern drawl. "Quite fetching!"

Kieran reached up and took Magnus' hand. He pressed it tightly to his chest. They looked at each other for a long moment.

Kieran sat up on his haunches. "You know what?" He put his arms about Magnus' bare shoulders and Magnus pulled him close.

"What?"

"I'm having some very unclean thoughts myself," Kieran whispered breathily into Magnus' ear.

"Well." Magnus kissed Kieran's neck and then his cheek. "Are we just gonna go to hell thinking about it?"

"Hell no!" Kieran purred. He flipped Magnus over onto his back in the bed and straddled him.

Magnus lay back laughing. He ran his hands down Kieran's chest across his hardening nipples.

"You have rather good upper body strength for a sissy."

"Baby!" Kieran bent over Magnus' face. "You have no idea." In a series of quick, fluid motions he had Magnus' jean's unbuttoned and pulled them off. He was back straddling Magnus in an instant.

"Damn, boy!" Magnus was impressed. "And how long have you been practicing *that* move?"

"Well. I accomplish a lot of my practice through mental imagery. I've been known to learn entire pieces that way." Kieran snapped the waistband of Magnus' checkered boxers.

"Ouch!" Magnus laughed and snapped the rear waistband of Kieran's briefs.

Kieran stretched out atop Magnus and took his face in his hands. They kissed, long and unhurried. Suddenly Magnus rolled Kieran over onto his back and sat astride him. He threw his hands up in a mock stadium cheer having gained the upper hand.

"I like a man who takes charge," Kieran said unfazed. He pulled Magnus' face to his own for another kiss, a harder, more urgent kiss. Their lips finally parted and they were left staring into each other's eyes, panting.

"Well." Magnus smiled, his eyes locked on Kieran's. "I guess this is where we figure out who does what to whom."

"Well, you know what they say?" Kieran said, circling

his legs about Magnus' hips.

    "What?" Magnus asked.

    "Just do it!" Kieran said.

    And so Magnus did.

CHAPTER 12

Magnus woke first. He was surprised he had actually gotten some sleep. He looked down at Kieran, still sleeping, nestled against Magnus' chest. Magnus stroked Kieran's hair. He felt changed, but couldn't quite figure out how. He chuckled to himself at how quickly inexperience could turn to confidence . . . fear to desire. Magnus wondered if he should wake Kieran, but he was sleeping so soundly.

"I do love you," Magnus whispered, kissing Kieran's hair.

He decided to let Kieran sleep. He obviously needed it. But Magnus had wakened fully rested . . . exhilarated . . . hungry. He wondered if it was past time for dinner, and if so, would he be able to wrangle another snack from Henry.

Carefully, he slid out from under Kieran's head, leaving a pillow behind in his stead. He shook his head at

Kieran. The boy was completely out of it. He leaned over and kissed Kieran's lips several times. A smile broke over Kieran's face, but it was an unconscious one.

Magnus grabbed a quick shower and dressed. Kieran slumbered undisturbed. Dressed and still hungry, Magnus stood by the bed silently, watching Kieran's peaceful sleep. He bent over to kiss Kieran several more times.

"Love you," he whispered in Kieran's ear. Saying those words affected him deeply. He had never said that to another human being . . . save his mother. But now, the words took on a whole different meaning.

He slipped out of the room quietly and headed for the stairs. He stood for a moment on the landing, watching for any signs of life below. He descended the stairs self-consciously, wondering if he shouldn't have waited until Kieran was awake. The gnawing in his stomach, crying out for carbohydrates, kept him pushing forward.

He stopped at the bottom of the stairs and looked about. Nothing. A shuffling sound from the music room caught his attention and he headed across the marble tiled floor to the door, hoping that Henry would be amenable to providing some sort of pre-dinner sustenance.

"Henry?" He called out, breezing into the room. An unfamiliar figure sat behind the desk on the far side.

"Can I help you?" The man stood.

"I'm so sorry!" Magnus stopped in his tracks. "I thought you were . . . I didn't know . . ." Magnus caught himself. "I'm Magnus Kroft." He tried to look relaxed. "I'm a friend of Kieran's."

The man stood silently, looking Magnus over. His face was angular and the eyes were a dull grayish-blue. He moved from behind the desk.

"I'm Kieran's father." The man beckoned Magnus closer. "Aaron Matheson."

Magnus strode confidently across the room to stand in front of Kieran's father. "It's a pleasure to meet you, sir." He extended his hand. The man looked nothing like Kieran.

Mr. Matheson looked at the proffered hand. He took it only after Magnus began to exhibit some discomfort. "How do *you* do?" He gave Magnus' hand a subtle squeeze and released. "I was not aware that my son would be here this weekend."

"I think it was . . . a last minute decision," Magnus said, covering. "I don't think he was expecting you either."

"I'm sure he didn't." Mr. Matheson slowly smiled. He looked Magnus over once again. "You must be one of my son's," the corner of his mouth arched, "friends from school."

Magnus nodded uncomfortably. While Kieran's eyes were magnetic, his father's were oddly salacious. Magnus stepped back. "You have a beautiful house," he said, turning his attention to the room beyond.

"You look a bit more athletic looking than I would have expected from a friend of Kieran's." Kieran's father's stare did not falter.

"I'm a dancer," was all Magnus could think to respond.

The older man's lips turned up at one corner again.

Magnus tried to shrug off his apprehension. "Kieran's playing on a few of the selections I plan to use in recital at the end of the semester," he added quickly.

"Of course." Mr. Matheson finally took his eyes off Magnus. "To what do I owe this . . . last minute visit?"

Magnus struggled for a response. "There was a problem at school and Kieran wanted to get away for a short time."

"Really?" Mr. Matheson's greying eyebrows arched again. "A problem." He almost sneered. "What kind of . . . problem?"

"A student died . . . one of Kieran's friends."

"I see." Mr. Matheson considered this. "Poor Kieran." He inched closer to Magnus. "But it's good to know that Kieran has . . . other friends to support him." He put an arm about Magnus' shoulder. "So, Magnus is it? Come over to the sofa and tell me about yourself."

The thought of resisting crossed his mind, but Magnus allowed himself to be led to the large sectional sofa in front of the desk.

Mr. Matheson gestured for Magnus to take a seat. "It's rare that I get to meet one of Kieran's . . . friends." He chuckled at the final word. "I'm afraid Kieran's still at that age where parents are more of a nuisance than anything."

Magnus wasn't sure what to make of Kieran's father. He sat down and scooted over to maintain some distance as Mr. Matheson sat down beside him.

"Do you mind if I smoke?" Mr. Matheson extracted a silver cigarette case from his inside coat pocket.

Magnus only shrugged and sat back trying to look more at ease. In moments a halo of pungent smoke surrounded Mr. Matheson's visage.

"And where is my erstwhile son?" Kieran's father asked with a yawn.

"He's taking a nap," Magnus said, pointing upwards. "I think the flight tired him out."

"Really?" Mr. Matheson flicked his ash into a crystal

dish on the side table. "And I thought he would be anxiously awaiting my arrival."

A noncommittal smile was the best response Magnus could concoct.

"No matter." Mr. Matheson leaned back onto the overstuffed sofa and crossed his legs. "You'll be charming enough company before dinner."

The double doors opened and Henry appeared. "Will you be having a cocktail before dinner, sir?"

"Absolutely!" Mr. Matheson became more animated. He turned to Magnus. "We're having martinis, right Henry?"

"Very good, sir." Henry started to leave.

"If it's all right, Henry, I'd like a bottled water." Magnus sat up straight. "And some crackers or cheese or whatever you might have handy."

"Oh, how disappointing," Mr. Matheson said. "Henry usually makes a pitcher for me." He nodded to Henry and waved him off. "Now I'll have to drink it all myself."

Again Magnus only smiled.

"So." Mr. Matheson relaxed again. "How long have you and my little Kieran been . . . friends?" The corner of his mouth arched suggestively.

"Only a couple of weeks . . . since the start of the semester." Magnus tried not to look at him.

"Ah." Mr. Matheson nodded. "I suppose things . . . develop faster for boys your age."

Magnus didn't like the tone of the conversation. "This is a very nice beach house," he said quickly. "Kieran said it's been in your family for some years."

Mr. Matheson cocked his head to one side. "Oh, yes. The old girl's been around for some time." His mouth arched again. "She's seen a lot of scandalous things." He chuckled again. "But she never tells."

Again Magnus didn't know how to respond. "The beaches where I'm from are hot and humid," he said quickly. "This is a very mild climate. I was surprised."

"Oh." Mr. Matheson shifted position in Magnus' direction. "It can get quite hot here too."

The double doors opened to Magnus' relief and Henry entered carrying a tray of drinks.

"Just sit those down here," Mr. Matheson said, gesturing to the coffee table. Henry complied silently and left just as unobtrusively. Mr. Matheson filled his martini glass from the large silver shaker. "Are you sure you won't have one with me?" He asked, plaintively.

"No thanks." Magnus reached for the bottled water on the side of the tray. "Water's fine for me." He frowned in disappointment that the tray held no solid nourishment.

Mr. Matheson took a long drink from his glass, half-emptying it. "Damn good!" he said, coming up for air. "Bless that Henry."

Magnus took a tentative sip from the unfamiliar, imported bottle of water. Satisfied that it was just water, he took a large swig. Mr. Matheson emptied his own glass and poured himself another.

"How inhospitable of Kieran to leave you alone in a strange place," he said, once more eying Magnus.

"I don't mind. I'd rather he rest up."

"Indeed." Mr. Matheson studied Magnus, who tried not to squirm under such intense scrutiny. "My dear, Magnus." Mr. Matheson's smile made the hair on Magnus' arms stand on end. "You have the blondest hair I think I've ever seen. You must have very close, Nordic ancestry."

Magnus studied his bottled water silently.

"I do like the Nordic races," Kieran's father continued. "There are too many fakes around, don't you think? They appear to be blonde at first, but, later on . . . you find out differently!" He chucked suggestively. "Right?"

Magnus sat his water down and stood. He walked over to the book shelves, relieved to put a little distance between himself and Kieran's father. "Kieran said you collect first editions," he said, trying to redirect the conversation.

"I collect many things," Mr. Matheson said, emptying his glass. He sat it down on the tray with a flourish and got up to join Magnus. "I like the leather coverings on old books." He closed in on Magnus. "But I do like the crispness of new ones as well." He stood beside Magnus smiling down at him. "Yes, I can definitely see what's behind Kieran's attraction to you."

Magnus tried to step away, but Mr. Matheson threw an arm about him. He squeezed Magnus' shoulder. "You are well-developed for such a young man."

Magnus' heart was pounding. He tried to shrug the unwelcomed arm from his shoulder. "I should probably check on Kieran," he said, struggling unsuccessfully.

"Kieran will be just fine." Kieran's father grabbed Magnus from behind, reaching down for Magnus' crotch.

"What the hell!" Magnus grabbed the older man's hand before it made contact.

Kieran's father stumbled backward, breaking his hold on Magnus.

"Hello . . . Daddy!" Kieran's voice boomed across the room.

"Kieran," Kieran's father stammered. He quickly

regained his composure and returned to the sofa and his pitcher of martinis. "What a pleasant surprise."

"I see you've met my friend, Magnus." Kieran walked across the parquet floor slowly, his eyes flashing. He looked at Magnus, his expression a mixture of pain and shame.

Magnus shuddered, shaking off the shock and disgust. He took a deep breath and met Kieran's pleading gaze. "Hi," he said, managing a smile. "Am I glad you're up!" Magnus' smile, forced as it was, reassured Kieran.

Kieran strode up to face Magnus with his back to his father. "I missed you," he whispered, putting a nervous hand to Magnus' chest.

Magnus relaxed. He looked down into Kieran's eyes. "I damn sure missed you." He put his hand to Kieran's and squeezed it reassuringly.

"I'll handle this," Kieran whispered. He turned to his father. "I wasn't expecting to see you this weekend." He walked over to his father and looked down at him with undisguised disgust. "How's mother doing?"

"I'm sure she's doing just fine," Mr. Matheson said, fidgeting with his martini glass.

"I was thinking about calling her . . . you know . . . let her know what's going on in my life."

"I'm sure she'd like that," his father said, smiling up at him nervously. He downed his martini. "Give her my love."

"I'll do that." Kieran looked back at Magnus. "My father and I try to keep mother happy. After all . . ." He gave his father a frozen glare. "She pays for all this."

Kieran's father ignored him and poured the last drops from the silver martini shaker.

"Yes," Kieran continued, returning to Magnus. "My

father's family went bankrupt and so he was lucky enough
to marry my mother. Her family was quite ...
comfortable." He took Magnus' hand. "My father has a
very difficult job ... keeping both my mother and me
happy." He turned another withering glare at his father.
"Don't you, daddy?"

Mr. Matheson's mouth twitched.

Kieran cocked his head at him. "Do you really think I
should call mother?" he asked as if it were a threat. "I
wouldn't want to upset her for any reason." His tone
grew more ominous. "For your sake, right daddy?"

Mr. Matheson grabbed up his empty martini glass and
jumped up agitatedly. "I need a refill." He started for the
door.

"Just a minute, daddy." Kieran wasn't finished with
him. "You don't have to stay here on my account. I know
you'd be more comfortable in your Manhattan apartment.
You can probably just catch the train ... if you hurry."

Mr. Matheson turned slowly. He met Kieran's glare.
"Perhaps you're right, my dear boy." He pulled open the
double doors. "It was good seeing you again," he turned
back with a bored expression, "son." He left Magnus and
Kieran alone.

Kieran's whole body seemed to fall in on itself.

"Not to worry," Magnus said, pulling him close.

"I'm sorry." Kieran sounded drained. "I probably
should have warned you."

"I can take care of myself." Magnus turned Kieran
around to face him. "Are you alright?"

Kieran collapsed against Magnus chest. "I hate him!"

"I know." Magnus embraced him. "And I think he
knows it."

"You just thought you knew how screwed up I am."

"I don't think you're screwed up." Magnus kissed Kieran's forehead tenderly. "But I am pretty sure you're family is screwed up."

"Still," Kieran said, dropping his eyes, ashamed. "I'm sorry you had to experience that."

"Kieran?" Magnus put a hand under Kieran's chin and pulled the smaller youth's face up to his. "I . . . did . . . What I mean to say is . . . did he ever . . . hurt you?"

Kieran smiled up at him, shaking his head. "No. I'm sure he's thought about it . . . but, he was too afraid of mother."

"Now her I would like to meet."

"You might be disappointed there, too."

"Poor little rich girl." Magnus kissed Kieran lightly.

"And we have to fly back tomorrow evening."

They embraced.

"Enough melancholy!" Magnus gave Kieran a sharp slap on the butt. "We can't let yesterday or tomorrow spoil today!"

"That's right."

Magnus stretched, throwing his arms into the air. "What other attractions does this old, run-down beach shack have to offer?" he asked.

"You mean besides me?" Kieran pushed him away playfully.

"Including you." Magnus pulled him back into his arms.

Kieran lolled against Magnus chest. There was no artificial scent about Magnus. Kieran once again pressed his face into the nape of Magnus' neck and breathed him in deeply. "Well," he began, struck with an idea. "There is the Jacuzzi by the pool. It's very hot, very bubbly, and very relaxing."

"Sorry." Magnus' face fell. "I didn't bring any trunks with me. I had this idea it would be cold up here—too cold for swimming."

Kieran slipped his hands under the back of Magnus' shirt to better feel the warmth of him. "You silly, unspoiled treasure," he said, smiling up at Magnus as suggestively as he knew how. "You will have absolutely no need for a bathing suit in the Jacuzzi."

"You are a nasty little boy, aren't you?" Magnus bent down to rub his nose against Kieran's. "Let's . . ." He straightened. "Wait a minute." He looked at Kieran with a sheepish grin. "Could we get some supper first?"

"Apparently this man will not live on love alone." Kieran rolled his eyes and poked Magnus in the stomach. "Come on. We'll grab something in the kitchen and take it out to the deck with us."

"Let me finish my bottle of water first." Magnus broke away from Kieran to retrieve his water from the coffee table. "I'll be right there."

Kieran did not object. "Don't keep me waiting!" He disappeared into the outer foyer.

Magnus took a deep breath, thinking. He sat the bottle of water back down and went over to the desk. As he had hoped, Kieran had left the computer up. He sat down and studied the screen. It was Mr. Matheson's e-mail. Magnus clicked on the contacts button and studied the list of unfamiliar names until one caught his eye.

"Bingo!" He clicked on the contact and dashed off a quick message. He read it over hastily and then hit the send button. "Good." He stood again but never took his eyes off the monitor. After a moment, satisfied, he broke away and started for the door. "Here we go," he muttered to himself and headed off to find Kieran.

CHAPTER 13

"We are not safe! None of us!" Kieran's whisper, laden with fear and urgency, swept over the small group of listeners.

Sitting next to Kieran, Magnus nodded in vigorous agreement, staring down at his tightly clasped hands. Kieran looked from one teen to the other, searching for some sign he was being heard.

"These people are murderers," he said sharply. "Which one of us will be next?"

"You're sure it was Alex?" Tommie asked. "I mean, it was dark and . . ."

"It wasn't dark!" Magnus said, squeezing Kieran's hand supportively. "The lights were on. There was no mistake. It was Alex. Dead!"

"They had cut him open!" Kieran's voice broke into a sob.

"Okay, okay!" Tommie said. "We believe you." He

turned to Magnus. "It's just hard to accept that Alex is . . . dead."

The group sat for a moment in silence.

Gail drummed her fingers on the table. "Well?" she said to Allison."

Allison refused to meet her gaze.

"You tell them or I will!" Gail said, her level of agitation rising.

Everyone's attention turned to Allison.

"What's going on?" Kieran looked from Tommie to Allison. "Allison?"

Tommie sat like a beaten puppy.

"Tommie?" Kieran persisted.

"I guess this is where she tells everyone we're breaking up," Tommie said, putting his face in his hands.

"What?" Magnus sat up. "I don't believe it."

"This is my fault!" Kieran looked devastated. "My stupid mouth!" He groaned, face in hands.

"Everyone put a cork in it! This is about Allison," Gail ordered, hammering the table with her fists.

The others sat back. Disbelief clouded their faces.

"It's no one's fault but mine." Tommie looked down at the table. "I . . ."

"Shut up, dickhead!" Gail jumped up and went behind the suffering boy. She bent over him, hands akimbo. "This is not about you! Now get over yourself?"

Tommie leaned away from her, but didn't speak. His own self-imposed guilt robbed him of any defense.

"Tell them!" Gail demanded, moving up behind Allison. She put her hands on Allison's shoulders. "They need to know."

Allison clasped her hands, eyes closed, as if praying. Finally she took a deep breath. "Fine." Her voice was shaking. "I got called down to the infirmary just before the weekend started." There was shocked silence. "I've been started on a new pill by Dr. Turner. They want to test its . . . effectiveness on a girl athlete."

"The bastards!" Gail sank back into her chair. "Fucking bastards!"

Kieran and Magnus took each other's hand, to stunned to speak. Tommie raised his head slowly, his face contorted by painful emotion. He could not bring himself to look at Allison. Sammy sat, sobbing softly beside him.

"Well?" Gail's voice was hoarse. "Somebody say something, goddamn it!"

"There's not much to say, Gail," Allison stated flatly. "We all know what it means."

"That's not good enough!" Gail clenched her fists. "We need a plan. We've got to deal with this." Her anger exploded. "We've got to do something for Christ's sake?"

Kieran made an unintelligible sound into his hands and bounded up from his chair. He paced the length of the table, back and forth, pounding the palm of his hand against his forehead.

Tommie slowly turned to face Allison. His mouth opened but he could utter no sound. His devastated expression affected Allison deeply. Tears streamed from his eyes and his whole body seemed to quake ominously. "No!" screamed from his mouth, carrying all the guilt and rage into a prolonged wail. He exploded from his chair, slamming it back against the wall. "Screw this shit!" He stumbled blindly for the door.

"Tommie!" Kieran cried out.

Tommie continued, oblivious. "I'll kill every goddamn—"

"Stop!" Magnus sprung from his chair and almost

tackled Tommie before he reached the door. "You're not going!"

He and Tommie wrestled until Magnus locked him in a bear hug, pinning Tommie's hands to his sides.

"Let me go!" Tommie wailed.

"I will not!" Magnus said through clenched teeth.

Gail bounded over to them. "Stop it!" She swung the back of her hand, slapping Tommie across the face. The sound echoed through the room. "Straighten up!" She boomed directly into Tommie's face.

The fight drained from Tommie's body as quickly as it had erupted. He slumped back against Magnus, sobbing.

"You didn't have to hit him, Gail!" Allison cried out.

Gail rubbed the back of her hand, almost in tears herself. "I didn't hurt him," she insisted. "His jaws like a rock." She held her hands out pleading. "I just wanted to get his attention!"

"All right, all right." Allison took Tommie's face in her hands. "I've got him," she said to a relieved Magnus. "Come here." She pulled Tommie to her. "Come back and sit down, before everyone in the school hears you."

Tommie calmed down at her touch. He looked up at her, a pleading look. Allison sighed and patted his cheeks.

"Okay, okay," she cooed. "I'll stop punishing you. I know you love me."

Tommie embraced her with a clumsy urgency, as if Allison might change her mind. He stepped back, his mind a little clearer. "Allison, you didn't take the pill, did you?" He asked.

She tried to look away, but he nudged her face back to his.

"Allison?"

Allison pulled away and went back to her chair, leaving Tommie with his hands up in a silent plea.

"Allison?" Tommie called again, stumbling over to her.

"I didn't have much of a choice," she said softly.

"Why, Allison?" Tommie asked in disbelief.

"I think they're catching on to us. It's not a pill anymore." Allison met Magnus' eyes. "Now they give you something to drink. Not like you can hide it under your tongue now."

"Damn it to hell!" was all Magnus could manage.

"We're all screwed!" Sammy rocked back and forth in his chair.

Kieran rushed over to Tommie. He stood in front of the boy, hand to mouth.

Tommie gave him a detached look. "We're in the same boat again," he said.

"I'm shit!" Kieran cried out. He dissolved into sobs and threw himself into Tommie's waiting arms. Tommie glanced up at Magnus and tried to smile.

"Excuse me, but I believe this shit is yours."

"He's really sorry about what he said to you and Allison," Magnus said. "Before ... you know ... that virginity thing."

"Hit me!" Kieran cried. "I deserve it!" He stood up stoically, drying his tears. "Go ahead. It'll make you feel better."

Instead Tommie wrapped Kieran in his arms. "It won't make me feel any better than it will you," he said.

"What are we gonna do?" Kieran wailed, taking Tommie's face in his hands.

Tommy shook his head and released Kieran. He sat down in the chair next to Allison and took her hand.

"This is ridiculous!" Magnus made a wide gesture. "I'm not doing this anymore. They can't make us!"

"We're just kids to them," Allison argued. "They're in control, not us."

The group settled into chairs about the table. Kieran remained on his feet, a funny look on his face.

"Come sit down by me," Magnus said to him, patting the seat beside him.

"No!" Kieran stood his ground, looking at each of them. "Magnus was right. This is ridiculous."

"What are you going on about," Tommie asked in disgust. "We've got serious planning to do!"

"Don't you see?" Kieran waved a hand in the air. "I don't know about you, but I'm no kid!"

"So *you're* a man now?" Tommie snorted with a helping of sarcasm.

"Aren't you?" Kieran gave him a hard look.

Everyone looked at him, confused.

"I am not a child anymore," Kieran continued. "I will not be told what I have to do by anyone—not my father, not a teacher, no one. I can say no. *We* can say no! Loud and clear!"

"What do you mean?" Magnus reached out for him.

"It's simple!" Kieran broke into a euphoric smile and threw himself into the chair next to Magnus. "Refuse the medication. Tell them you don't want it and you won't take it."

"Just say no to drugs!" Gail said, mocking.

"Wait a minute." Tommie held up his hand. "He's right. We've been thinking like kids—doing everything we're told." He turned to Allison. "Don't take anymore, sweetheart. Tell them no! What can they do?"

"Dr. Powell will be pissed," squeaked Sammy from

the corner.

"Eventually," Gail said, "you know they'll come around to forcing us . . . somehow."

"Maybe." Magnus put an arm about Kieran. "But this'll throw a big wrench in their current methods and plans. It'll buy time . . . create confusion."

"Hell, yeah!" Tommie raised a hand and Magnus returned a high five. He grinned at Kieran. "Come over here you little smart-ass smarty. I'm gonna kiss you!"

Kieran threw his hands up in defense. "Stay, dog!"

"If you don't mind," Magnus said, pulling Kieran toward him. "I'll take care of that myself."

He kissed Kieran, suppressing a laugh, knowing all the others were watching.

Tommy let out a howl and gave Allison a kiss.

"Get a room!" Gail groaned. She turned to Sammy. "And stop rocking! What's wrong with you, anyway?"

Sammy looked shell-shocked. Cringing at Gail's rebuff, his hands began to shake.

"Come here, Sammy." Tommie motioned to Sammy to come sit in the empty chair next to him.

Sammy looked afraid to move.

"Come here," Tommy repeated softly. "It's okay. Come talk to me."

Sammy gave Gail a cautious glance and circled the table in the other direction. Gail rolled her eyes but, aware of Allison's stony glare, thought better of it. Sammy plopped himself down beside Tommie.

"Now, what's wrong?" Tommie asked, putting a protective arm about the boy.

Sammy tried to speak, but began to shake even more.

"Whoa, whoa!" Tommy wrapped his arms about the smaller boy.

Sammy pressed against Tommie. He looped his arms about Tommie's neck and sobbed softly into the collar of Tommie's shirt.

Tommie tightened his embrace. "Come on, little one," he said soothingly. "I'm not gonna let anyone hurt you."

Magnus leaned across the table at the two. "Sammy, we're all your friends," he assured the boy. "Tommie's right. No one here is gonna let you down."

Sammy wrestled a slip of paper from his pants pocket. He held it up for Tommie's inspection. "I . . . got . . . this . . . ," he managed between sobs, "in . . . English . . . this morning." He relinquished the paper to Tommie.

Tommie shook it open with a free hand and studied it. His face darkened. "It's a hall pass for this afternoon," he declared, his voice low and edgy. "Powell wants him to report to the infirmary at two."

"Oh my God!" Allison gasped.

"That's three of us." Kieran massaged his temples. "They're accelerating the whole process."

"We've made them nervous," Magnus agreed.

Tommie grabbed Sammy's chin and pointed the boy's face up to his own. "Don't worry, Sammy." He held the young teen tightly. "Just tell them you don't want it and you won't take it."

"Say no, kid!" Gail bellowed. "Sons of bitches!"

Sammy was quiet for a moment. Allison handed him a napkin and he snorted into it.

"I'm not as old as all of you," Sammy said, his chest heaving in stifled sobs. "Not as big. Dr. Powell'll make me take the medicine."

"No!" Tommie shook Sammy's chin for emphasis. "No one can make you unless they hold you down and force you." Sammy started to speak, but Tommie put a hand over his mouth. "I said, no," he repeated. "No one's gonna force you 'cause we won't let 'em? We'll go to the infirmary with you."

"Of course we will," Allison cooed soothingly.

"But all of you'll get in trouble," Sammy said, trying to brighten at this turn of events. "You'll have to miss class. Dr. Powell'll—"

"No!" Tommie shook Sammy's chin once more. "We could care less about that. You're not taking that medicine! Am I clear?"

Sammy looked up into Tommie's eyes and nodded. He buried his face into Tommie's chest.

"Here's the plan," Tommie said, turning to the others. "Very simple. We go down there with Sammy and we tell that son-of-a-bitch we're not taking any more crap from him. No more experimenting on us!" He tapped his fist on the table. "We all stand together!"

Allison, Gail and Magnus nodded.

"That won't put an end to it all," Kieran cautioned, biting his lower lip. "Like Gail said, eventually they'll come to the conclusion that they'll have to force us."

For a moment no one spoke.

"Then we'll have to fight," Tommie said evenly. "Bottom line!"

Gail stood, fists clenched at her side. "Now that's what I'm talking about," she said. "I'm done with this shit. Bring 'em on!"

"Not yet!" Kieran furrowed his brow, thinking. "Remember what the Godfather said. Never let them know what you're thinking. We'll have to be very low key at first. Just a polite refusal to cooperate. We'll escalate our response based on theirs."

"Don't you see?" Sammy sat up drying his tears. "We can't win a fight. They've got the means to win and we don't!"

"Sammy, don't underestimate your big brothers and sisters," Tommie said, and tussled the boy's hair. "And don't underestimate yourself either, little bro!" His confidence made Sammy relax a little. Tommy looked up at the other teens. "I don't want him going down there by himself. I say we all go together—one united front."

"Agreed." Kieran nodded.

"You're not taking anymore vitamin garbage," Tommie ordered, grabbing Allison's hand. "Agreed?"

"I feel so stupid."

"No, baby!" Tommie shook his head vigorously. "That has nothing to do with it."

"He's right, Allison," Magnus agreed. "It may seem stupid now, but I never thought that saying no was an option either. It's a mindset. It would have been difficult to do alone . . . but not together!"

"Well let's get it over with!" Gail stood. "I can't wait to see old shit-face's face when we tell him." The resulting laughter cleared the air and even Sammy smiled.

"Come on, Sammy," Tommie said, lifting the boy to his feet. "You're taking your tribe with you to see Powell."

"Who's gonna tell him?" Sammy stammered. "Do I have to tell him? Couldn't . . ."

"I'll do the talking!" Kieran rose from his chair with an imperious wave. "I've been waiting to tell that ass where to get off for a long time!"

"Take it easy, Godfather!" Magnus stood beside him. "They really don't know for sure that we know anything yet. Like you said, let's not give away our whole hand until we're called on it."

"What do you suggest?"

"What I suggest is that we just say we've decided to take charge of our own health; that we prefer a more natural approach to our . . . nutrition?"

"I like it." Tommie stood, pulling Allison up with him. "That's our story."

"We can say we've all become Buddhist or something," Allison said. "You know . . . vegetarian."

"I'm not becoming a vegetarian for anyone!" Gail pushed her chair back. "Let's just tell 'em that we've all decided to adopt an all-natural approach to health—something we've seen on television."

"Okay." Kieran started for the door. "But if he gets pissy about it, I'm telling him to kiss our asses!"

"That's my man!" Magnus grabbed Kieran's shoulders and followed behind.

"And don't you forget it!" Kieran said, giving Magnus a sly over-the-shoulder glance.

They paraded out into the hall and headed down toward the elevator. Gail took over the lead, walking as fast as her short but muscled legs would go, forcing Magnus and Kieran to power walk to keep up. Allison walked between Tommie and Sammy holding their hands. All the other students were already back in class, and the daring move to skip class further fueled the ever growing hyperactivity of the small, rebel group of teens storming through the empty halls.

Gail assailed the infirmary door first, rapping loudly and repeatedly on the metal door. The group gathered behind her, panting from the exertion, watching the door for some sign of life. As if in anticipation, the door swung inward.

"Yes?" A middle-aged woman peered out at the teens.

"We're here to see Powell," Gail stated flatly.

"Are you referring to *Dr.* Powell?" The older woman brushed the wrinkles from her ankle length skirt.

"Oh, you know the guy," Gail retorted with undisguised sarcasm. "Calls himself a doctor, does he?"

"Young lady, I don't like your tone."

"Yeah, well I'm no lady!" Gail pushed past her. "And I don't think much of your Holy Ghost hairdo either."

The group of teens nervously followed Gail into the room.

"What's going on here?" Dr. Powell looked up from the counter covered with an array of medical charts he was writing on. "Ms. Gordy?" His eyebrows rose as he studied the group before him. "I don't think I asked to see all of you."

Kieran stepped forward. "But Sammy had an appointment," he stated, his voice almost syrupy with sweetness. "We thought we'd all come down with him."

"I see." Dr. Powell adjusted his eyeglasses and looked down at Sammy. "I think that Sammy is old enough to see his doctor on his own."

Sammy sidled closer to Tommie.

"Of course he is," Kieran responded. "But we thought we all needed to see you."

"Indeed?" Powell settled back onto his stool by the counter.

"We've all made a decision together," Kieran said. "And, since it also involves Sammy, we thought we should all fill you in now."

Dr. Powell stared at the group. He stood, taking off his glasses. "Well," he said. "This sounds important."

"Not really." Kieran smiled disarmingly. "We thought

this would be easier than your having to make time to hear us individually."

"I see." Dr. Powell sat back down. "Very considerate of you all since I am very busy. What is it you all need to tell me?"

"First of all," Kieran gestured to his friends, "We want to thank you for your concern about our physical well-being."

Dr. Powell only nodded.

"But," Kieran continued, "After doing some reading and speaking to our families and former teachers, we've decided to take a more natural . . . a holistic approach to our health and performance enhancement."

Magnus could not help but grin at Kieran's verbal ingenuity.

"For these reasons," Kieran paused, "and others, we must regrettably decline any more of your . . . vitamin therapy."

"I see." Dr. Powell's face betrayed no concern.

"We think it best to try and get all our vitamin requirements from natural foods and, with your permission of course, I'll make some suggestions to cafeteria staff." Before Dr. Powell could respond, Kieran continued, "and of course, you can continue to monitor the health aspects of our performance and we'd welcome any suggestions you have about diet." He beamed a confident smile.

Dr. Powell sat silent. He put his reading glasses back on and studied each student individually over the top of the glasses. Kieran detected a slight twitching at the corner of Dr. Powell's right eye. Powell focused his gaze on Sammy.

"I believe we have an appointment, Sammy," he said,

narrowing his eyes at the boy.

Sammy cringed against Tommie and Tommie put a protective arm about him. He met Dr. Powell's nervous glare.

"Sammy's terrified of Doctors," Tommie said. "He's asked me to be here with him during your exam, right Sammy?"

Sammy nodded vigorously, refusing to look at the doctor.

"That would be highly irregular," Dr. Powel said, clearing his throat. "And a violation of doctor-patient confidentiality."

"Nonsense!" Kieran gave a dismissive wave. "There's no violation if Sammy says it's okay." He adopted an expression of parental concern. "You know how prone Sammy is to panic attacks in situations like this. Tommie's presence will keep him calm—will make your exam much easier."

"Very well, then." Dr. Powell's face was devoid of expression. "But I think I'll postpone Sammy's appointment now for when I have more time available."

"Not a problem," Kieran said cheerfully. "Just let Sammy and Tommie know when." He signaled to the others to leave.

The group piled out the door. Kieran was last out and shut the door quietly. Everyone was breathing heavily, as if they had been holding their breath before.

"I guess that went well," Kieran said, hands on his hips.

Sammy rushed over to him and threw his arms about Kieran, hugging him clumsily. "You're a genius, Kieran!" His young pubescent voice broke.

"You *were* rather amazing," Magnus said, giving

Kieran's shoulder a squeeze.

"He didn't look very happy about this, "Gail said frowning.

"He'll get over it," Tommie said, laughing.

"That's what I'm afraid of," Gail retorted.

"He can eat shit and die!" Kieran said, breaking free of Sammy. He took Magnus' hand and pulled him toward the elevator. Magnus glanced back at the others.

"Looks like we have a revolution," he said.

The other's laughed, following behind.

The mood in the infirmary was very different. Dr. Powell sat staring at the door. The nurse stood fidgeting with her lab coat by the door. Dr. Powell's face was no longer a blank canvass. Instead, a dark anger had painted itself across his demeanor. After a moment, he turned back to the stack of charts on the counter. He dug through them, pulling out six.

"Harriet," he said to the nurse. "Call the Committee. We need to meet this evening."

"Yes, Dr. Powell." Harriet almost curtsied. "Shall I reschedule an appointment for that boy?"

Dr. Powell's look shut her up quickly. She nodded quickly and headed to the back of the infirmary to put away the unused exam equipment. Dr. Powell sat, thumbing through the six charts, tapping his annoyance on the metal counter with the nail of his index finger.

Suddenly, his face relaxed. A sardonic smile broke free, released by some epiphany. He gathered up the charts and headed for his office. "We'll see!" was all he said, shuffling out the door.

CHAPTER 14

"You've got to be kidding!" Kieran let the basketball bounce past him. "I do *not* play basketball."

"Come on girly-man," Gail called out heading after the ball. "It's about time you learned a sport." She lobbed the ball over to Tommie who promptly sank a shot cleanly through the hoop.

"At least pretend," Tommie said, shaking his head at Kieran. He began strutting about the center court waving at the applause from the imaginary crowd.

"I . . . do . . . not . . . play . . . sports!" Kieran repeated venomously.

Magnus finished lacing up his sneakers and headed out onto the court. "But, Kieran, this was the only room we could risk being spied on but not heard," he said. "Remember, you said we were all going to get healthier."

Kieran crossed his arms and stood his ground. "I'd rather eat turtle dung!" he announced defiantly.

"Turtle wha . . . ?" Tommie sighed with exasperation. "You are hopeless."

He started after Gail who had caught the rebound and was charging the net. She dribbled the ball aggressively about the court, but Tommie kept up his press, keeping her from the net and a clear shot.

"Take the shot, Allison!" Gail passed the ball across to center court where Allison had positioned herself.

In a quick, fluid motion, Allison sprang into the air, arced the ball high. "Two points!" she yelled as it fell through the net without touching the rim.

"Damn, girl!" Tommie stood stunned.

"Get over it, *boy*," Gail hollered running over to Allison. The two girls exchanged a high five. "You X chromosome's don't have any monopoly on the game." She blew Tommie a raspberry.

The action stopped as Sammy came bounding into the gym. "Hey guys!" he called out.

Tommie saw the excitement in the boys face. "Okay, kid, what have you gone and done?"

"I'm a genius, too!" Sammy grinned broadly and picked up the ball, dribbling it clumsily.

"Nerd boy, you can't even dribble!" Gail taunted him from side court.

Sammy ignored her. He tried to dribble around Tommie.

"Careful, little girl," Tommie said laughing. "You could hurt yourself." He moved to block Sammy's progress toward the net.

"I did it," Sammy managed to say between pants for breath. He tripped over Tommie's foot, but somehow managed to regain his balance.

"Did what?" Tommie feigned a few slaps at the ball,

letting Sammy retain control."

"I broke the encryption!" Sammy tried unsuccessfully to pass Tommie on the right.

"What encryption?" Tommie asked, letting Sammy keep control of the ball.

"The wireless surveillance system." Sammy made a lunge to the left. "I can access all of it!"

"What?" Tommie stopped in his tracks. His eyes widened.

Sammy pushed past Tommie's frozen arms toward the net. He took the shot and, to the amazed attention of the others, the ball banked off the backboard through the net. "I made it!" Sammy hopped about excitedly. "Two points! I should go to the pros!"

"Whoa, whoa!" Tommie motioned the others over. "Take it easy, bro."

"God, you're pathetic," Gail said to Tommie. "You let the little dweeb take you!"

"Gail!" Allison slapped Gail on the arm. "Be quiet. Something's happened."

Kieran and Magnus ran over to join the group.

"What did you do?" Kieran asked breathlessly. "What's happened?"

"Shhh," Tommie silenced the group. He held Sammy by the shoulders. "Are you sure?"

"Uh huh," Sammy said ecstatic.

Tommie commanded, "Bounce the ball, Gail. Loudly!"

Gail pounded the court with the ball, dribbling furiously, covering the sound of their voices. Tommie smiled up at the others.

"The kid's broken into the surveillance system."

Kieran's hand went to his mouth. "Powell has mikes

and cameras everywhere. Even in his office."

"Oh!" Sammy grabbed Tommie's arm. "I almost forgot. Dr. Powell's meeting with some people in his office now."

"What?" Kieran stopped dead in his tracks. "Where?"

"In the board room," Sammy said, sheepishly.

"Is there surveillance in the board room?" Tommie asked, pulling the boy around to face him.

Sammy looked like he had been slapped.

"I'm not upset with you," Tommie assured him. "I'm just excited about your breakthrough."

"There's no camera," Sammy said, brightening. "But Powell does record everything that's said. I have a feed coming into the computer lab, and . . . Oh, I almost forgot, I'm recording the meeting now. Hope it doesn't go on too long 'cause the disk space . . ."

"That's my boy!" Tommie cried out. He grabbed the boy up in a bear hug, swinging Sammy about in a circle. "I love this kid!"

"He means as a friend, sweetheart," Kieran said, patting Sammy's arm. "He shook his head at Tommie. "Stop confusing him."

"You're not confused, are you, bro?" Tommie asked, setting Sammy back on his feet.

"No," Sammy giggled, shaking his head. "You're a breeder."

The group broke into laughter.

"You tell him, Sammy," Magnus interjected.

"Yeah," Tommie said suggestively. He took Sammy's face in his hands. "But if the kid can set us up to listen in the next 15 minutes, I'm gonna personally teach him how to French kiss!"

"He's good at it, too!" Allison said, giving Sammy a

knowing look.

Sammy looked like he might faint. Just as suddenly, he broke away and made a run for the door. "Everyone to the computer lab," he yelled over his shoulder, almost tripping over his brief case on the floor. He turned back to Tommie, startling the group with his own suggestive grin. "I'll have everything ready in 10 minutes!" He grabbed up his case and dashed out the door.

"Our little boy is growing up." Kieran said. He took Tommie's hand and brushed an imaginary tear from his eyes.

Allison whooped and gave Tommie a sharp slap on the butt. "Looks like I may have a little competition," she said.

"Competition's a good thing," Tommie said with a peacockish swagger. He started for the door. "Come on! You know I like an audience."

The group followed him out, laughing.

Sammy was nowhere in sight. They ran down the hall into the maze of classrooms toward the computer lab. A security guard stepped out of a doorway behind them.

"Stop!" He yelled gruffly. The teens spun on their heels to face him. "Where do you trouble makers think you're going?"

"None of your business, Hardcastle," Tommie said, stepping up into the guard's face. "We're on our break time."

Hardcastle grabbed Tommie by the arm and slammed him up against the wall.

"You watch your mouth, punk! I . . ."

Hardcastle stopped short, looking down at his crotch. Gail's hand held his gonads in a tight clench.

"Let go of him now, Hardcastle," she said evenly.

"Or I'll rip your goddamn puny little balls up over your head?"

Hardcastle broke out in a cold sweat.

Magnus leaned in. "You'd better worry more about what we'll do to your ass when she's through with you," he said, leering.

"You punks'll pay for this," Hardcastle sputtered. "You're being watched. There'll be ten other security down here any minute."

Gail gave a good squeeze, dropping the guard to his knees grunting. "Funny," she said directly in the man's face. "I don't hear anyone coming."

Kieran looked up at the every present cameras. Still, no sign of rescue for the incapacitated guard. He chuckled. "Sammy," was all he needed to say.

Gail gave another good squeeze and butted her head into the side of the guard's head. A loud crack resonated through the hall and the guard fell out cold.

"Ow!" Gail rubbed her forehead. "That felt good!"

"Hurry!" Kieran called out, starting back down the hall.

The group galloped after him.

"You okay?" Magnus saw Tommie massaging his neck.

"He caught me off guard," Tommie said with a shrug. He sped up behind Gail and took her by the shoulders. "Thanks, Big Mama!" He gave her shoulders a squeeze. "Guess I'll have to kiss you, too."

"You try it," Gail said, escaping his massaging, "and I'll head butt you in those marbles you call balls!"

Allison shrieked with laughter.

"Feel the love, girl!" Tommie continued to tease Gail. "It might change you." He poked her in the small of the back.

Gail took a good natured swing at him, missing by a wide margin.

"Keep up!" Kieran ordered, rounding the next corner.

Magnus caught up to him. "What's wrong?" he asked, sensing Kieran's worry.

The fast pace was making Kieran's breathing hard. "I don't know." He grabbed Magnus hand. "Something doesn't feel right."

They turned into the technology wing that held the computer lab. Magnus could see the lab door standing open and the lights were on. Kieran pushed ahead and dove into the doorway with Magnus right behind him. They stopped dead in their tracks.

"I'm very disappointed in you, Kieran." Dr. Powell was standing behind one of the computer monitors, an armed guard by his side. He had a very frightened Sammy by the collar.

The rest of the teens tumbled into the lab behind Kieran and Magnus.

Tommie held Allison behind him, trying to keep her hidden. "Get out!" he whispered loudly over his shoulder.

"Nonsense!" Dr. Powell gestured to the door. "Come in Allison. All of you."

"Let him go!" Magnus said, pointing to Sammy.

The others were suddenly pushed further into the room by two more guards carrying large, black semi-automatic pistols.

"I'll give the orders here," Dr. Powell boomed. "I'm afraid you kids are in a lot of trouble." Sammy broke away from Dr. Powell and ran into Allison's arms. Dr. Powell motioned one of the guards over and began giving instructions, his voice too low for the rebel teens to hear.

Magnus looked down at Kieran. "Where's Gail," he mouthed more than said.

Kieran shook his head, not understanding.

"Gail," Magnus said in a whisper.

Kieran looked around quickly. He raised his eyebrows at Magnus and shrugged. Sammy and Allison stood embracing directly in front of them.

Magnus leaned into Sammy's ear from behind. "Where's Gail?" he whispered, putting his hands on Sammy's shoulders.

Sammy looked back, frowning. He scanned the group. A smile broke over his face. Magnus smiled back.

"All right!" Powell's voice bounced off the room's hard surfaces. "We'll restore a little discipline to this place!"

"We haven't done anything!" Sammy protested.

The others started to object as well.

"Quiet!" Dr. Powell silenced them. "You're all moving down to the Playhouse in the basement." He waved the pistol. "No more arguments!"

"Playhouse?" Magnus eyebrows went up.

"He means solitary lockup in the basement," Kieran replied.

"What about our classes," Sammy squeaked, pressing closer to Allison.

"Classes?" Dr. Powell laughed. "That will be the least of your worries." He gestured to the guards. "Get them out of here!"

The guards pressed in and corralled the kids into the hall. The young protestors were hustled reluctantly down the hall toward the familiar elevator. They were taken down two at a time with a guard. Tommie was the last to disembark into the dimly lit basement. The boys were then pushed into a ten by ten room with two sets of bunk beds. The heavy metal door was locked shut behind them.

Tommie rushed the small window in the door. "Allison?" he called out.

"It's okay!" Allison called back before being locked in her own cell.

Tommie watched through the window as the guards sat up a table outside in the hall.

"I got first shift," one of the guards said and plopped down in a chair next to the table. "Change every four hours."

A familiar figure came up to the table, rubbing his head. "No! I've got first shift," the other man said.

Tommie stared into Hardcastle's cold expression through the window.

Hardcastle walked slowly over to the small window. "You punks get comfortable," he said to Tommie through clenched teeth. He slammed a metal cover over the window.

Tommie turned back to the other boys. Magnus started to speak, but Tommie shushed him. He put a hand to his ear and then pointed up at the ceiling. Magnus looked at Kieran.

"Bugs," Kieran mouthed. Magnus nodded, understanding.

Sammy stood in the middle of the room, surveying the walls, corners, and overhead light fixture. He turned to Tommie, pointing at the overhead light. Tommie gestured to Magnus for assistance. They dragged one of the bunk beds to the center of the room. Tommie gave Sammy a boost up to the top bunk. Sammy removed the plastic light diffuser and studied the interior edges of the fluorescent fixture. His eyes widened and he pointed to a small black attachment in the fixture's casing.

Tommie climbed up to the top bunk beside Sammy. He studied the black box before nodding down at Kieran. Kieran reached out as if to grab something and jerked his hand back. Tommie smiled and grabbed the offending contraption. He jumped off the top bunk, pulling the box out of the light fixture, wires and all. His weight snapped the wires, freeing the small electronic listening device.

Sammy scrambled down beside him and took possession of the device. He turned it over in his hands.

"Wired," he commented with professional disdain. "Very primitive," he sighed.

"Technology snob!" Tommie said, giving Sammy's hair a tug.

"All right, then." Kieran sat on the bottom bunk. "But just in case, let's keep it down."

"Huddle!" Tommie ordered, sitting on the bunk next to Kieran.

Sammy sat on Tommie's knee and Magnus took a seat at Kieran's other side.

Kieran took a deep breath. "We don't know where she is," he said.

Tommie started to speak, but Kieran held up a hand.

"We don't know if she's in any position to help us," Kieran said evenly. "We can't count on that until we know for sure."

The others nodded.

"And at this point," Kieran continued, "I don't know what to do."

"We'll think of something," Magnus said, throwing his arm over Keiran's shoulder. "We just need a little time."

Sammy jumped up and headed for the door. He studied the lock. "The door's steel," he said, shaking his head. "The deadbolt goes at least two inches into the door casing which is also steel."

Tommie followed him. He hammered his fists on the door. "Allison!" he yelled. "Allison!"

"I'm okay!" Her voice was almost inaudible, but the sound seemed to relax Tommie.

"Shut up in there!" Hardcastle boomed from the hall.

"Kiss my ass!" Tommie retorted.

"She sounds okay, huh?" Sammy looked up at Tommie, his eyes wide.

"We're okay right now," Kieran said. He pressed into Magnus who wrapped his arms tightly about him.

"I hope Gail is okay." Magnus raised an eyebrow at Tommie. "Do you think she might have gotten outside?"

"With Gail, there's no telling," Tommie responded without excitement. "They could have captured her by now."

Kieran put his hands over Magnus' which were still clasped about his chest. "As long as she's not next door with Allison, we can assume she's still out and free," he said.

Sammy plopped down on the other bottom bunk. "I bet she'll be down here soon and kick that bastard's ass out there," he said, savoring the image in his mind.

"You think Gail can take him?" Tommie asked, grinning down at the boy.

"She's tough," Sammy nodded. "And I'm certain they haven't caught her yet. She's planning her next move."

"I hope you're right." Magnus relaxed his grip on Kieran who leaned heavily against his chest. "Come on, Kieran." He pushed Kieran back on the bunk. "You lie down and rest. I want your brain working on this problem, too."

"This has been exhausting." Kieran said. He sank his head into the uncovered pillow." I don't feel very smart right now. I've made a mess of things."

"Stop it!" Magnus stretched out beside him. "Your idea was the right thing. We needed to stand our ground. We *need* to stand our ground!"

CHAPTER 15

Gail watched from around the corner as her friends were transported down to the basement. At first, she had cursed the sneaker that had forced her to stop for a moment and tie it. Now she realized how lucky she had been. Now what? She shook her head. Her first instinct was to rush the guards and body-slam them, but better judgment told her that there may be more of them in the computer lab . . . and they had guns.

"Shit, goddamnit," Gail muttered to herself and raced down the hall she had just come from. She needed to get away and think.

She paused in the next hall to catch her breath. The sound of a lone violin caught her ear and she panned her eyes down the hall—the music studios. She thought a moment, realizing alone she might not be able to help her friends or herself. The decision made, she ran over to the source of the violin playing and peered into the classroom window. A flutter of movement by the large window caught her eye and she watched the figure tapping a long bow on the top of a music stand. She turned the knob and slid silently into the room, closing the door behind her.

"Can't you see I'm practicing?" The angry figure, silhouetted by the sun, turned sharply.

"Can it, Conner!" Gail ordered, shutting the door behind her. "I need your help."

"You need my what?" Conner lowered his violin and shook his brightly dyed, rainbow hair. "Well, I've never given love advice to a dyke before."

"If you could cut the camp for about five minutes?" Gail did not look amused. She listened at the door. "We have a big problem."

"We?" Conner returned his instrument to its case on the chair beside him. "I don't think *we* have anything in common, much less a problem."

"Look, Mary. This is about the gay students here," Gail said, trying not to get angry. "Haven't you been curious as to why there are so many of us here?"

"Sweetie," Conner said, with a dramatic wave. "I think you're referring to the whole flaming student body here."

"Exactly." Gail cast a momentary glance over her shoulder. "The whole school's gay ... well, except for Carter ... and he's a little gay."

"What are you getting at?" Conner raised an eyebrow at Gail.

"Has Powell started you on his so-called vitamin therapy yet?"

"I don't need any ..."

"Do you know anyone who is taking the drugs?" Gail

interrupted.

"Well, there's . . ."

"How are they feeling lately?"

"There's a virus going round . . ."

"Bullshit!" Gail's fists clenched. "There ain't no goddamn virus. Powell's experimenting on us!"

Conner turned away to fit his bow next to his violin. "Don't be an idiot," he said, looking down his nose. "If you don't want the vitamins, you don't have to take them."

"Again, bullshit!" Gail's hands went to her hips. "We tried that. Allison, Kieran, Tommie, Magnus, and Sammy have been locked up in the basement for refusing."

"What?"

"You heard me!" Gail rocked on her heels. "I got away by luck. If you refuse the drugs, the same thing will happen to you!"

"Again, what do you want me to do about it?"

"Help me!" Gail thundered. "We've got to help the others!"

"You're full of shit," Conner said. "The problem's drugs all right, like . . . what have you been smoking!"

"You realize, of course, that if I didn't need your help right now, I'd be pounding your sorry little ass into the tile." Gail's eyes burrowed into his.

"Right." Conner thought for a moment. "So you're saying those vitamins are making people sick."

"They're not vitamins," Gail said, closing her eyes to fight back the growing frustration. "And yes, they're making people sick."

Conner started to reply, but Gail silenced him.

"You remember Alex and Bart?" she asked.

Conner nodded.

"Well," Gail continued. "They weren't runaways like Powell said. You know they wouldn't do that. And we know it's a lie because Magnus and Kieran saw Alex's body . . . dead body . . . in the basement lab."

"Wha . . . ?" Conner stumbled backwards. "You're lying!"

"Why would I lie to you?"

"You're punking me! You're . . ."

"Screw this!" Gail wanted to punch him, but thought better of it. "I've never given you the time of day before. Why would I bother?"

"Kieran put you up to it."

"Goddamn it, Conner!" Gail's face was almost purple. "Kieran doesn't tell me what to do. Are you gonna help me or not?" Tears broke out the side of her eyes and she brushed them away angrily.

Conner studied Gail's face. Something was definitely wrong. Tears were a foreign substance to Gail's face. The gravity of her story began to gain a foothold in his mind.

"This can't be," he said. "I don't . . ." His hand went to his other arm and massaged the bicep. Tears started down his own cheeks.

"Shit!" Gail's hands went to the top of her head. "What's wrong now? I didn't . . ." She stopped at the sudden realization. Her features dropped. "You've taken the vitamins haven't you?"

Conner nodded, suppressing a sob. "This morning," he said hoarsely. "They announced over the intercom this morning. Everyone went to the cafeteria for shots." He put his hand to his mouth. "Why don't you know that?"

"We were all in the gym," Gail said, losing all her anger. "The intercom only goes to the classrooms."

"This is stupid!" Conner said, shaking off his tears. "I

don't feel bad. There's no way . . ."

"Conner!" Gail stepped forward. "Listen to me! You won't feel it right off the bat. It takes several days of treatment. Alex was taking the shit for several weeks before he got so sick. You remember how sick Alex was before we heard that lie about his running away?"

Conner looked down.

"Are you supposed to get more shots?" she asked. "What were you told?"

"Every week," Conner croaked, the tears starting again.

"Shit!" Gail circled him, thinking. "Look. I don't care if you believe any of this. Believe it . . . don't believe it! But my friends are locked up in the basement. I need to get them out." She held up a fist. "I'm scared shitless! Do you understand?"

Conner sighed heavily and wiped his face. "Okay, I'll help," he said without reservation.

"You will?" Gail's mouth fell open.

"I don't believe everything," Conner said. "But you're not that good an actor." He tried to smile at Gail. "You're really scared and . . . if you're scared . . . then something is definitely wrong." His posture straightened. "What do you want me to do?"

"You'll really help?"

"Duh!" Conner closed his violin case and hoisted it over his back by the shoulder strap. "Even if you're full of shit and punking me, this will break the boredom around here. I'm in. What's the plan?"

"Plan." Gail thought a minute.

"You do have a plan, don't you?" Conner signed again. "Unbelievable!"

"I've got a plan," Gail protested. "I just have to add

you into the equation now." She headed for the door and checked for movement out in the hall. "Okay," she said, making a decision. "Here's the deal. I've got a little errand to run first. When can you get free?"

"Well, I have string ensemble in about fifteen minutes," Conner said. "I really shouldn't miss that."

"Oh no." Gail's sarcasm dripped. "That wouldn't do, would it?"

"Suck my dick, Ms. Sappho!" A hand went to Conner's hip.

"Okay, okay." Gail looked at Conner with a greater sense of appreciation. "Ballsy little princess, aren't you?" She slapped Conner on the back."

"Ow!" Conner staggered into the door.

"Sorry," Gail said, steadying him. "Look. Meet me by the basement elevator at three. I need you for a distraction."

"Can I bring a date?" Conner blinked suggestively.

"You got someone you can trust?"

"I can create a distraction for you much better with an accomplice."

"Okay, but just remember." Gail looked hard into the boy's eyes. "If you or your . . . accomplice don't show up, or screw me over on this . . . I'll get you before they get me."

"Don't be such a dominatrix," Conner said, pursing his lips. "I'll be there."

Gail nodded and opened the door. The hall was full of students changing class. Gail ducked out into the stream and disappeared.

Conner stepped into the hall just as the swim team came barreling by on their way to practice. He recognized someone. "Danny?" He called out.

A tall muscular boy stopped and caught Conner's eye.

"Hi, Aquaman" Conner called to him again. "Come over here a second."

The boy hesitated. "Conner? What's up?" the boy asked.

Conner smiled seductively. "I need you."

Gail kept her head down and moved with the flow of students heading to the dorms during the class break. She ducked into one of the dorm rooms, praying that the camera monitors did not find her suspicious or identifiable. She immediately went to work and extracted a small pocket knife she kept in her brassiere. She opened the flathead screwdriver attachment and quickly unscrewed the wall plate covering the light switch.

"Please be there," she muttered to herself, peering into the wall cavity.

She grasped the almost invisible paper clip that had been pulled open and hooked over the wall board. She heard the keys jangle as she lifted the paper clip, carefully wresting the keys out of the confined space.

"Yes!" She said triumphantly, examining her find. She pocketed them and moved on to her next task.

A small television set rested on the top of Allison's chest of drawers next to an old, bulky VCR player. Gail checked it over, satisfied that no screws were holding the VCR player together. She lifted the top up carefully.

"Little son of a bitch!" She whispered. It was there.

She laughed to herself. The player didn't work as most all of its insides had been removed. Instead, inside was a small, compact tabliet computer . . . Sammy's backup. The boy had long ago hacked into the schools wireless network and had unfiltered and unmonitored access to the internet. Attached to the small tablet were two solid-state hard drives connected to the computer via USB connections. Sammy backed up all his software here.

Gail unplugged it carefully and extracted it from his hiding place. She slid it into the front of her jeans and pulled her shirttail out and over the small bulge. "Sammy, boy," she said, vowing to be easier on the kid.

Satisfied, she stretched out on Allison's bed to wait for the next class change. Before she got too comfortable, she spotted Allison's two carbon steel tennis rackets propped up against the wall by the chest of drawers. Gail hopped up and retrieved one, turning it over in her hands and checking its weight.

"This'll do nicely," she said with a smile. She reclined back on the bed and fingered the tight strings crisscrossing the racket head. "You're not a baseball bat, buddy," she said relaxing into the pillow. "But . . . yeah . . . you'll do just fine."

CHAPTER 16

Despite the oppressive quiet, the unwilling cell-mates had a troubled night. Unable to discern night from day, the boys had relied on Tommie's watch to go to bed, but there was no alarm to wake them up.

Magnus flexed his left arm to restore the circulation challenged by the weight of Kieran's sleeping head. He leaned over to kiss Kieran's cheek and watch his slumbering—slumber that had not been particularly peaceful. With great care, he slid his arm from under Kieran's while at the same time tucking the pillow into the space to cradle his friend's head. He sat up and dropped his bare feet onto the cold concrete floor. He could hear Sammy's muffled snoring and tried to recall his bearings in the darkness. The only way to tell if it was morning yet was to get a look at Tommie's watch.

He stood up and inched across the floor toward Sammy's rhythmic breath sounds. Stretching his arms out ahead, he felt for the top bunk as he moved closer. Finally his fingers found the soft mattress. As his eyes began to adjust to the dark, he squinted into the dim space of the upper bunk. Nothing. He cocked his ear downward. Sammy was on the lower bunk ... but. Magnus smiled. Suppressing a chuckle, he went down to one knee and tried to make out the lower bunk's occupants. Tommie was in the middle with Sammy clasped in his right arm against his chest.

"Damn it," Magnus mumbled under his breath. Tommie's watch was on his left wrist, encircled by Sammy's hand. Magnus leaned into the lower bunk, reaching out to peel Sammy's fingers off the watch face.

"What are you doing?"

"Shit!" Magnus started at the sound of Tommie's voice, banging his head on the top bunk rail. "Why didn't you tell me you were awake?"

"Shhh," Tommie hissed. "You'll wake him."

"What time is it?"

Tommie lifted his free arm. "If you push the button in the top, the face will light up." He extended his arm to Magnus.

"It's seven a.m.," Magnus said, following instructions. "What time should we wake everyone?"

"Let them sleep," Tommie whispered. "I thought this little one was never gonna fall asleep." He rolled Sammy over onto the pillow.

"Of course he couldn't sleep," Magnus said. "He was in bed with the man of his dreams." He could see Tommie's grin in the light of the fading watch dial.

Tommie sat up and spun around on the bunk to face Magnus. "That would be sleep in the literal sense of the word, thank you very much."

"Says you," Magnus responded, chuckling.

"I'll just let that become part of the myth that accompanies the legend that is me," Tommie whispered.

"Whatever!"

Magnus took Tommie's hand and pulled him up from the bunk.

"Did you hear anything last night?" Tommie asked quietly.

Magnus could see his concern. "Don't worry, Tommie," he said. "I think she's fine. Everything was quiet."

"I need to know for sure." Tommie made his way to the door.

The metal plate still covered the small window above the knob. He put an ear against the door, listening intently. He turned to say something to Magnus but was startled to find Magnus standing behind him.

Tommie leaned back against the door. "Nothing," he said desperately.

"If I were in your shoes, I'd be just as . . . scared." Magnus put a hand on the boy's shoulder.

Tommie nodded, suddenly unable to speak.

"I know she's okay," Magnus continued. "When the lights come on we'll try to call for her."

Again Tommie could only nod, looking down at the floor. "I can't stand this," he managed through clenched teeth. He pounded his temples with his open palms. "I should have done something."

Even in the dark, Magnus could see the tears glisten on Tommie's cheeks. "What? What could you do?" he asked.

"Something!"

"Stop!" Magnus pulled Tommie into a tight embrace.

"We'll figure this out."

Tommie's whole body shook like a tight spring. Magnus worried he might explode at any moment. The lights came on at last.

"And what's going on here?" a voice called out behind them.

Magnus and Tommie jerked their heads around.

Kieran stood, arms crossed, tapping his foot. "You heard me!" It was obvious to both boys that Kieran was pulling their chain. "Is this what goes on when I'm asleep?"

"Okay, Tommie," Magnus said, rolling his eyes. "We can't hide it anymore."

For a moment, Tommie's anxiety lifted. He tried to smile.

"It's no use, Kieran," Magnus lamented. "This thing between Tommie and me . . . we can't pretend anymore . . . it's too strong!"

Magnus pulled Tommie's hand to his lips and kissed it. "Ours is a love that can no longer be ignored."

He laid his head on Tommie's shoulder and Tommie reciprocated, cocking his head over onto Magnus'.

"Sorry, kid," Tommie said, giving Kieran a pitying look. "The boy wants a real man. You're just too girly."

"Oh, really?" Kieran raised an eyebrow emphasizing his sarcasm.

"What's going on?" Sammy's head popped up from the bed. He tried to sit up, still half asleep. "What did I miss?"

"Well," Kieran said, throwing his hands up. "Magnus and Tommie have given into the love that dares not speak its name."

Magnus and Tommie choked with laughter.

Sammy spun his feet around onto the cold, concrete floor. "The what?" he asked, not sure what Kieran meant.

Kieran wagged his finger at the other two boys. "Magnus has dumped me for this . . ." He gestured to Tommie. "This prissy soprano!"

Hey!" Tommie dove at Kieran. "That's gonna cost you!"

He pulled Kieran over onto the bed next to Sammy, tickling him mercilessly.

"Stop it! Stop!" Kieran cried, falling back against Sammy. Tommie abandoned him as quickly as he had attacked.

"What's going on?" Sammy asked, steadying Kieran. He was fully awake now.

"I caught Tommie and Magnus making out in the dark," Kieran lamented, regaining his composure.

Sammy's eyes widened.

"You liar," Magnus threw at him with a broad grin. "We were not making out . . . much."

"True!" Tommie extended his arms out to the side and bowed humbly before his audience. "We we're making," he stood, savoring the imaginary drama, "sweet love."

"Kieran," Sammy said, finally catching on. "That means you and I can finally be together."

Kieran looked at the younger boy with undisguised delight. "Why you smart-mouthed little hussy!" He gave Sammy a hug. "I'm promoting you to princess-status in our little soap opera."

"Wheeeee!" Sammy clasped his hands to his heart.

"Okay, okay." Tommie sighed, grateful for the momentary lightening of his anxiety. "The lights are on." He returned to the door. "Allison?" he called out. He hammered his fists on the unyielding door. "Allison, can you hear me?" He pressed his ear to the grey metal. After a moment he shook his head at Manus. "Nothing!"

"Let's both try," Magnus offered, joining Tommie at the door. "Allison?" he yelled.

"Allison?" both boys trumpeted. Tommie pounded the door.

Sammy and Kieran joined in. "Allison?" they all cried out.

Again, Tommie pressed his ear to the door. He heard a muffled, female voice yell, "I'm okay!"

"I can hear her," Tommie said, straightening. "She's okay." His whole body seemed to unwind. "Thank, God!" He covered his face with his hands.

"She's okay," Kieran whispered, hugging Tommie reassuringly.

Magnus threw his arms about the other two boys as they clung together in silence. Sammy, feeling left out, ran over to them and wriggled under Magnus' arm, joining the group hug. They remained that way for some time until stirred by a rattling noise coming from beyond the door.

Sammy's head popped out of the group embrace excitedly. "Do you think they're bringing us some food?"

The others laughed.

"You must be starting another growth spurt," Kieran said, slapping the boy atop his head. "You've been eating like a pig lately."

"*My* butt's not big." Sammy smirked up at him.

"Wha ... ?" Kieran pulled away, hands on his hips. "You little bitch!"

"I'm sorry, Kieran," Sammy said, regretting his outburst. "He clasped his hands under his chin, pleading.

"I didn't mean it!"

Kieran rolled his eyes. The anger he was trying to fake flickered on his face. He gave Tommie a cutting glare. "I blame you for this."

"Me?" Tommie tried not to laugh.

"It's not his fault, Kieran," Sammy sputtered, fearing more conflict. "I don't know why I said that."

"I know why you said it!" Kieran grabbed the young teen's shoulders. "You said it 'cause you thought it, and our people tell it like it is—no filtering needed." Sammy grinned tentatively. "But," Kieran continued, "if you ever say something like that to *me* again," he leaned into Sammy, face to face, "I'll cut you!" He gave Sammy a peck on the cheek.

Sammy hugged him. "I love you, Kieran," he said, giggling.

"I know," Kieran responded with a long sigh.

"Awwwww," Magnus and Tommie chanted mockingly.

They started at the sudden scraping outside the door. All eyes focused on the doorknob as the definite sound of a key turning the lock snapped to its conclusion. The boys stepped back, not knowing what to anticipate. The door swung open and two security guards charged in with weapons drawn. They corralled the boys back to the beds.

"Chill out!" Tommie snapped at one of the guards when he was pushed.

"Sit down, all of you!" Powell's voice boomed.

Kieran stood to speak.

"Silence!" Powell ordered.

He stood with file in hand, glaring at the boys over the top of his eyeglasses. He gestured at Magnus.

"Bring him."

"Wha . . . ?" Magnus was jerked forward by the two guards.

"Leave him alone!" Kieran almost screamed. He grabbed for one of the guards and was thrown back into Tommie.

"What's this about?" Tommie stood to his full height, fists clenched. "What do you want with Magnus?"

Powell shook his head, the edge of his mouth arched sarcastically. "That is none of your business. Stay where you are and you won't get hurt!" He turned back to the door. "Bring the boy and make it quick!"

"Magnus!" Kieran cried out, trying to follow.

"No, Kieran!" Tommie grabbed him by the arm.

"Magnus!" Kieran screamed, struggling against him.

Magnus tried to look back as he was dragged out the door. "I'll be okay!" he called out, trying to reassure his friends.

The door was slammed shut behind the intruders. The remaining boys stood in shocked silence

"I don't understand," Kieran sobbed. "What do they want with him?" He caught his breath in a panic. "What are they going to do to him?" He turned to Tommie in desperation.

Tommie embraced him, stroking his friend's hair reassuringly. "I don't know, Kieran." He looked over to Sammy who stood trembling and in tears. "I don't know."

CHAPTER 17

Magnus stood defiantly despite the fact that his arms were clamped in the tight grip of Dr. Powell's goons. He looked about the lab, suppressing a shudder at the memory of finding Alex's body there just a few days ago. Powell had donned his lab coat and busied himself giving instructions to his nurse.

"What do you want?" Magnus shouted at him. "Why am I here?"

Dr. Powell ignored him and took a seat by the lab table that was piled high with files and notebooks.

"You're not going to get away with this!" Magnus continued to shout.

One of Powell's men almost jerked Magnus' shoulder out of socket in response.

Dr. Powell gestured for calm. "Don't hurt him," he commanded. "He's too valuable a specimen."

Emboldened by the order to do him no harm,

Magnus struggled against his captors, managing to kick one of the hapless guards squarely in the kneecap. Finally Dr. Powell looked up from his paperwork and signaled the guards to put Magnus in a chair across from him. The guards positioned themselves behind and Magnus was relieved that, at least, they no longer had their hands on him. He sat, arms crossed, glaring at Dr. Powell.

"Mr. Kroft," Dr. Powell began. "Magnus," he added with a syrupy smile. "Let me reiterate the obvious fact that you and your little friends are not in charge here. You are not at liberty to self-determine either your bad behavior or the choice whether or not to cooperate with my research. Your parents agreed to this when they placed you in the program."

"Bullshit!" Magnus said. "My mother would never have agreed to you conducting experiments that might hurt me in anyway."

"You don't know what you're talking about," Dr. Powell responded. "My research will be a benefit to all of mankind."

"Bullshit again," Magnus said, interrupting. "You're so-called experimenting has already killed two students!" He sat forward for emphasis. "We know that for a fact! You can't deny it."

"Very well then," Dr. Powell said with an icy smile. "You *have* been snooping." He took off his eyeglasses. "But it changes nothing. Let me assure you that the importance of the work I am doing here will not be interfered with by you or your little . . . friends."

"You're too late," Magnus said before he could stop himself.

"Really." Dr. Powell chuckled, cleaning his glasses before putting them back on. "I am well aware of your email to Kieran's mother."

Magnus caught his breath.

"I spoke to her briefly the other day," Dr. Powell continued. "We had a nice chat. I let her know how her son had been attempting to sneak off with you for . . . God knows what?"

Magnus started to speak, but Dr. Powell held up a hand for silence. "I let her know that we had other student runaways for the same reasons," he continued. "After all," he said, adjusting the papers on the counter, "you're almost adults. If you want to run off and sink further into your perversion, there's very little I or my staff can do about it."

"You're a liar and a murderer," Magnus said hotly, no longer able to keep his anger in check.

Dr. Powell once again raised a dismissive hand. "You kids have such imaginations." His voice was almost laughing. "Mrs. Matheson was very understanding and encouraged me to do the best I could in the situation."

Magnus was overcome with a feeling of helplessness. "You're lying," was all he could say.

"And," Dr. Powell continued, ignoring him, "do the best I can is exactly what I'm going to do."

"We won't take any more of your treatments!" Magnus insisted.

"Really?" Dr. Powell stood. "Whether or not your friends become," he smiled, "runaways themselves all depends on you."

"What?" Magnus didn't understand.

"My work has progressed to the point that I am now able to identify the subjects most likely to withstand our current level of treatment. I have new technology arriving today that will make the difference in the success of my work."

"Treatment," Magnus said. "Treatment for what?"

"Exactly." Dr. Powell picked up one of the folders and handed it to the nurse. "Let me fill you in," he said to Magnus. "Perhaps if you understand what it is we are trying to accomplish, you might be more, shall we say, cooperative."

"I doubt it," Magnus responded before being silenced by Dr. Powell once again.

"You have a disease, Mr. Kroft . . . a disease I have been working to eradicate from the gene pool for a number of years now . . . and, I am very close to a final solution."

"There's nothing wrong with me!"

"Oh, but there is." Dr. Powell approached the boy, standing over him with an intimidating stare. "You are a homosexual, boy. That is an illness . . . a blight on humankind and the moral fabric of this society."

"You're fucked up!" Magnus said angrily.

"No," Dr. Powell said. "You are . . . how did you say . . . fucked up! My work has identified a physical component . . . a cause if you will . . . one of several. You're like an autistic child, or a congenitally blind or deaf person, all of which should and would welcome a cure for their condition."

"That's a load of crap!" Magnus said. "There is nothing wrong with being gay."

"Yes there is!" Dr. Powell insisted. "It's abnormal. It serves no evolutionary purpose." He returned to his seat. "Magnus," he said, trying to sound concerned. "Wouldn't you like to be like everyone else? Wouldn't you like to live a normal life . . . have a home, children, a normal relationship with the opposite sex?"

"Who are you to tell me what's normal," Magnus said with disgust. "All you've said is that I'm different from the majority of people. Difference is not a disease. It's a gift, like my talent for dance, and I don't see any reason to want to change it."

"You are deluded. How can you call something so vile a gift?"

"There is nothing vile about it and it's part of who I am. Change that and everything else changes."

"Very sad." Dr. Powell took off his glasses and massaged his eyes. "I can see that reason is not going to sway your immaturity."

"You have no reasons—"

"Enough!" Dr. Powell commanded. "We're wasting time." His demeanor darkened to an impenetrable glare. "Let's try this a different way. My work is going to be completed with or without you. With you, your friends live. Without you, I can guarantee that . . . at least some . . . will not survive."

"What are you saying?" Magnus asked, stunned.

"You are my strongest specimen with respect to the treatment I've developed," Dr. Powell said. "You have all the genetic markers my research is seeking to understand and change. If you agree to cooperate . . . cooperate fully with my treatment regimen . . . then your friends will be irrelevant to my research." He paused to let his words sink in. "The lives of your friends . . . and many other students . . . are in your hands. It's that simple."

The fight drained out of Magnus. He thought of Kieran, Tommie, Allison, and the others; his life, all their lives. "They won't accept this," Magnus said, shaking his head.

"You have to give them no choice," Dr. Powell said.

"You have to tell them they are mistaken about everything. You have to convince them that you don't want to be a part of their little gay cabal any more. If you can do this . . . reject them and get them to reject you . . . then I will expel them from the school, and they will be free to return to their former lives."

"What are you going to do to me?" Magnus asked, staring at the floor. All emotion drained from him.

"The research we are doing here is a form of stem-cell therapy." Dr. Powell sat back with a self-satisfied smile. "We have long known that neurological diseases like Parkinson's, Alzheimer's, and Huntington's can be reversed using stem cell therapies. In re-directing brain activity, the use of neural stem cells is essential. Our first trials involved intravenous administration of the stem cells, but we found that there was a danger of the injected cells lodging in other vital organs such as the lungs, resulting in potentially deadly side effects."

"So that's what happened to Alex and Bart," Magnus said, narrowing his eyes at the doctor.

"They played a valuable role in refining our methods of stem cell delivery," the doctor said with a shrug. "Their deaths were unfortunate, but necessary in the overall scheme of the research."

"How can you sit there and justify that?" Magnus said angrily. "Necessary? You killed them. How can you morally justify that? You sit there and tell me how I am immoral because I'm gay, and yet you don't even blink at killing otherwise healthy young . . ."

"Healthy?" Dr. Powell boomed. "They were not healthy. They were diseased . . . their lives headed toward a useless, unhappy existence."

"How do you know they were unhappy?" Magnus

asked, further incensed. "You're just projecting your own bigotry onto us!"

"They were better off dead!" Dr. Powell slammed a fist onto the stack of charts in front of him. "If they couldn't be cured, they were better off dead. It was not murder, it was euthanasia and humanely administered. I put them out of their misery, and an even greater misery that would have resulted if they had been allowed to continue as they were."

Magnus sat in shocked silence. He realized the man in front of him was no more than a raving lunatic—a lunatic with a very dangerous set of killing skills. He forced himself to relax. It was important to find out the full scope of what was going on.

"You were telling me about the therapy," Magnus said flatly.

Dr. Powell nodded, satisfied that he had cowed the boy. "I have genetically engineered a type of stem cell that is biased in favor of the genetic markers that I believe affect sexual orientation in favor of normal heterosexual behavior," he said, his face becoming more animated and expressive as he went on. "One breakthrough came when that boy, Tommie, was studied further."

Magnus' head shot up.

"Oh yes," Dr. Powell continued. "We are very aware that he is heterosexual. Did you think we are so easily fooled by your little games?"

"What's Tommie got to do with this?" Magnus asked. "If, as you say, he is straight, then why involve him?"

"Very simple," Dr. Powell interrupted. "He afforded us the opportunity to further refine our sense of the genetic markers we needed to focus on. His genetic material gave us greater confidence that what my therapy will alter is sexual behavior and without losing ... how shall I put it ... the creative, artistic dimension that is not sexually defined."

"You can't be sure of any of this," Magnus said. "There's no way you can narrow it all down so easily. You can't reduce a human being to just a bunch of cells. Ms. Julie had it right. I am more than the sum of my parts, and my art is even more than that. You can't *fix* me. Whatever Frankenstein monster you want to make out of me is not going to be me. It'll be something else. It will be less!"

"Ridiculous!" Dr. Powell insisted. "You will be everything you are now. You are more than your sexual orientation as well. Changing that will not change you."

"It will!" Magnus stood angrily. "You change any part of me and you change me."

"Impossible!" Dr. Powell sighed heavily. "Children your age are impossible to argue with. Think whatever you like, but in the end you will see that I am right." He motioned for Magnus to sit down.

Magnus realized it was useless to continue arguing. He regained his seat, sitting with his arms crossed, scowling at the row of cabinets over Dr. Powell's head. "You haven't told me what your so-called ... treatment ... consists of," he said finally.

"Indeed," Dr. Powell said. "It is a four step process. First, you will be started on a course of powerful immunosuppressants." He smiled. "The ones you have been refusing to take. This ensures that there will be little chance of a potentially dangerous immune response to the foreign, cells that will be introduced. Second, while your body's defenses are slowly shut down, there will be several days of special brain monitoring ... what we call brain mapping. I have developed a very specialized form of quantitative electroencephalogram using a combination of electromagnetic and photon emission sensors. You will undergo visual, aural, and nerve ending stimuli and the areas of your brain that are affected will be mapped and the particular wavelengths of the resulting electromagnetic activity will also be thoroughly measured and mapped. This becomes very important in the fourth step, but let's not get ahead of ourselves."

He chuckled to himself as if he were discussing his favorite book. "The third step is the most delicate. I have had to develop a set of very specialized tools and apparatus for this phase. My genetically engineered stem cells will be injected directly into the areas of your neural network where we identify your sexual response is generated . . . especially the hippocampus region of the brain."

"You're going to stick needles in my brain?" Magnus was horrified.

"Not to worry," Dr. Powell said with a dismissive wave. "You will feel nothing, even though you will be fully conscious during the entire procedure."

"I'll be awake?"

"Completely," Dr. Powell said. "After the cells have been introduced, we move into the fourth phase of the treatment. While these engineered stem cells begin to take hold and replace the damaged cells that produce your aberrant homosexual behavior, you will be placed in a special kind of hyperbaric chamber of my own design. In addition to the concentrated oxygen therapy to enhance brain activity, this fully enclosed isolation chamber will bombard the new, growing neuron structures with audio and visual stimulation along with positive and negative reinforcements depending on the type of stimulation presented."

"What?" Magnus asked. "Are you talking about brain washing . . . electroshock treatment?"

Dr. Powell dismissed Magnus' comments with a wave. "That would be barbaric," he said. "The form of positive and negative reinforcement I'm talking about takes place on the cellular level. It would be too complicated for you to understand."

"Whatever," Magnus said with undisguised sarcasm.

"In any event," Dr. Powell continued, "this is going to happen with or without your cooperation. Your cooperation would be of benefit to the overall process which is why I am willing to negotiate your cooperation with the release of your friends. It is your decision and I need your answer now."

Magnus looked down at his hands, accepting what he had to do . . . what was required of him. "There will have to be a guarantee."

Dr. Powell sat back. "I cannot—"

"Not about the experiment," Magnus said. "I don't hold out much confidence in that. I want a guarantee that my friends will be released to leave this place. I will agree to cooperate fully with you, but all that will end if you don't keep your part of the bargain. If I'm as important as you say, my cooperation is essential to your success."

Dr. Powell studied the ceiling for a moment. "Agreed," he said. "But understand this . . . all of you will be kept under surveillance, intense surveillance. Any more trouble and not only will I complete my treatment trial with you," he leaned forward, "but I will autopsy your friends for neural tissue samples for further study."

"That won't be necessary." Magnus felt his gut

tighten to the point of pain. "If you release my friends, I won't fight you any further."

"I know you are ... worried about the overall outcome, but I want you to know I have every confidence that my process will be completely successful with you," the doctor said. He sat back in his chair. "The benefits to you will be incalculable ... the chance at a normal life. As I said, in the end, you will see that I am right."

Magnus felt drained and helpless. This insane man had the upper hand and there was no one else to help him or his friends. He fully realized that there was no alternative. He would just have to find a way to make sure his friends were free. "When do I get to see my friends," he asked, unable to look up at Dr. Powell.

"Tomorrow morning," Dr. Powell said. He stood, satisfied with his work. "You've made the right decision—for yourself and for your friends."

Magnus did not respond. He stood and allowed himself to be escorted out of the lab by Dr. Powell's guards. They deposited him into a small hospital-like room just outside the lab. He looked about the stark, white room, the hospital bed, and the nondescript landscape print that hung on the wall opposite the foot of the bed.

Magnus heard the door shut behind him and the deadbolt lock snap into place. He sat helpless on the bed, staring at his hands. So this was it. This was how it was all going to end. The memory of his last encounter with Alex flashed into his mind. How sick the boy had been. How apparently accepting of his fate he was. Tears flooded Magnus' cheeks, falling onto his trembling, clasped hands in his lap.

Magnus shook himself. "No!" he cried out, wiping

the tears away. He clamped his jaw, demanding that the tears stop, refusing to feel sorry for himself. He shut his eyes, remembering Kieran's face, his soft hands, his easy laugh. He let the warmth of his love for Kieran wash over him. Magnus knew where he would find the strength to do what he had to do. Kieran and the other friends he had grown to love would have to be put first. Magnus smiled to himself, surprised at how happy it made him feel that he could save them.

"Thank God," he whispered into the air.

After a moment of quiet peace, the other reality broke through. He knew he would have to hurt Kieran in order to save him. It was a hard truth to realize. He tried to convince himself that Kieran was strong and resilient . . . that Kieran would be okay. He would have his whole life ahead of him and would have the support and friendship of Tommie, Allison, Sammy, and yes, even Gail.

Magnus lay back on the bed, hands behind his head, staring up at the dull, textured ceiling. He thought about what he would have to do tomorrow. He would have to convince Kieran. He would have to bury the love he had come to crave and rely on. He closed his eyes and prayed . . . prayed that he could do this . . . prayed that Kieran would not be too hurt.

"I love you, Kieran," he whispered. "I love you enough to let you go."

A heavy, salty tear broke free from his tightly clenched eyelids and trailed down the side of his face onto the pillow.

"But now you have to hate me." He covered his face with his arms.

CHAPTER 18

The Powell Institute presented an imposing silhouette against the orange backdrop of sunrise. The cool Colorado air preceded a front of thundershowers that was quickly snuffing out the pied morning sky. Before its occupants had risen, the rain had enveloped the Institute and the surrounding landscape, and the occasional rumble of thunder accompanied it.

The occupants of the concrete basement of the Institute could know nothing about the stirrings of Mother Nature beyond their small, sterile cells. The surrounding bedrock that cradled the basement realm allowed no sound to intrude from beyond the walls.

In the absence of any sense of day or night, Tommie had relied on the distant noises that accompanied the change of shift for the guards just outside the steel door that imprisoned him and his friends. Although exhausted, he had been unable to sleep and instead, kept watch over

Kieran and Sammy who slept restlessly in each other's arms in the bottom bunk.

He watched them as he had for most of the night, except those times when he plastered his ear to the door listening for shift change or for any sound that might be from Allison's cell. He ached to call her name, but didn't want to wake her in the event that she, too, had managed to escape into sleep.

He watched Kieran stir restlessly once more, and the tears that seemed to accompany each episode. Tommie clenched his fists against the real pain he felt watching Kieran even in his sleep, sob and cry out. The feeling of hopelessness, the total void of any possible way to help or console his friend, was almost more than Tommie could stand. Each time Kieran stirred this way, Tommie would find himself close to tears of his own and he would quietly hammer the solid concrete walls the soft inside of his fists . . . refusing to let a single drop fall . . . anything to keep from screaming his anger.

Shift change had just begun and Tommie knew that the door would soon be opening so the guards could bring in the breakfast cart. He though seriously about jumping on them, wanting to seriously hurt someone. He knew he stood little chance, but if they beat him unconscious or worse shot at him, at least he would be freed from the agony of helplessness.

He pressed his cheek against the door and listened. The squeaking of a metal car's wheels on the floor beyond let him know that they were about to serve breakfast. Deciding it would be better to softly wake his friends himself than to let them be jarred awake by the sudden onslaught of light and noise, he hurried over to the bed.

Kneeling beside Kieran, he reached over and gave his friend's shoulder a slight nudge. "Kieran," he said softly in his friend's ear. "Kieran, it's morning."

Kieran's swollen eyes opened into narrow slits.

"Kieran," Tommie said again, running his fingers over Kieran's hair. "They're bringing breakfast."

Kieran bolted up in the bed. "Magnus?" He looked around the room, trying to focus as the lights came on.

Tommie put a hand on Kieran's shoulder, not sure what to say. "Magnus hasn't come back yet, Kieran."

"No word about Gail or Allison?" Kieran's face clouded with disappointment.

"It's been quiet all night," Tommie said. He took Kieran's hand. "Maybe no news is good news."

"Dammit!" Kieran fell back onto the pillow. "Tommie, I don't know how much more I can stand."

"I know," Tommie said, giving Kieran's hand a squeeze. "But we have to. We need to be ready to act on a moment's . . ." He stopped as the door to their cell swung open.

Two guards entered, one pushing the wobbly cafeteria cart, and the other who remained by the door with his weapon drawn. Tommie stood, assessing the situation, flexing his fingers.

Kieran instantly recognized the signs that Tommie was about to do something reckless. He put his hand on Tommie's arm until the guards had exited. "Sit down by me," Kieran said. He spun his legs around to sit on the edge of the bed. "We'd better wake Sammy."

"I'm awake," Sammy said, raising up on his elbows. "Are they going to let us go now?"

"Fraid not, baby," Kieran said, shaking his head. He motioned for Sammy to sit on his other side. "They've just brought some breakfast."

Tommie pulled the cart over to the bed. "You didn't eat any supper," he said, taking his place on the bed by Kieran. "Now I want you to eat something."

Kieran frowned at the trays of prepared food. "I can't, he said. "I'll just throw it up."

"Don't be silly," Tommy said. "You need something. You've lost half your body weight in tears."

"I just can't," Kieran said. "Let Sammy have it."

"I'm not eating unless you eat," Sammy said, watching for Kieran's reaction.

"There," Tommie said, throwing the younger boy a warm smile. "You see? You have to eat for Sammy's sake. You know what he's like when his blood sugar gets low."

"What are they serving?" Kieran sighed.

Tommie reached for one of the trays before Kieran could change his mind. "Our favorite breakfast casserole," he said, uncovering a tray and putting it on Kieran's lap.

"Ugh!" was Kieran's response.

"Now eat up, so Sammy won't waste away, Tommie said. He gave Sammy a tray and then took one for himself. He watched as Kieran took a small bite of the requisite English muffin.

"Hey," Sammy said, pausing mid-bite. "Who's the extra tray for?"

The boys stared at the cart and the last remaining tray it held. Kieran caught his breath, dropping the muffin back onto the tray in his lap.

"Shit!" Tommie put his tray on the floor and embraced Kieran who had once again dissolved into tears. "Don't start this again, Kieran," he said, pleading. "It doesn't help anything."

"The tray is for me," a familiar voice said from across the room.

The occupants of the bed froze, mouths agape. The guards left the room quickly, slamming shut the door to the small prison.

"Magnus!" Kieran rose from the bed slowly. "Oh my God. Magnus?" Tears of a different kind flooded his cheeks. He threw his arms out and rushed toward the object of his joy.

Magnus held out his hands as well, but not for an embrace. His hands clearly said, stay back.

Kieran stopped, confused. "What's wrong?" he asked, taking a tentative step back. "What did they do to you?" Kieran looked Magnus over for some sign of injury.

"Magnus?" Tommie said, not sure what to make of Magnus' blank expression.

"I'm okay," Magnus said to them. He had steeled himself for this, but his arms ached to hold Kieran. The pain he saw in Kieran's eyes squeezed his heart to the bursting. "I just wanted to let you all know that I am fine and all this will be over soon."

He turned his attention away from Kieran and picked up the remaining breakfast tray. He carried it over to the other, empty bunk and sat down, taking the time to reinforce his resolve to do what he knew he had to do.

"Wha . . ." Kieran stuttered, frozen.

"What's going on, Magnus?" Tommie asked, standing by Kieran. Magnus was clearly acting strangely.

"Look." Magnus took a bite of his food and chewed thoughtfully. "We've had some fun," he said, "but it's time to get serious. Dr. Powell's work is very important and he's explained it all to me. I need for you all to accept the fact that I'm a part of it now."

"Oh my God!" Kieran grabbed for Tommie's arm.

"What are you saying, Magnus?" Tommie threw an arm about Kieran. He pushed Kieran behind him and signaled for Sammy to stand by his stunned friend. He faced Magnus squarely. "Why are you acting like this? If you're giving into Powell then we're all doomed."

"Don't be silly," Magnus said. He infused his voice with a chilling calm. "You all are not needed now. Powell's gonna send you home. You'll be fine."

"No!" Kieran said, pushing his way past Tommie. "You can't mean this. I'm not leaving without you!"

"You have to Kieran," Magnus said, shaking his head. "You don't have a choice." He looked down at the cold food before him. "And I want you to go."

"No, no!" Kieran paced the floor in front of Magnus, his arms flailing about in anger and frustration. "Powell's done something to you already," Kieran said. He turned to face Magnus. "You're drugged, or under hypnosis, or something. You wouldn't say things like this if you were thinking clearly!"

Magnus dropped the piece of toast and sat the tray on the bed beside him. "You don't understand, Kieran," he said, standing. "I've made my decision. This is the way it's going to be." He started for the door. "You're not going to change my mind. Dr. Powell can cure me . . . give me a chance at a normal life."

"Normal!" Kieran rushed after him. "You *are* normal!" he said, grabbing Magnus' shoulder and spinning him around. "There's nothing wrong with you. I don't know what's happened, but I'm not letting you go through with this."

"This isn't your choice," Magnus said. "It's mine and I've made it. We can't be together anymore. It was wrong" He folded his arms across his chest as if to shield himself from his own necessary lies. "I don't want to be with you anymore. You're too fucked up! This whole thing is fucked up! You were perfectly happy without me before and you will be perfectly happy without me now."

"No I won't!" Kieran said, pleading. "You don't mean this. You don't mean any of this. You can't!" He reached to embrace Magnus.

"Stop it!" Magnus said, holding Kieran at arm's length. "Accept it! This is how it's going to be. We can't see each other anymore. Go home!"

"Magnus," Kieran said, dissolving into sobs. "Please don't do this!" His voice dropped to a weak whisper. "I love you, Magnus, please . . ."

"Tommie!" Magnus pushed Kieran into Tommie's arms. "Please take him home!"

Tommie folded his muscular arms about Kieran tightly, refusing to let the sobbing boy free. His glare cut across the room to Magnus. "I warned you if you hurt him," he said, his voice shaking with anger. "Someway, somehow, I am going to hurt you!"

Magnus swallowed hard, unable to meet Tommie's hard stare. He grappled with his emotions, wanting to tell them his real feelings—why he was doing this, but he knew he couldn't—not and keep them safe.

He turned to the door and hammered his fists against it. "Let me out! I'm done in here!"

The door latch released and Magnus pulled hard, swinging the door out, crashing it into the door stop on the opposing wall. He stopped inside the door for a moment, needing one last look. He turned sharply. Kieran had buried his face in Tommie's neck, unable to watch Magnus leave. Magnus looked at him, trying to burn his first love's image into his brain, an image so strong that not even Powell's best efforts could remove.

Tommie watched Magnus start to leave. For a moment, he was overcome with the unremitting wave of hatred that had erupted at the betrayal of his best friend. His eyes spat daggers across the room as Magnus turned in the doorway. Tommie wanted Magnus to look him in the eyes—to know the depth of his hatred—to know that this was not over by a long shot. But Magnus didn't even notice him, and Tommie was taken aback by the change in the boy's demeanor—by the strange expression that crossed Magnus' face as he looked back at Kieran. And then the expression changed again—the look of someone in great pain—a look that did not fit the words that had just been spoken. And then it was gone.

Magnus turned and fled out the door. One of the guards reached in and pulled the door closed. The sound of the deadbolt slipping into its sheaf echoed about the hard walls of the small white cell, mingling with the wracking sobs from Kieran's throat.

Tommie held Kieran tightly in his arms. He looked back at Sammy who stood paralyzed and in shock. Tommie held an arm out to him and the smaller boy rushed into his arms as well. Tommie embraced the two tightly, his mind racing to understand what had just happened. He bent his head to kiss the top of each friend's head.

Tommie clenched his eyes shut and tried to focus on Kieran's pain and Sammy's fear. Something, he didn't know what, had wrestled his own anger into the background. He chastised himself. Try as he did, he couldn't hate Magnus. His gaze returned to the securely locked door. What was he not seeing?

CHAPTER 19

Gail pushed the boxes out from under the bed where they had hidden her from view. She clicked the small tablet computer shut and stretched out on her back, starring up at the box springs overhead. It had taken some manipulation to get Sammy's camera links opened but she had managed it. Some, like the hallway by the basement elevator, had backup systems and could only be diverted for about thirty seconds. But, Sammy was a stickler for the simple—the shortest path to the most utility. Even her own, self-imposed computer illiteracy was not a handicap to negotiating Sammy's cartoon-like icons. She hadn't seen all that went on in Dr. Powell's lab, but she had caught the last part, and that was enough to make sleeping through the night very difficult.

She reached up and pulled the plug out of the socket behind her head, hoping that the overnight lack of use had left the small computer with a full battery—just in case. She had thought about making her move when everyone was asleep, but the surveillance cameras had held her at bay and she had not wanted to raise any alarms yet by disabling the cameras until the last necessary moments. She had decided on the more prudent and efficient course of moving about with the student body during class changes. A little bit of disguise, a baseball cap and an ace bandage about her bosom, and she could easily pass for a guy. She checked her watch. It was almost time. Another few moments and the cafeteria would be emptying into the halls for morning classes.

She slid from under the bed and carefully placed the tablet on the mattress. She pulled open the bottom drawer of Allison's bureau, pleased to find the array of braces and ace bandaging that one would expect in the effects of an ace, female tennis player. She knew that Allison also liked to wear one of Tommie's baseball caps when she was out on the courts and a little rummaging found one of the caps for her own special use.

She took a moment to don the various parts of her costume before checking things out in Allison's full length mirror on the back of her room's door. She checked out her new profile, more barrel-chested than bosomed—not that she didn't like her breasts. It's just that the binding would keep them out of harm's way should she need to pound a few heads together. That thought made her smile. Pummeling a few heads would improve her mood greatly.

The sound of loud voices caught her ear and she cracked the door open for a peek. A wave of students was just beginning to pour down the hall and Gail watched intently, waiting—and there he was as promised. Almost forgetting, she grabbed up the two tennis rackets, slipped them quickly into their carrying case and hoisted them onto her back by the case strap.

Conner strolled down the hall, in no hurry, arm-in-arm with a tall, nervous looking boy Gail recognized from the swim team. Conner looked like he could care less what those rushing past them thought about their apparent intimacy, but the swimmer was not as sure of himself, and looked about sheepishly for any sign of disapproval. As they passed Allison's dorm room, Conner caught Gail's eye in the crack of the door and nodded slightly in her direction.

Gail slid the baseball cap down over her forehead, shielding her face from any overhead surveillance. She manipulated the tablet computer into the back of her pants struggling to keep from dropping the tennis rackets at the same time. Waiting for a small group of young gymnasts to pass by, she slid out into the middle of them, keeping her head low. The group was moving fast enough that they caught up with Conner and his nervous companion in no time.

Gail left the group as quickly as she had joined it and insinuated herself between Conner and the swimmer. "So, you got my message?" she asked.

"Yes," Conner said, annoyed at her intervening presence. "It wasn't hard to miss. How did you get on my Facebook page anyway? You're not on my friend's list."

Gail threw her arms about the two boys and led them down a different hallway. "Oh, she said. "There's not a site on the internet that Sammy hasn't hacked."

"Nice," Conner said, rolling his eyes.

"So, who's your little friend here?" Gail looked the tall boy up and down. "Nice biceps," she said, and gave the swimmer's upper arm a squeeze.

"Hands off!" Conner said, cattily. "He's not your type."

"What's *not* your type?" Gail laughed.

"Ha, ha," Conner responded, pushing Gail over to the other side of the swimmer and taking his friend's arm again. "What's the drill?"

Gail caught the swimmer's eye and rolled her own.

"I'm Daniel," the boy said, extending his hand to Gail.

"You have my sympathies," Gail said to him, cocking her head in Conner's direction. She gave him her customary firm handshake.

"Again . . . ha, ha!" Conner said flatly. "I didn't know dykes had a sense of humor."

"Right back at ya!" Gail said. "Anyway, are you both ready for this?"

"We're ready," Conner said. "What, where, and when?"

"A diversion in the basement and as soon as we get there," Gail said. "Have you been filled in?" she asked, hooking her arm over the tall swimmer's shoulder.

"Yeah," Daniel said, nodding. "It sounds kind-a farfetched, but it sure fits in with what I've experienced around here. One of our team members started Dr. Powell's nutrition plan and the next thing you know he's left the school—supposedly a runaway."

"That excuse's getting kind of old," Gail said in agreement.

"Yeah," Daniel continued, "I mean . . . everyone at this school is gay."

"Or . . . gay-ish," Conner interjected.

"Right," Daniel said, laughing. "This is gay teenage paradise compared to other private, much less public high schools. Why would anyone want to run away?

"Exactly!" Gail slapped him on the back. "You've got a good head on your shoulders to be hanging with this prissy queen."

"You want our help or not?" Conner glared at Gail.

"Calm down, sister," Gail said. "Just making light conversation."

The group finally approached the basement elevator.

"This is it," Gail said, looking about. She checked her watch again. "Now listen." She stopped the group on the opposite side of the hall from the elevator at a classroom door. She pulled them close. "Okay, I need you to stand between me and the cameras."

The other boys side-stepped around to block the camera line of sight. Gail pulled out the small tablet computer, and tapped on its touch screen frantically.

"I can shut the camera down for about thirty seconds," Gail said. "When I say go we need to get to the elevator and get on it before the backup systems come on line."

The other two boys nodded nervously.

Gail slid the small tablet back into the rear of her jeans waistband. She turned to Daniel. "Wait for the blinking red light on the camera to go off." She gave Conner a shove. "You fags are so useless!" she called out loudly and started back down the hall at an angle toward the elevator.

"Who you calling a fag, you pencil-dick!" Conner said, assuming his role seamlessly to play to Gail's new male persona. He charged Gail and pushed her against the elevator door. The encased tennis rackets tumbled from her shoulder. Deftly, Gail pressed the elevator button as she backed into it. Conner pressed Gail's shoulders against the elevator door.

With her back to the hallway camera, Gail whispered, "Keep it up!"

"I'm gonna rip your balls off," Conner yelled out.

"Back off, bitch!" Gail said. She pushed Conner backwards and reached down to grab up the tennis rackets.

"Camera's off!" Daniel said excitedly. He charged into the two of them. At the same time the elevator door opened and Daniel shoved the others through the door. In a second, it closed behind them.

Gail quickly pushed the button to keep the door closed. "Good job," she said, slipping the rackets over her shoulder. "Okay, now here's what's up. It'll take about fifteen seconds for this elevator to take us down."

"What about cameras in the basement?" Daniel asked.

"Aren't any," Gail responded. "We're not supposed to be going down there."

"What now?" Daniel swallowed.

"You two get off first and start brawling ... or whatever it is you two fairy princesses do in a fight."

"Don't worry." Conner turned on Daniel dramatically. "This slut has given me a sexually transmitted disease."

"Really?" Gail's eyebrows went up.

"Acting!" Conner groaned.

"Well ... knowing you ..."

"Watch it!" Conner said. He turned again to Daniel. "Is it okay if I slap you?"

"That's fine." Daniel laughed nervously. "I can take it."

"Here we go!" Gail released the elevator hold button

and pushed the down button for the basement.

They caught themselves as the elevator jerked and started down. Gail eyed her companions closely for any sign of hesitation. If they didn't do their part, Gail knew her chances would be very slim against a full-grown male. She was strong and fully capable of physical aggression, but she was also a realist.

A small bell sounded, signaling their arrival at basement level. As if on cue, Conner stretched his arms out dramatically and took several deep, panting breaths as if preparing to go on stage. The elevator door slid open and Conner grabbed Daniel's hand, violently slinging the bigger boy out into the hallway beyond.

"You son of a bitch!" Conner screamed storming out of the elevator in pursuit. "You are lower than roach shit!"

Daniel steadied himself trying not to laugh. "Don't be such a drama queen, Conner!" he yelled back. He threw his hands into the air and headed away from Conner toward the small desk down the hall.

The burley security guard stood warily, putting his hand on his holstered pistol. Gail stayed in the elevator, one finger on the button holding the door open and grasping one of the tennis rackets in her other hand. She waited for her moment out of the guard's sightline.

"Don't you walk away from me!" Conner screeched, bearing down on Daniel.

Daniel was now almost sprinting toward the security desk. "Where's Dr. Powell, please?" he called to the guard.

"You two have no business down here," the guard said, facing them menacingly.

"Dude, that guy is crazy!" Daniel said, panting heavily

as he reached the guard. "Do something!"

"What's going on here?" the guard said, looking somewhat unsure.

Conner stood his ground halfway between the elevator and the guard's desk. "I wouldn't get to close to him if I were you," he called out to the guard. "He's got herpes!"

"You lying little cunt!" Daniel turned back to face Conner. "Don't blame me cause you're such a slut. There's no way you can blame this on me."

"How can you say that?" Conner dissolved into tears. "I have only been with you. I haven't cheated. Not once!"

"You two need to take this back upstairs," the guard said, moving from behind the desk. "You have no business being down here."

"Of course I need to be down here," Conner said, sobbing loudly. "I need to see Dr. Powell." He sank to his knees. "No one cares about me here."

Daniel rushed over to Conner. "Don't say that, baby." He reached down and pulled Conner up into his arms. "I do care about you. You've just let this get out of control."

"I'll probably die!" Conner said shrilly.

"Dr. Powell's not down here, boys." The guard moved closer to them, hoping to corral them back into the elevator. "Make an appointment with his secretary."

"Make an appointment?" Conner fell against Daniel's shoulder sobbing.

"Don't be so insensitive," Daniel said angrily pointing at the guard. "Can't you see he's upset?"

"Look," said the Guard. "I don't care what the problem is. You two get back on that elevator." He holstered his weapon to grab their arms. "Come on."

Conner shook free of the guard's grasp. "Take your filthy hands off me you Cretan!" His eyes were blazing now.

"Come on, Conner," Daniel said soothingly. "Let's go back up. We'll get you an appointment."

"No!" Conner's hands went to his hips. "I want to see Dr. Powell now!"

"That ain't gonna happen," the guard said. "Now move it!"

Conner once again dissolved into loud sobs.

"Conner," Daniel said. "Come on. Let's go."

Conner reached out and pushed Daniel forcefully, sending the gangly boy reeling past the guard. "You did this to me!" He pushed the guard aside. "You had your fun and now you think you can just walk away!"

"Would you just chill?" Daniel regained his balance.

"You asshole!" Conner swung hard, catching Daniel on the side of the face with a thunderous clap.

Daniel fell back into the guard whose back was now to the elevator.

"Settle down!" the guard yelled, stepping back and pushing Daniel away from him. "That's enough!"

A loud *whack* echoed through the hall. The guard crumpled to the floor. Gail stood over him, tapping the business end of one of the tennis rackets against the palm of her hand. Satisfied, she knelt down and rifled the unconscious man's pocket for his keys.

"Is he dead?" Conner asked, his voice trembling.

"Not yet," Gail responded, extracting the keys from one of the man's pants pockets. "And if he knows what's good for him, he'd better stay down." She started to rise, but paused. "One more thing." She slid the man's pistol from its holster and stood, shoving it into her waistband.

"Now we're in business!"

"Pretty good distraction, huh?" Conner said proudly.

"Not bad," Gail agreed with a nod.

Daniel rubbed the side of his face. "Boy, you sure can hit hard," he said to Conner, managing a grin.

"Sorry, sweet cheeks," Conner said, reaching up to pat the taller boy's face. "Just acting."

"Oh my God!" Gail said with mock surprise. "You mean you don't have herpes?"

"Again," Conner responded, shaking his head. "More trite lesbian humor."

"I don't know," Daniel said. "For a minute there, I wasn't sure myself."

Conner puffed up like a peacock. "Ladies and gentleman," he said to the imaginary audience. "The Academy Award for best actor . . ."

"Put a sock in it!" Gail said with a dismissive wave. "We've got work to do."

"Gail?" A voice called out.

Gail turned to the metal door, across from the guard's desk, searching for the source of the muffled cry. "Tommy?" she shouted.

"In here, Gail!" Tommy's resonant voice overcame the intruding metal and sound proofing.

"Allison?" Gail shouted. "Allison?"

"Over here!" Allison's voice called from the door opposite.

"Okay," Gail said with purpose. "Ladies first." She fumbled with the keys, trying several in the door before one finally engaged. "Bingo!" she said and swung the door inward.

"Gail!" Allison stood in front of Gail, almost in tears, hands clasped under her chin.

"My lady," Gail said, spreading her arms. "Your knight in shining armor is here."

Allison dove at her, wrapping her arms about the shorter girl's neck, giggling. "Gail, thank God!"

Gail glanced back at her two co-conspirators. "Take a good look, boys. See what you pansies are missing?"

"What we've been missing?" Conner asked, linking his arm through Daniel's. "What's there to see?" He cast Daniel a sideways glance. "Lesbianics is pretty much like two watermelons bumping in the night."

Daniel choked with laughter.

Allison released her hold on Gail. "Queer chauvinist pigs," she said, shaking a finger at the two boys.

Gail pushed past the boys into the hall, pulling Allison along with her. "Fags," she said, turning to the boys. "What they lack in imagination, they make up for in . . ." She gestured to the two boys' heads. "Weird hairdos."

"Boooooo!" the two boys said in unison.

"Come on!" Gail pulled Allison over to the other door. "Okay, boys," she called out. "The women . . ." She glanced back at Conner and Daniel. "The real women . . ." She shook her head at them. "Are gonna save your asses once again."

"Open the goddamn door!" Tommie yelled in muffled tones.

"Keep your pants on," Gail responded, fumbling once more with the keys. Finally she swung the door inward. "Okay, boys," she said, beaming triumphantly at them. "Grab your condoms and let's go!"

"I told you she'd get us out!" Sammy said with a self-satisfied nod as the heroes swarmed into the cell.

Gail's attention immediately went to Kieran, and she

didn't like what she saw. "What's got into . . ."

"Gail!" Tommie said, stretching out his arms. "I'm gonna kiss you!" He lunged at her.

Gail stepped back. "You keep your goddamn hands . . ." Her voice disappeared as Tommie's lips planted themselves firmly on hers. He released her just as quickly before she had a chance to regain her wits and punch him in the stomach.

"Hey, babe!" Tommie said, hurriedly side-stepping the sputtering, spitting Gail for his true love. "I was worried about you." He pulled Allison into his arms, kissing her passionately.

"You asshole!" Gail said, landing a kick squarely on Tommie's buttocks.

"Ow!" Tommie rubbed his bottom. He smiled down at Allison. "She has definite intimacy problems," he said.

"Don't be so insensitive," Allison said, smiling up at him. "You've got to remember, you kissing Gail is like a guy kissing you."

"Well," Gail said. "We all know Tommie Tune here wouldn't have any problem with that."

Allison caught a glance of Kieran. "What?" She broke free from Tommie's embrace. Kieran was blank-faced and exhausted looking. Sammy stood by him looking exceptionally afraid.

"Hi, sweetheart," Allison said, opening her arms to Sammy.

Sammy didn't need a second invitation and rushed into her embrace.

Allison kissed him on the forehead. "What's going on?" she whispered in his ear.

"They . . ." Sammy stiffened "They took Magnus."

Allison turned to Kieran, fully aware of what that

meant. "Kieran," she said softly and took his hand. "Oh, Kieran."

Kieran couldn't look at her. Tears again streamed down his smooth cheeks.

"Damn it!" Tommie embraced Kieran from behind. "Kieran, you've got to pull it together," he said, shaking Kieran slightly. "We need your brain power now more than ever."

"We're gonna end this shit today!" Gail boomed. She shook her tennis racket in the air. "Now there are more of us."

For the first time, Tommie noticed Conner and Daniel hanging back at the door. "Conner!" he said, leaving Kieran. "Welcome to Fags Gone Wild!" He reached out to hug the boy.

Conner held up a hand. "Hug your girlfriend, straight boy."

He circled around Tommie to Kieran. "Everyone, that's Daniel," he said, pointing to the tall boy behind him. "Say hello to him."

With the others distracted, Conner turned his attention to Kieran. He stood looking at him, hands on hips, hoping his presence would pull some sarcastic response. Except for the tears, Kieran's face was blank.

"I can't believe I'm gonna do this," Conner said, jerking Kieran into his arms. "I know you're not much to look at, but Christ!" He pushed Kieran away, gripping the boy's shoulders. "If you'd just stop bawling and . . ." He flicked a hand through Kieran's hair. "And washed your hair or something."

Kieran looked up at him for the first time.

"Girlfriend." Conner cradled Kieran's cheeks in his hands. "Magnus needs you." He gestured to the group.

"And we're here to help."

"Damn right!" Gail said. "We've got strength in numbers now." She tossed the tennis racket in her hand to Allison. "And now we've got an equalizer!" She pulled the heavy pistol from her waistband. "And I intend to use it!"

"Holy shit!" Tommie said. "We've got a loaded lesbian on our hands."

"Well?" Conner asked, squeezing Kieran's shoulders.

Kieran blinked and wiped his eyes. He looked at Conner. "You have a lot of gall talking about my hair," he said weakly. He waved a finger at Conner's rainbow spiked hair. "You look like some baby ate a box of crayons and crapped on your head."

Conner turned to the others. "He's back."

The group laughed, relieved. No one looked more relieved than Sammy. He smiled broadly, hugging himself.

"Hi," Daniel said from behind.

Sammy turned sharply.

"I'm Daniel Rhodes," the tall boy said shyly. "You're Sammy, aren't you?"

Sammy nodded, tongue-tied.

"I was in your English Lit class first semester." Daniel smiled down at Sammy. "We all had books but you had that . . . that . . ."

"Kindle," Sammy said, afraid to look the other boy in the eye. "I'm . . . I'm a technology nerd."

"It was cool," Daniel said, laughing. "Everyone was jealous."

"They're easy to use." Sammy smiled up at Daniel. "A lot of kids have them now."

"True, but you started the fashion here."

"There you have it. I'm on the cutting edge of . . .

something." Sammy batted his eyes at Daniel, trying to think of what Kieran would do. "You're a swim jock, right?"

"Well," Daniel said, shuffling nervously. "I don't think anyone considers swimmers jocks."

"I do," Sammy said quickly. "I admire anyone physically coordinated. Apparently all my coordination's up here." He tapped the side of his head, thinking quickly, "and here," he added, wiggling his fingers in the air.

"You look perfectly coordinated to me."

Sammy's jaw dropped.

"You're arms are long enough," Daniel continued. "You'd probably make a good swimmer."

"Really?" Sammy cocked his head at the tall boy. "That's so sweet," he said, unaware that the rest of the group was watching him and Daniel closely.

"Okay!" Tommie said loudly.

Sammy started, suddenly aware of Tommie looking at him. "What?" he asked innocently.

Tommy hulked over to the two younger boys. He stood eye to eye with Daniel, trying to look menacing. "So," he said and turned to Sammy. "Do I need to be jealous?"

"Wha . . . ?" Daniel stuttered.

"Yes," Sammy said, pushing Tommie away and laughing. He took Daniel's arm. "Ignore him," he said flashing Daniel his brightest smile. "He's just playing with you."

"Well," Daniel said, his smile returning. "Can't say I'd blame him for being jealous."

Sammy seemed to inhale all the air in the room.

"Poor Conner," Kieran said. He seemed more

himself. "Dumped for a younger man."

"Honey, I've never been dumped," Conner replied, pursing his lips. "To me boyfriends are like Kleenex. You blow, then you pull a fresh one out of the box."

"You really are a slut," Gail said, snickering.

"An out and proud slut, thank you," Conner said, snapping his fingers through the air.

"What about Magnus?" Kieran asked weakly.

"Don't worry," Tommie said. "We'll get him out."

"What happened to Magnus?" Allison asked.

"They took him to be their new lab rat," Tommie answered. "But we'll get him."

"They didn't take him," Kieran said. He looked down at the floor. "He went willingly."

"What?" Allison couldn't believe what she had just heard. "I don't believe that."

"Well, it's true," Kieran said, anger replacing sadness. "He doesn't want to be gay. He's decided to take . . . the cure." He almost spat the word.

"He's just confused, Kieran," Tommie said. "Fear is keeping him from thinking straight."

"Oh, I think straight is exactly how he's trying to think," Kieran said, his voice rising. "Used again!   I should be use to it by now, I guess."

Tommie tried to embrace Kieran, but the angry boy pushed him away. "Let him rot in the lab!" Kieran broke away from the group. "I don't need to waste my time on someone that screwed up!" He was almost shouting through the renewed tears.

"Kieran!" Tommie said.

Kieran stomped a foot for emphasis. "I mean it!" he said, but too weakly to be taken seriously.

"Hold your horses there, missy," Gail said, waving the

tennis racket for emphasis. "You're way off the deep end."

"You weren't here," Kieran said, turning away from her. "You didn't hear what he said." He rubbed his swollen eyes. "You didn't hear how he said it to me!"

"Bullshit!" Gail paraded to the front of the group. "I may not have seen what went on in this room, but I saw what went on in the lab before and . . ." Her hands went to her hips. "If you'd let go of the personal drama long enough to listen to me, I think you'll see things differently."

"What are you talking about?" Kieran covered his face with his hands.

"Well," Gail said. "For instance, I assume that Magnus came in, delivered some spiel about not wanting to be gay anymore, and how you couldn't see each other anymore, blah, blah, blah."

Kieran's eyes widened.

"Jeez!" Tommie said, impressed. "Are all dykes psychic?"

"I don't know," Gail replied, rolling her eyes at him. "Are all straight boys stupid?" She dismissed him with a wave. "Look," she said, returning her attention to Kieran. "Magnus was dragged into the lab. Powell told him to cooperate or we would all be killed. If he cooperated, we would all be sent home, alive. He had to convince you he was serious so you wouldn't question . . . you'd just leave and forget about him."

Kieran sank onto one of the bunk beds, his face clouded and pained.

"And I guess you all bought it, lock, stock, and barrel." Gail sighed and dropped her arms to her side. "Come on, Kieran," she said. "Magnus loves you. Can you really believe he said what he said just to hurt you?"

"I'm too stupid to live!" Kieran buried his face in his hands, sobbing.

"No, you're not." Tommie plopped down beside Kieran and threw an arm about him. "We all should have known something was up." He gave Kieran a shake. "Now, cheer up! Magnus still loves you and, for God's sake, he was willing to sacrifice himself for you." He looked at the others. "For all of us."

Kieran's head shot up, the flow of tears suddenly halted. "I'll be goddamned if that's gonna happen!" He shook off Tommie's arm and jumped to his feet. "I am fed up with this shit!" he bellowed.

"Watch out, people!" Tommie looked up at the group wide-eyed. "Queen Matheson is loose once more!"

A groan filtered in from the hallway just outside the door.

"Looks like dip-shit's waking up," Gail said, hoisting up her tennis racket.

"Give me that!" Kieran snatched the tennis racket from her. "We're getting out of here now!" He headed for the door and everyone parted, giving him a wide birth.

"Shall we?" Tommie motioned to the others to follow. He grabbed Allison's hand. "Stick close, babe. We don't want any friendly fire accidents."

"He looks more pissed off than I've ever seen him," Allison whispered.

"To know him is to fear him," Tommie replied with a smile.

Outside the cell, the battered security guard had roused. He sat on the floor holding his head and moaning. He finally oriented himself enough to reach for his radio.

"I don't think so!" a voice roared from behind.

The guard turned his head sharply, just in time to catch the full force of the tennis racket Kieran swung with all his might. A loud crack echoed down the hall and the guard smashed back onto the hard floor, rolling a few feet into unconsciousness.

"Damn, boy!" Tommie said, keeping his distance. "That's some back hand!"

The others crowded forward. Kieran stood triumphantly over the fallen guard. Gail was laughing, enjoying the scene.

"Sammy," Kieran commanded.

Sammy rushed forward, wringing his hands. "Yes, ma'am!" He almost saluted.

"Just get the radio from him." Kieran couldn't help but smile at the boy's new-found audacity. "You should be able to monitor what the other goons are up to."

Sammy grabbed the two-way radio and fiddled with the dial.

"Now what?" Conner asked.

"Armageddon!" Kieran responded, hoisting the tennis racket onto his shoulder.

"Fall in, troops!" Tommie said, laughing.

"It's about time!" Gail pulled the pistol from her belt. "Let's kick some ass."

"You know anything about shooting that?" Tommie put a hand on her shoulder.

"What's to know," Gail said with a smirk. "Point and pull the trigger, and I'll probably be more accurate than you are at the urinal."

"Ha, ha," Tommie said flatly. "How about I take that other racket off your hands?"

"Sure." Gail pulled off the other racket that had been

slung over her shoulder by its carrying strap. "I need both hands free for my pistol grip." She assumed a crouched position like a TV cop, gun held in both hands, pointing down the hallway above Kieran's head.

"You just keep that thing pointed up and away," Tommie said.

"Yeah, yeah, and you do the same," Gail responded.

CHAPTER 20

The rebel teens crowded around the heavily reinforced door to the infirmary. Sammy hung back adjusting the radio frequency, listening intently to the traffic of garbled conversations going on between the Institute's security staff. Daniel inched over beside Sammy, leaning over his shoulder to watch. Sammy became aware of the other boy's hand on his shoulder. He smiled to himself and willed his hands to remain steady.

"There," Sammy said, as a clear voice came over the radio. "Got it."

"What are they saying?" Daniel asked.

Sammy could feel the boy's breath against his ear. "Nothing important," he said, turning his eyes up to Daniel's. "Just small talk."

"You sure are good with electronics, aren't you?" Daniel smiled down at him.

Sammy looked into the boy's dark eyes. All he could think was *what would Kieran do?* "I'm just good with my hands," he said finally, batting his eyes at Daniel for good measure.

The tall boy's eyes widened and then crinkled into a grin. "You're a lot different than I thought you'd be," he said.

"Really?" Sammy returned his gaze to the radio, blushing. "I hope I've surprised you."

Daniel leaned into Sammy's ear again. "Completely," he whispered breathily.

"Jesus Christ!" Gail said, thumping the side of her head with her fist. "We're all about to die and these two are making goo-goo eyes at each other."

"We're not about to die," Kieran said, completely serious. "So leave them alone."

"Whatever!" Gail pulled the small tablet out of her pants. "Here nerd-boy!" She shoved it at Sammy.

"My computer!" Sammy grabbed it from her excitedly. "How . . . ?"

"Don't you worry about how," Gail said. "You just take care of business before you do anymore googly eyes at fish-boy there."

Sammy giggled and turned on his favorite toy.

"What now?" Tommie asked.

"Storm the citadel!" Conner said excitedly.

"Keep your voice down," Kieran warned. "We have the element of surprise. Gail, you've got the gun. You'll need to go in first."

Tommie gingerly tried the door knob. "Locked," he said. "How do we get in?"

"Gail?" Kieran asked, looking at the stocky girl.

"Again," she said. "No prob." She reached into her

jeans pocket and pulled out the familiar ring of keys. "I certainly remembered to bring these."

"Excellent!" Kieran smiled, taking the keys from her.

"God," Tommie said. "I'm going to have to kiss her again."

"I wouldn't advise it," Gail said. She jerked the pistol's cocking slide back. "Lover boy!"

An ominous click rang through the hallway as a bullet was chambered for firing. She raised an eyebrow at Tommie.

Tommie looked back at Allison with a grin. "God, she makes me hot!"

"My next boyfriend's gonna have better sense." Allison said, rolling her eyes.

"Aw, babe," Tommie said, donning his hurt puppy look. "Lesbos need love, too."

Gail started to respond.

"All right, all right!" Kieran interrupted. He selected one of the keys and slid it into the lock. He turned it slowly, trying to minimize the sound as the deadbolt pulled free of the metal door sill. "Okay, Gail," he whispered. "Get ready."

Gail gripped the pistol in both hands and held it at the ready.

Kieran held up a hand. "No shooting unless it's absolutely necessary!"

Slowly Kieran opened the heavy door a crack. He peered into the room. The familiar, big-haired nurse was sitting in a chair, crocheting, in front of a large grey, metal tank of some sort.

Kieran turned back to the others. "One," he mouthed and held up 1 finger to indicate the number of persons in the room. He nodded to Gail and looked back at the others. With a deep breath, he jerked the door open and burst into the room. He bore down on the nurse with Gail right beside him. The nurse was oblivious to their presence.

"Don't move!" Gail pushed ahead and pressed her pistol muzzle into the woman's temple. "Don't even think about it!"

Despite the warning, the stunned woman stood instinctively. "What are you doing in here?" she said, dropping her crochet to the floor.

"Goddamn it!" Gail swung the heavy pistol, striking the woman hard across the face.

The nurse spun in a circle before falling like a limp puppet back into the chair.

"What about don't move did you not understand?" Gail asked, breathing heavily.

"Well," Kieran said, throwing up his hands in exasperation. "I guess we won't be asking her any questions. You know, like where is Magnus?" He glared at Gail, hands on his hips.

"Hey," Gail said with a shrug. "At least I didn't shoot her."

The others had crowded into the room, looking ready for battle.

Kieran waved to Conner. "Find something and tie her up." He looked down at the nurse. "And gag her too."

Conner rushed over to the nearby lab counter and began rifling through drawers and cabinets.

"What the hell is this thing?" Tommie asked, rapping on the massive tank-like structure with his knuckles.

"To hell with this thing," Kieran said with growing agitation. "Where the hell is Magnus?"

"Not far, I'd say," Gail responded, pushing the pistol

back into her waist band. "I'd say he's inside this thing."

"What?" Kieran's voice broke.

"After shooting him up with their poisons," Gail said. She tried to remember what Powell had said to Magnus in the lab. "The next stage in the so-called treatment was an isolation tank of some sort."

"Let me have a look," Sammy said, handing the radio to Daniel. He circled the tank, studying every bolt and seam. "There," he said, pointing to a stream of hoses connecting the metal behemoth to an array of oxygen tanks on the far wall. "It's some sort of hyperbaric chamber." He tapped on a line of needle gauges at the intake point. "It's also pressurized."

"Get him out of there!" Kieran was to the point of screaming.

"Calm down, Kieran," Tommie said. "Let Sammy do his thing."

Kieran buried his face into Tommie's chest.

Conner returned from his foraging. "I found some ace bandages and tape. He motioned to Allison. "Help me truss up this turkey."

"Gladly," Allison said, kneeling beside the unconscious nurse.

"It's like a deep sea decompression chamber," Sammy said excitedly from behind the large tank. "Here's the entrance!"

Kieran's head jerked up and he pulled Tommie around to the back of the tank with him. "Where?" He asked, excitedly.

Sammy pointed to the round porthole-like doorway, sealed like a bank vault by a large metal wheel.

"Open it!" Kieran said, grabbing for the wheel.

"Wait!" Sammy caught Kieran's hand.

"What are you doing?" Kieran said angrily.

"You can't just open it," Sammy said. "If you do and Magnus is in there, it will decompress too quickly and Magnus will be killed!"

Kieran stepped back, angry at himself more than anything. Sammy stood frozen, afraid to do anything more.

"Ignore me, Sammy," Kieran said, closing his eyes. "You know what you're doing. Just tell me if there's something you need me to do."

Sammy looked at Tommie.

"Figure it out, kid," Tommie said, giving him a reassuring nod. He took Kieran's hand, pulling him out of Sammy's way.

Sammy returned his attention to the tank. He rechecked the overall configuration, trying desperately to find a control point. He went back to the array of hoses. Braided in among them was a thick black strand.

Sammy dropped to the floor, fingering the cable looking for some sort of imprint that would confirm his suspicions. "Bingo!" he cried out, jumping back to his feet.

"What?" Kieran asked.

"Data cable," Sammy replied, tracing the path of the cable back to the wall below the oxygen canisters.

He followed it with his eyes along the baseboard. It ended at a freestanding cabinet fitted into the corner of the room. Sammy darted to the cabinet and pulled it open. A keyboard rested on a pullout extension just below an oversized monitor. The screen was black. Sammy extracted a small stool from a niche below the keyboard and plopped down.

"What have you found?" Tommie asked.

"Can we get him out?" Kieran asked, joining Tommie behind Sammy.

"That may take me a little time," Sammy responded, sliding out the keyboard. "I think this may be the control point for the tank. I just need some time to check it all out."

"Take all the time you need," Tommie said. He squeezed Kieran's hand. "Let us know if we can help."

"Guys!" Daniel said, coming around the tank into view.

"What's up?" Tommie asked noting the fear in the boy's face.

"I just heard on the radio," Daniel said, holding out the radio as if to prove a point. "They're about to do a security check down on this level!" He looked like he might panic. "What do we do?"

"Stay calm," Tommie said, taking command. "Kieran?" He put a hand to his friend's cheek. "Stay here with Sammy in case he needs something."

"I'm okay," Kieran said softly.

Tommie and Daniel circled back to the other side of the tank where Allison and Conner were finishing up their work on the unconscious nurse.

"All right, guys," Tommie said. "We've got a problem."

"What now?" Allison asked, getting to her feet.

"Can we get this thing opened?" Gail pulled her pistol out. "I can shoot a few holes in it."

"Settle down, girl. No," Tommie said, rolling his eyes. "Sammy's working on that angle. Daniel just picked up that the security goons are on their way down to check on things."

"How much time do we have?" Conner asked, tying

off the last knot at the nurse's feet.

"No way to tell," Tommie replied. "Gail, man the door. The moment they're on this level let me know."

Gail strutted over to the door carrying her pistol at her side.

"Next," Tommie said to the other three, "we need to come up with a way to barricade the door."

They all split up, heading for opposite corners of the room searching for heavy objects. Tommie headed back to the control point to check on Sammy's progress. As he rounded the tank, he could see the large monitor was now active and filled with various pop-ups and windows displaying undecipherable readouts.

"How're we doing?" Tommie asked, coming up beside Kieran.

Kieran's hands were to his mouth, his eyes wide in horror.

"What?" Tommie leaned over Sammy's shoulder, studying the monitor. The various graphs and readouts overlay a central video feed. "What are we looking at?" He asked.

Sammy looked up at him. He hesitated, seeing the look on Kieran's face. "Magnus," he whispered to Tommie.

"Where?" Tommie scanned the screen looking for any sign of Magnus.

Sammy pointed to the central video feed window and outlined a human form with his finger.

"Oh, shit!" Tommie said. He realized it was an overhead shot of a human form, head encased in a form-fitting cap from which streamed a flood of wires like a Medusa's hair. The features were covered with a mask over the nose and mouth, but Tommie was able to recognize Magnus' closed-eye features.

Tommie leaned his head down next to Sammy's and whispered, "Is he alive?"

Sammy nodded, pointing to what looked like a heart monitor readout.

"I'm standing right here," Kieran said from behind them. "I know he's alive. Just get him out!" He put a hand over his mouth, suddenly aware that he was screaming.

Tommie kept his attention on the monitor. "What do you think, Sammy?" He said, no longer trying to keep Kieran from hearing.

"Just a second," Sammy was squinting at a small window overlay at the bottom of the screen. "Just checking something on the internet," he said, reading quickly. "Based on this level of pressurization, we'll need at least twenty minutes to safely equalize the pressure in the tank to the outside."

"Get to it!" Tommie ordered. He turned to Kieran. "Twenty minutes, Kieran," he said. "Hang in there."

"I'm sorry, Tommie," Kieran said, nodding weakly, trying to look brave.

Tommie embraced his friend and kissed him on the cheek. "You're doing fine," he said, and quickly headed back to the others.

"How's it going over there?" Allison asked the moment Tommie rounded the tank.

"Tricky," Tommie replied, "What's our progress on barricading the door?"

"Not very good," Daniel said. "Those lab tables," he said, pointing at the long row of metal tables, "are about all there is, and they don't look very heavy."

"No they don't," Tommie said, studying the room's

contents for himself. "Nothing." He went over to one of the tables, grabbed it under one corner and lifted it effortlessly. "Useless!" He muttered to himself.

"What do we do?" Allison asked, wringing her hands.

Tommie shrugged. "We've got to come up with something."

"Let 'em come," Gail said sharply, waving her pistol.

"Just remember, Tommie said, giving her a stern look. "They have lots of weapons. We only have your pistol and a couple of tennis rackets."

Gail's bravado slipped a little with that reminder.

"We may have to hold up in here," Tommie said. "This may be our Alamo."

The friends looked at each other, understanding exactly what that meant if history was any guide.

"We have got to barricade that door!" Tommie put his hands on top of his head and clenched his eyes shut in anger.

"Jesus Christ!" Conner said. "The biggest thing in the room is that damn tank and it must weight a ton."

"At least," Daniel agreed.

Allison eyed the huge tank, hopelessly shaking her head. "How the hell did they get that monstrosity in here in the first place?" She asked.

"Shit!" Tommie looked at the tank in a new light. He slapped the side of his head. "Stupid, stupid, stupid!" He rushed over to it and fell to the floor, studying the structure's base. "Damn it!" he said, almost laughing.

"What?" Allison asked worriedly.

"Has he lost his marbles under there?" Gail asked, watching from the door.

"The damn things on wheels," Tommie said, sitting back up.

"So what?" Conner said. "We still can't move it." He shook his head. "Even if we all pushed . . ."

"Don't you see?" Tommie interrupted. "It's motorized. There's some sort of drive assembly under there. Sammy . . ." He paused.

Tommie jumped to his feet and ran around the tank with the others in pursuit.

"Sammy!" Tommie called out, bearing down on the boy who sat in rapt concentration over the control panel. "Sammy!"

"Huh?" Sammy looked up. "What?" he asked, as if unsure where he was.

"Sammy," Tommie said. "We have to move the tank!"

"Move the . . . ?" Sammy adjusted his glasses looking about confused.

Tommie took the boy's face in his hands and turned it up to face him. "We . . . need . . . to . . . move the tank," he said slowly. "To barricade the door. It's the heaviest thing in the room."

"It weighs 3200 pounds. Are you insane?"

"It's on wheels," Tommie said, rolling his eyes.

"Wheels?"

"And they're motorized," Tommie added, patting Sammy on the head.

"What?" Sammy turned back to the control panel, clicking the mouse feverishly.

"I'll be damned," he said. "It is, and I can drive it from here."

"Then move it to the door and pronto," Tommie said.

"What about Magnus?" Kieran asked, his voice shaking.

"Well?" Tommie asked, turning back to Sammy. "Will this interfere with your decompression of the tank?"

Sammy pursed his lips, studying the monitor. "No," he said confidently. "The two operations are independent. We just need to make sure that none of the hoses and wires get tangled in the process."

"Excellent," Tommie said. He turned to Kieran. "Everything's gonna be all right, okay?"

Kieran nodded silently.

"Everyone get on the wires and hoses connecting the tank to everything else," Tommie ordered. "We don't want any problems while Sammy moves the tank into position against the door." He rushed around checking all the connections himself. "No tangles, no snags, nothing. Call out if you see a problem developing so Sammy can stop the damn thing."

The other teens obeyed without question, each one manning an area of wires or tubes not covered by someone else. Tommie looked over the tank that held his friend. In that same instant, the selfless willingness of his other friends to follow his instructions touched him in a way he hadn't expected. The weight of leadership hung over him and the realization that his decisions from there on out might mean the difference between life and death for Magnus—for all his friends—and for himself, produced a strange tightness in his chest.

Tommie looked back at Kieran standing alone by the wall, helpless with fear and mental exhaustion. It was Kieran's role to lead the group mind—to make the important decisions that affected the others. A resolve took hold of Tommie's will, strengthening his mind and body—a resolve to not fail his friends, no matter what.

"All right," he said, seeing that everyone was in place.

"Are you ready, Sammy?"

"Ready," Sammy called out. "It's a pretty straight run to the door and the tank even has a video feed from the front for guidance."

"Are you sure you can do this?" Tommie asked, already knowing the answer.

Sammy's head jerked around. "Does the Pope wear red Prada shoes?"

"And a pretty lace dress," Conner added from his position behind the tank.

Renewed laughter rippled through the tension.

"That's how we do the Vatican drag," Tommie said lightly. "Okay, let's get this show on the road. You have the con, Mr. Harper."

"Aye, aye, captain," Sammy said, returning to the control center.

A hum of electricity surged through the base of the tank structure, and it shuddered ominously. Kieran's hands returned to his mouth anxiously, and Tommie motioned to his friend to join him. Kieran threw himself into Tommie's arms and they watched together as the mammoth tank began an agonizingly slow movement across the floor."

"Heads up!" Gail called out from the door. "We have incoming!"

"Shit!" Tommie said, leaving Kieran for the doorway. "Shut it and lock it!" He called out, reaching the door as Gail closed it. "Where's the key?" He asked frantically.

Gail pulled the set of keys from her pocket.

Tommie fumbled with them. "Which one?"

Gail pointed out one of the keys and Tommie jammed it into the two-way deadbolt assembly. With both hands, he jerked back on the key, breaking it off in the lock.

"Gail," Tommie commanded. "Get to the side of the tank and follow it. Keep the door in your sights and . . ." He looked at her hard. "If that door opens, you start shooting."

Gail nodded and rushed over to a position beside the tank as it crept toward the door. Her hands held the pistol steady, aimed at the door. Her eyes met Tommie's for an instant and he nodded to her. She nodded back, her face a mask of steel.

"Okay, everyone," Tommie said, satisfied. "Keep your eyes on those wires and tubes. Gail's got the door covered. "Mr. Harper?" He called out. "Can this damn thing go any faster?"

"Nay, captain!" Sammy yelled back in what might have been a Scottish brogue. "I'm giving her all she's got!"

"Okay." Tommie took a deep breath. "Steady as she goes," he said in his best Captain Kirk impression. "How much longer on the decompression?"

"Five more minutes," Sammy called back.

"How are we doing with wires and hoses?" Tommie scanned the others.

"Everything's good," Conner replied from his position at the array of oxygen tanks. "Allison's got the wires under control."

"Baby?" Tommie called to her.

"We're okay," Allison called back.

Tommie returned his attention to the door as the knob was turned noisily from the outside. Was there anything he was forgetting? He looked up at the video camera hanging from high in the front corner of the room.

"Shit!" Tommie tightened his grip on the tennis racket he was still carrying and bore down on that corner of the room. He lifted the rack to test the distance and jumped taking a swing at the camera. It was too high.

"I can reach it," Daniel said, coming up beside him.

"You sure?"

"It may take a couple of tries," Daniel said, eyeing the camera, "but I'll get it."

Tommie handed the boy the racket. "Knock the shit out of it," he said returning to the door.

He looked back at Gail. Beads of sweat were trickling down the side of her face and her nerves were starting to tell. "Give 'em hell, boyfriend," he said, giving her a thumbs up.

She stuck her tongue out at him and the worst of the tension seemed to evaporate. Her aim was still steady.

Tommie pressed his ear to the door. He could hear several attempts to jam a key in from the other side and felt a sense of accomplishment for his decision to break a key off in the deadbolt. He could also hear the angry mumbling of the men outside, but not clearly enough to understand what they were saying—or planning.

"Good," Tommie said, clapping his hands. He started back for the control center. "That ought to hold them off long enough . . ."

The sound of metal hitting the floor caught his ear. In his peripheral vision, he saw a small piece of metal skipping across the floor tile.

"Shit!" Tommie said, realizing the key tip he had broken off in the door was now dislodged. He turned sharply to the door. The wieldy tank car was a good two yards from the door. "Gail!" He called out.

"Get behind the tank," She yelled back, squinting

down the pistol sight line at the door. "I've got the door."

Tommie cast a quick look of desperation in Sammy's direction.

"Hurry, Sammy!" Kieran's voice went up an octave.

Tommy heard the door knob turn. "No!" He cried out and charged the door, slamming against it with his shoulder.

A cry of pain beyond let him know that someone's finger had not prevented the door from closing. He slid down to the floor, his back wedged against the door and his feet braced against the bumper of the tank car. A loud crash sounded from the corner.

"Got it!" Daniel yelled as the remains of the offending video camera danced across the hard surface of the floor.

The door knob turned again and Tommie cried out in pain as multiple human battering rams slammed against the door from the outside.

"Tommie!" Allison shouted, rushing around the tank.

"Stay back!" Tommie commanded through clenched teeth.

The tank continued its relentless progression to the door, bending Tommie's legs at the knees in its course.

"Fuck!" Tommie cried out again as his spine absorbed another slamming onslaught from behind the door. His body continued to retract like an accordion at the knees and waist.

A pair of hands suddenly grabbed Tommie's ankles and jerked his feet off to the side. His head hammered against the door as he was spun around and dragged across the slick, porcelain tile floor away from the doorway. Tommie heard the door start to open and he could hear the shouts of the men beyond.

"Goddamn it!" Tommie clenched his eyes shut and almost screamed. He hammered the floor with his fists overcome by his sense of failure.

The shouts from the doorway disappeared as the mammoth tank closed in, preventing the door from opening more than a foot. In a few seconds, its relentless push caused the intruding arms and hands to withdraw and the door clicked shut.

CHAPTER 21

"Tommie!" A voice called out.

Tommie heard the electrical whine of the tank's motor stop. He opened his eyes.

"Tommie!" Daniel said again, trying to pull Tommie to his feet.

Tommie glanced back at the door. The tank was firmly seated against it. He breathed a sigh of relief. "Thank God," he said, massaging the small of his back.

"Are you okay," Daniel asked. His hands still gripped Tommie's ankles. "Sorry," he said, letting go quickly.

"No problem and thanks," Tommie said.

Daniel helped him to his feet.

"Status report, Sammy!" Tommie called out.

"Decompression is complete," Sammy called back. "I'm releasing the airlock."

All eyes went to the oval door at the rear of the tank. The wheel, centered on the door that locked it into place, was spinning counterclockwise as if by magic.

"You rock, Sammy," Tommy said, as a short hissing sound signaled the door's opening.

"It's a pretty user-friendly system," Sammy said from the control panel. "I've already stopped the sedation and . . . I wasn't sure what these other inputs were, but I shut them down as well. "You'd better unhook Magnus from everything, just in case, especially the breathing mask. They've been pumping in pure oxygen."

"Tommie?" Kieran's voice rose through renewed tears.

"Stay put, Kieran," Tommie said, swinging the door open the rest of the way. "Let me check on him first."

Tommie climbed up into the tank. Magnus lay unmoving on the bare metal table in the center of the tank, covered by a thin white sheet. Tommy knelt beside him and quickly removed the mask covering Magnus' nose and mouth.

"Magnus?" Tommie said, softly.

The unconscious boy's lips were blood red and his skin an eerie pink that seemed to glow in the fluorescent lighting inside the tank.

"Magnus!" Tommie lightly slapped his friend's cheek, trying to rouse him.

Magnus stirred slightly and a weak moan escaped his lips.

"He's alive!" Tommie shouted over his shoulder.

Kieran scrambled into the tank and fell to his knees beside Tommie. He looked over the still, prone Magnus, clad only in his boxers. "Why isn't he moving yet?" he asked in a panic.

"It's okay," Tommie said gently. "He's still a little sedated. Give him time."

"Will he be all right?" Kieran sank into Tommie's side and the strong arm that quickly encircled his shoulders.

"I think so," Tommie said, unable to think of anything more positive. "I hope so."

"What if they damaged him?" Kieran began to tremble. "Damaged his mind?" A sob escaped his lips. "What if he doesn't even know me? My God . . ."

"Kieran!" Tommie shook Kieran slightly. "Until we know differently, he's fine." He pressed his head against Kieran's. "And you're not that easy to forget."

Despite the tears, Kieran tried to smile up at Tommie.

"Is he okay?" Allison asked from the doorway.

"Come in, babe," Tommie said, motioning for Allison to join them.

She climbed in and settled on the opposite side of Magnus. Kieran's hand was on Magnus' and Allison put her hand over both. "He looks fine, Kieran," she said, giving his hand a squeeze. "He's gonna be just fine."

Kieran met her eyes, trying to believe what she said.

"Stay with them, Allison," Tommie said. "You two work to wake him up. I've got to find us a way out of this."

He stood to leave, but Allison caught his arm. "Tommie," she said, pulling him across Magnus' body. She took Tommie's face in her hands. He looked into her eyes, eyes that told him unequivocally that she believed in him. He smiled, kissed her, and hurried back out to join the others.

The small group stood around him, waiting.

"Good job, Sammy," Tommie said, giving the younger boy's hair a tousle.

"You're awesome," Daniel said, changing position to stand next to Sammy.

"It's what I do," Sammy said, smiling up at the tall swimmer. "Especially since I can't jump as high as you can." He nodded to the corner of the room that once housed the now mangled video camera.

"That?" Daniel shrugged. "You're . . . that's nothing."

"Yeah, yeah, yeah!" Gail piped up loudly. "You're both fucking fabulous! Now if we could just . . ."

"Gail," Tommie interrupted.

She glared at him.

"I'm sorry you didn't get to shoot anyone." Tommie smirked.

She blinked at him.

"But," Tommie continued. "We're not done, so you still have a chance."

Gail seemed to brighten at that thought.

"We need a way out." Tommie stood, hands on hips. "We can't sit here cut off from the rest of the world."

"We're in a solid building's cellar with one door," Conner said, throwing up his hands. "That's our only way out."

"Well," Sammy said, his voice trailing off.

"What?" Tommie asked quickly. "What has you're beautiful mind come up with?"

"Well, nothing really," Sammy replied. "It's just . . ." He paused looking about.

"Just what?" Tommie pulled the boy to him at arm's length. "Say it! Please!"

"It doesn't make any sense." Sammy took a deep breath.

"Jesus Christ!" Gail almost screamed.

"Shut up, Gail!" It was Tommie's turn to glare at her. "Come on, little boy," he said, giving Sammy a little shake. "Out with it. Give me something good and I'll give you that kiss I've been promising."

Sammy thought about that. "Ew!" he said, wrinkling his nose. "That'd be like kissing my older brother."

"What?" Tommie's eyes widened. He eyed the younger boy, sensing a change ... a new maturity. "Okay," Tommie said with a smile, taking it in stride. "Give me something good and . . ." He glanced at the tall swimmer. "Daniel will give you a big wet one!"

"What?" Daniels face turned a bright crimson. "I . . ."

"What, nothing!" Tommie replied. "If Sammy finds us a way out, you'll have to give him a kiss ... a *big* kiss for all of us."

Daniel sputtered nervously.

Sammy took the taller boy's hand. "Don't worry," he said. "It won't hurt a bit."

Daniel broke into laughter. "Hey," he said, recovering his composure. "You have to find us a way out first."

"That's the ticket," Tommie said, slapping Daniel on the shoulder. "Okay, Sammy. What have you got?"

"Well." Sammy nodded. "It's really more of a question."

"Jeez!" Now Tommie was exasperated. "Out with it!"

"Okay, okay." Sammy pointed to the tank. "That tank wasn't here before."

"Yeah," Tommie said.

"So," Sammy continued. "If that's the only door to the lab . . ."

He pointed to the metal door firmly barricaded by the tank.

"Then how did they get this massive tank in here?"

"It has four-wheel drive, remember?" Tommie said.

Sammy's eyes rolled. "Yes, I know, but how did they drive it into the lab?"

"What?" Tommie asked, confused.

"Well, it certainly wasn't constructed in here. Too much welding, sandblasting, rust-proofing. No! This was built on the outside by professional fabricators. That being the case, how the hell did they get it down here? It's too big for the elevator in the hall, too big to get through that door. I'm just saying."

Tommie pulled the boy into his arms. "There's that beautiful mind again," he said. "You are a fucking genius!"

"It still doesn't solve the mystery." Sammy pushed away, laughing.

"Bullshit!" Tommie said. He clapped his hands together. "It means one thing. There's another way in. There's another, *bigger* way in!"

"So," Sammy said, turning to Daniel. "I'm read—"

"Oh no!" Tommie said, spinning the boy back around. "You don't get that kiss just yet."

"But—"

"Not until you find the door." Tommie released the boy. "Find the door. How hard can it be? It must be at least as big as the tank!"

"Damn!" Sammy darted to the center of the room. He turned slowly in a circle, his eyes focusing in an intensity that took in every detail of the walls of the lab. He scanned the rows of cabinets and shelves. His concentration became more difficult as the pounding at the door resumed. He could also smell the acrid scent of an acetylene torch cutting metal. He forced his mind to shut off to all but visual stimuli.

"What's he up to?" Gail asked, sneering.

"Hush!" Tommie commanded. "He needs to focus."

"Do you really think Sammy can find a way out?"

Daniel whispered.

"If he can't," Tommie responded, "then no one can."

Sammy's concentration broke suddenly. He headed for the back wall that contained the morgue refrigerator units. The wall was lined like a checkerboard with small square metal doors, latched shut. He stood studying the perimeter of the array of individual cooling pods.

"What is it, Sammy?" Daniel joined the boy in front of the coolers. "What do you see?"

"No facing." Sammy muttered, inching up to the unit and running a finger down the joint between metal and concrete.

A loud hiss jerked everyone's attention to the door. A bright, orange flame had burst through at the edge of the door jamb and began a slow pirouette around the top hinge.

"Shit!" Gail ran to the fire extinguisher on the wall by the door. She pulled it free and fumbled with its working parts.

"Let me!" Conner ran over to her.

He took the extinguisher, quickly jerking the sealing pin out. He aimed at the door seam and released a spray of foam. There was no effect on the flame.

"You just pull the trigger," Gail said, pulling the hose from Conner's hand. "I've got this covered."

Conner pulled the release trigger on the extinguisher and, beginning at the flame's starting point, Gail pressed the end of the hose into the seam between door and wall at the top hinge. The flame died out, but only for a moment. Gail threw a desperate look at Tommie.

"They're trying to cut the door off its hinges!"

"Sammy!" Tommie called out.

"Oh!" Sammy started from his concentration.

"Anything?" Tommie asked, trying not to sound too overanxious.

"Got it!"

Sammy darted about the wall containing the refrigerator units whose only purpose was to store human cadavers. He ran a hand along the crevice between the stacked, individual units.

His eye caught something on the floor in the corner. "I knew it" he hollered excitedly, hurrying to the corner.

The others stood back, watching him.

Sammy pressed his foot against a small pedal-like lever in the corner. A loud click sounded and the whole wall rolled inward opening a small crack at the corner.

Sammy dug his fingers into the crevice and pulled. "It's too heavy!" He cried.

Tommie and Daniel rushed forward, reaching in above Sammy's head.

"On three!" Tommie said. "One, two, three!"

They all pulled together. The wall spun on its opposite, hinged side. The actual depth of the refrigerator units came into view as the wall opened half-way out into the lab.

"That's enough!" Tommie said, slapping the other boys on the back. "Good job, again, Sammy!"

Sammy shrugged, aware of Daniel beaming down at him from the side.

Tommie ran to the tank that held Magnus.

"Allison!" he called out, climbing up into the restrictive space.

Allison sat on the edge of the metal table. Magnus was sitting up—barely. He leaned back against Allison, moaning softly, still too drugged to respond in any meaningful way. Allison clasped him against her breast.

"Allison," Tommie repeated, tenderly. He slipped his arm around her. "Thank God," he said looking at Magnus.

"Tommie," Kieran said weakly, still holding Magnus' hands. "We can't get him to wake up all the way."

"He will," Tommie replied. "We need to get him out."

Allison nodded and laid Magnus' head back onto the table gently. She climbed out first to make room for the other two. Kieran and Tommie each took a side of the gurney and rolled the table to the tank's exit.

"Daniel!" Tommie jumped down to the floor of the lab. "We need some help over here."

Daniel rushed over. Kieran was busy cranking the handle at the back of the gurney that was slowly tilting it up and forward. Daniel climbed up into the tank on the other side of the metal gurney.

"Okay," Tommie said, reaching his arms upward. "Steady him on the table and slowly slide him down to me.

"Magnus," Kieran said, softly. He bent over his friend and kissed him lightly on the lips. "We'll get you out." He laid Magnus back onto the cold, metal gurney.

As the table tilted ever upward, Magnus' body began to slide downward. Kieran and Daniel grasped him across the chest and slowed his controlled fall.

"Kieran." Tommie held Magnus' legs. "Can you hold him by yourself?"

Kieran nodded and wrapped his arms tighter about the table and Magnus.

"Down here, Daniel," Tommie said.

Daniel leapt to the floor. He reached up and took hold of Magnus' waist.

"Okay Kieran," Tommie said. "We've got him. Let him slide down our way. Daniel, get him under the arms and hold him up."

Tommie hoisted Magnus' still limp form into Daniel's arms.

"I've got him," Daniel said, locking his hands behind Magnus' back.

"Hop down, Kieran," Tommie called to his friend. "You and Allison get into the elevator with the others."

"Elevator?" Kieran and Allison said in unison. They looked toward the others and instantly took in the situation.

"What about Magnus?" Kieran asked.

"I've got it covered," Tommie replied. He bent down, slipping one arm in behind Magnus' knees. "Let me have him, Daniel."

Daniel lay Magnus back onto Tommie and Tommie straightened, hoisting Magnus up and cradling him in his arms.

Suddenly Magnus' eyes opened full. He blinked up into Tommie's face. "Tommie?" he said weakly.

"I go you, bro'," Tommie said, smiling down at his friend. "Just relax."

"Magnus!" Kieran rushed up beside Tommie.

Magnus blinked, trying to focus on the sound of the voice. "Kieran?" He managed shakily.

Kieran reached out to embrace Magnus.

"Not now, Kieran!" Tommie said, pushing past him, carrying Magnus. The pounding on the door became deafening. "We need to get out of here!"

Kieran nodded acceptance and followed Tommie to the large service elevator. They joined Allison and the others who had already taken their places.

"Gail!" Tommie called out, shifting Magnus in his arms. "Give it up! Come on!"

"In a minute!" She ran over to the row of cabinets above the long lab counter and threw open doors until she found what she was looking for. "Ha!" She said, pulling out a large aluminum can.

"Gail!" Tommie called out angrily.

"Okay, okay!" She said, hauling the can over to the barricaded door.

The bright, orange flame was now slicing through the bottom hinge of the door. Gail unscrewed the cap on the can and began pouring its clear, liquid contents about the metal door and across the floor as she headed toward the elevator. The viscous liquid seemed to spread out with its own purpose. When emptied of its contents, Gail tossed the can out onto the tiled floor and dove into the elevator. Daniel pulled the elevator cage door across the expansive doorway and slammed it into the catch on the opposite side.

"Conner!" Tommie called out, nodding at the elevator control buttons.

Conner slammed a palm against the *up* button. A hammering crash sent the desperate group of teens defensively to their knees. They peered through the cage door as the elevator began its slow rise to whatever was above them. The metal door Gail had stood guard over now lay on the floor to the side of the now opened doorway. Black uniformed security officers squeezed into the room around the nose of the metal tank that had barricaded the opening before.

A click and its resulting, distracting light caught the entrapped group's attention. Gail tossed the burning cigarette lighter out of the cage into the liquid she had previously deposited in the room beyond. The guards in the room brought their guns up, aiming at the teens crouched like sitting ducks in plain view behind the cage door of the agonizingly slow elevator.

Suddenly, the room ignited into a blinding blue/orange explosion of fire. Screams erupted from its center. The teens lay on the elevator floor as random shots pinged off the elevator gate and its steel underbelly. As the floor of the elevator cleared the ceiling of the lab, Tommy shot up from the floor.

"Gail," he shouted.

"What?" she shouted back.

"You rock!" Tommy said, giving her a salute.

CHAPTER 22

"Magnus . . . Magnus!" Kieran shook Magnus by the shoulders. "Say something so I'll know that you're okay."

Magnus struggled to sit upright. "Kieran," he said, shaking his head to clear the lingering fog of sedation.

The sounds of ancillary explosions from the lab below added to his confusion. The steel floor on which he sat was strangely warm.

"Magnus," Kieran persisted. "Do you recognize me? Do you know who I am?"

"Give him time, Kieran," Allison said. She knelt on the floor beside Magnus.

Magnus strained to focus his eyes. "I . . ." A familiar shape loomed close to his face. "Kieran?" He repeated as before. "How . . ." He reached out to see if the apparition was real or imagined. His fingers brushed Kieran's cheek. "How did you get here?"

Kieran clasped Magnus' hand against his cheek. "You know me?" He exhaled his fear. "You know who I am?"

"I . . ." Magnus blinked. "Of course I know who you are," he said, confused by Kieran's question.

"Welcome back, Magnus," Allison said putting a hand on his shoulder. "You had us worried."

"Damn it!" Tommie's strong baritone ricocheted off the metal walls of the slowly rising elevator. "How long does it take for this thing to reach the top?"

"Just a little more," Sammy said, peering up through the cage door to the next floor that was slowly sinking below the top of the cage. "Just a few feet more."

"How is he?" Tommie called out, turning his attention to Kieran.

"He's making sense now," Kieran replied. He took Magnus' arm. "Can you stand?" He pulled Magnus shakily to his feet.

"Easy does it, Magnus," Allison said, taking his other arm.

"Dude," Tommie said. "You had us worried."

"I still don't understand," Magnus said, shifting unsteadily on his feet. "What are you all doing?"

"Saving your sorry ass!" Kieran said, releasing his hold on Magnus.

Magnus blinked again.

"Uh Oh!" Tommie said quietly.

"Saving . . ." Magnus rubbed his temples.

"Do you understand what I'm saying to you?" Kieran's voice rose an octave.

"Ye . . . yes," Magnus replied.

"Do you remember what happened to you before you woke up?"

Magnus looked at Kieran's face, flushed with anger.

"I . . . yes I remember," he said, lowering his eyes.

"Don't you *ever* pull that shit on me again!" Kieran smashed his fists into Magnus' shoulders, sending the unsteady dancer spiraling backwards into Tommie.

"Whoa there!" Tommie managed to say, catching Magnus under the arms.

Kieran pounced on Magnus, pulling him away from Tommie and wrapping his arms about the boy's neck. "Don't you ever do that to me again!" Kieran sobbed. "Don't you ever tell me you don't love me!"

"Kieran," Tommie said gently. "You're choking him."

"Back off!" Kieran said hotly.

"Backing off," Tommie replied, taking Allison with him a few steps backwards.

Kieran released his embrace about Magnus' neck. "Do you think for one minute, I'd just pack up and leave you to die here?"

"Well, Kieran." Tommie coughed. "Technically at first you were—"

"Shut up, Tommie!" Kieran's voice thundered.

"And . . . shutting up," Tommie replied, throwing his arm about Allison.

"What were you thinking?" Kieran continued through new tears. "What did you think you were doing?"

Magnus looked into Kieran's eyes, painfully aware of the hurt he had caused. "I was trying to save you, Kieran. I couldn't let anything happen to you." Tears filled his own eyes. "Do you hate me?"

"I hate what you did!" Kieran said, reaching up to take Magnus' face in his hands. "But I love you." He looked the boy straight in his eyes. "Do you hear me? I love you."

Magnus closed his eyes and touched his forehead to

Kieran's. "And I love you, Kieran."

Kieran pressed himself to Magnus. "You're damn right you do," he said, fully embracing his love.

"Okay," Tommie said. He sidled over to the elevator's cage door. "Now that that's settled . . ."

The elevator shuddered to a stop. Beyond the elevator cage door was another, but solid metal door. Daniel hoisted the cage door up, allowing Tommie access to the pull-handle at the bottom of the new door.

"Either they're waiting for us or they're not," Tommie said, pulling up on the door with a grunt. The flexible, hinged door slid upward.

Everyone squinted against the bright sunlight that greeted them. They exhaled as a group, relieved at the empty driveway before them stretching out along a cinder block wall that separated them from the view of the public landscapes beyond.

"We're at the back of the Institute," Sammy said, surveying the scene. "They can move things in and out of here with no worry about being observed."

"How do we get away?" Magnus asked, still relying on Kieran for steady support. He tested his balance. "I'm not sure I can walk very far yet . . . much less run."

"The garage should be somewhere to the left of us," Sammy said. "Maybe we can . . . borrow a car?"

"Great," Conner said, venturing into the sunlight. "Now we can add grand theft auto to our list of accomplishments today."

Allison slipped an arm about Tommie's waist.

"With security the way it is, I doubt we'll find that anyone's left their keys in a car," she said.

"No," Tommie replied. "You're right. We'll need to jack a car. Anyone know anything about cars?" He asked.

As if on cue, the whole group turned toward Gail.

"What's everyone looking at me for?" She asked, hands on hips. "Oh, sure! 'Cause I'm the lesbo, everyone just assumes I know how to build a house and repair automobiles."

"No, dear," Allison said with a smile. "Not repair, just steal." She pursed her lips. "Not like it'll be your first time, huh?"

"Wha ..." Tommie's eyes widened at Gail. "Dude! You've stolen a car before?"

"Thanks," Gail said, giving Allison a look. "Any other secrets you wanna air?"

"Girl, don't look at me like that," Allison replied, almost laughing. "You bragged about that all last summer."

"Whatever." Gail sniffed at the group. "At least someone ..." She cut her eyes at Tommie. "And that would be me. Someone around here has a useful set of skills."

"Oh, dyke-friend, let's get on with it," Conner said, putting a hand on Gail's shoulder. "And when you're done with this heist, I've got a little shoplifting I need you to do at the *Gap.*"

"Why do you guys have to be so touchy-feely?" Gail shook Conner's hand from her shoulder. "All right. Let's find the garage."

"Coast is clear!" Daniel called out, dropping from his hold on the top of the cinder block wall.

"Damn that boy can jump," Tommie said to Sammy with a grin. "Right." He had everyone's attention. "Let's move out."

"Stay close to the walls," Sammy said. "The exterior cameras are mostly aimed at the lawn areas."

Tommie nodded and led down a grassy berm away from the service elevator. Except for Magnus and Kieran, the group scurried single-file along the hedges that lined the exterior walls of the Institute. The garage was a metal building that nested to the back corner of the main granite structure. One of the many garage bays' overhead doors was up, and Tommy led the group of teens into the seeming safety of the enclosed space. He perused the contents of the space.

"There," he called out to Gail. He pointed. "That van." He turned to the girl. "Can you do it?"

"Piece of cake," Gail responded. "First, I need a screwdriver." She rushed to the workbench along the back wall and rifled through some tool chests.

"Daniel!" Tommie called to the tall swimmer. "Keep watch."

Daniel nodded and headed for the door.

"Stop right there!" an angry voice bellowed from the garage bay door.

The group of teens jerked their attention from Gail to the door. Four security guards stood with Uzi machine guns aimed to strafe their targets if necessary. One of the guards was reporting their discovery on his radio.

Tommie stood defiantly in front of his friends, trying not to show the overwhelming loss of the hope that had sustained his strength of leadership.

"Let's just kill the little bastards now!" said one of the guards. "They deserve it for what they did to the others."

"Settle down, Foster," said the guard with the radio. "Dr. Powell will want to autopsy them as healthy specimens." He grinned at the teens, baring his teeth ominously.

Tommie turned to face his friends, looking for

something to say. He stood mute. His shoulders drooped betraying his despair.

Allison left the group to take Tommie's arm. "It's okay, baby," she said softly. "We tried."

"For nothing," Tommie replied hoarsely. He focused on the guard, unable to look his friends in the eye.

"Tommie," Kieran chastised his friend. "You got us farther than I think any of the rest of us could have."

Tommie raised his eyes to meet Kieran's. "I . . ." His voice caught in his throat. "What did I miss? What should I have done differently?"

"Don't be silly," Allison said, kissing his cheek.

"Well . . ." Magnus said, flexing. His strength was almost fully restored. "You could have left me behind. You could be out of here by—"

"Magnus!" Kieran said in disbelief.

"No way, dude!" Tommie shook his head. "No way we would have done that."

"Damn right," Kieran said. "We stick together . . . no matter what!"

"And," Conner said, joining them. "May I remind you?" He glanced at the guards and back to his friends. "It's not over yet. I'm not giving up."

Tommie smiled at him. "Unless you've got some deadly fairy dust in your pocket, I don't see much that we can do."

Conner turned his back to the guards, facing Tommie and all his friends.

"Remember," he said, lowering his voice to a whisper. He mouthed a name. "Gail."

The group stared at Conner, not understanding. Conner smiled. Slowly, the dawning realization spread over the faces of the trapped teens. Gail was not with them. Once again she had escaped detection.

"Eyes forward," Tommie commanded.

He turned his back to the guards and pretended to console Allison. Instead, his eyes went to the van at the back of the garage. For a second the front driver's side of the van seemed to drop almost imperceptible lower over the tire and then back up. Someone was in the van. His face broke into an ecstatic smile, but only for a second. His thoughts raced. An idea formed—a chance—a slim possibility. He looked up at the garage door motor housing and the dangling piece of cord with the red, pull handle.

He caught Daniel's eye and raised his eyes to the emergency release cord. Daniel's eyes followed. When their eyes met again, Tommie looked questioningly at Daniel and the mouthed, "Can you reach it?"

Daniel looked up, mentally testing the height. He looked again at Tommie and the side of his mouth curled up in a confident smile.

Tommie took a deep breath and turned to Kieran. Nodding, he tested their psychic connection.

Kieran looked at him, confused.

"This is all your fault you little bitch!" Tommie yelled suddenly, turning on Kieran.

Tommie's body language said anger, but Kieran saw something different in his eyes.

"Don't yell at me," Kieran yelled back. "Hiding in the garage wasn't my stupid idea!"

"I told you we should have left your deadbeat boyfriend back in the lab?"

"Bitch fight!" Conner yelled out, hoping to raise the distraction quotient.

"Who are you calling deadbeat," Magnus said,

jumping into the fray. "And you don't talk to him that way or I'll kick your ass!"

"You wanna piece of me, Tinkerbell?" Tommie got in Magnus face. "Give it your best shot, Nancy!"

Magnus roared and dove for Tommie's midsection. They tumbled onto the floor of the garage, locked in mock combat. The rest of the teens circled to cheer on their favorite contender. The guards at the door kept their distance outside the door and watched in bemusement. Their weapons lowered in concert as they enjoyed the spectacle before them.

Suddenly from the back of the garage a car motor roared to life. Startled, the guards turned their attention to the van and its revving engine.

"Now!" Tommie shouted to Daniel.

In one deft leap, Daniel levitated off the garage floor and shot upward. Simultaneously, he extended his long arm and grabbed for the Garage door's emergency release cord. As his weight dropped, the cord jerked downward in his hand, releasing the garage door from the motorized assembly. The heavy, metal door's potential energy engaged and it began to slide downward, accelerating with the pull of gravity. Startled, the armed guards instinctively stepped farther back from the falling door which slammed violently onto the concrete drive, blocking the guard's access.

Inside, Tommie was already off the floor. In an instant he was at the garage door and turned the center handle clockwise, engaging the slide bar on both sides into slots that securely locked the door into the surrounding steel frame.

"Everyone into the van!" Tommie shouted.

The teens raced for the van, jumping in as Gail slid

the passenger door open. Tommie bounded into the driver's seat and jerked the gear shift into drive.

"What now!" Gail asked, settling into the front passenger seat beside Tommie.

"Get your gun out, girl!" Tommie responded breathlessly. "You're gonna get your chance to shoot someone!"

"Fucking yeah!" Gail rolled her window down with gusto.

"Get ready, everyone!" Tommie shouted above the engine roar.

"Seatbelts," Daniel called out, strapping himself in.

Everyone followed suit. They could hear the pounding on the garage door as the guards tried to pry it upward.

"Side door!" Tommie shouted. "Everyone get down!"

Gail jerked her aim toward the exterior door directly across from her window. It shook as someone outside pounded against it.

Tommie floored the gas pedal and shouted, "Ramming speed!"

Before being slammed back onto her seat, Gail got off a few shots into the wooden door across from her.

The tires spun against the concrete floor raising a cloud of acrid smoke before regaining traction. The van almost leapt for the garage door. Its back wheels smoking, the passenger van slammed into the segmented garage door, ripping it from its track and sending it flying outward onto the drive beyond. The line of guards trying to force it open from the outside, were flattened under it. Their situation worsened as Tommie gunned the van over the collapsed door into the sunlight.

The remaining guards recovered quickly, but not

before the van and its teenage carjackers had cleared the crumpled door, accelerating ever faster down the drive. Tommie struggled to control the steering, daring not to look back.

"Take the next right," Sammy called out from the rear.

Tommie glanced up at the rearview mirror to see the boy standing up and leaning over the seat in front of him where Magnus and Kieran crouched.

"Sit down, Sammy!" Tommie shouted over the screaming engine. He saw Sammy's head duck back down behind the seat as the rear window was blown out by gunfire. Tommie jerked the wheel to the right and careened through a gate in the high stone wall that now provided an impenetrable cover from the remaining guards' gunfire.

"Sammy's been hit!" Allison screamed.

"Gail!" Tommie threw the girl an urgent glance.

"Keep driving!" she shouted. "I'm on it!" She scrambled behind. "Stay down," she commanded Magnus and Kieran. Keeping low, she reached the back seat and crawled in next to Allison. Daniel was cradling Sammy in his arms, panic stricken.

"Sammy!" Gail reached out to grab the boy's trembling shoulder. "Sammy!"

"It's his arm," Daniel said, trying not to scream.

Sammy turned to face Gail, his eyes wide in fear.

"Fuck!" Gail managed to say, releasing the bulk of her anxiety, relieved to find the boy alive. "Let me see."

"I don't know how bad it is," Allison stuttered, afraid to release her grip on the source of the bleeding just above Sammy's left elbow.

"I've got it." Gail pried Allison's blood fingers away

and leaned in to examine the wound. "It's not a bullet wound," she said quickly assessing the injury. She looked at the shards of safety glass littering the floor. "Looks like he got hit with some glass."

She lifted the boy's shirt, nodding with satisfaction to see Sammy's ever present under shirt. She grabbed it with both hands saying, "This'll do," and ripped a large piece off the bottom hem. She fashioned a bandage and tied it tightly over the wound. "Keep pressure on it," she said, patting Allison's arm. She glanced down at Sammy. "You'll live, kid," she said.

"Are you sure he'll be alright?" Daniel asked, pulling Sammy closer to him.

Gail shook her head at the two boys. "Oh, you two'll be sodomizing each other in no time."

"Gail!" Allison slapped Gail on the back of the head.

"Just statin' the facts ma'am," Gail said, ducking the second slap. She was aware of Sammy grinning up at her. "Did you get that 911 off?" she asked.

Sammy met Gail's eyes. "I got it off while they were getting Magnus out of the tank," he said with a nod. "Now we'll see if anyone pays attention."

"They will," Gail said emphatically. "They have to." She put a hand on Sammy's chest. "Hang in there, you little bastard," she said, surprised at her own actions. "You're tougher than you look."

Sammy smiled up at her. Even the pain in his arm couldn't spoil this moment.

"Problem!" Tommie shouted from the front.

"Shit," Gail almost spat.

"What now!" Kieran stuck his head up. "What's the problem?"

"Stay down!" Gail ordered, scrambling back to the

driver's cab. She fell onto the seat next to Tommie, craning her neck above the dash.

"What should I do?" Tommie whispered to her. He pulled his foot from the accelerator and the van slowed quickly to a crawl.

Gail studied the situation. Five or six more security guards blocked the front gate which was uncharacteristically shut. They held rifles and shotguns at the ready, aimed at the slowly advancing van of teens. "Well, we can run it," she suggested without conviction. "We can try to crash the gate."

Tommie shook his head. "This van isn't bullet proof. With those weapons they'll rip us apart."

"Fuck!" Gail slammed the dash with her fist.

Tommie tapped his forehead against the steering wheel. "Oh, well," he said, trying to sound flippant. "I guess we could make the argument that we're going to die anyway if we don't try."

"Tommie," Kieran said from the side window where he and Magnus crouched, surveying the situation.

"What's your take on this?" Tommie asked, smiling back at his friend.

"Live and fight another day," Conner said, crawling up behind Magnus.

"Damn it!" Gail glared back at him. "What about stay down didn't you understand?"

Conner shot her the bird. "I'm not staying back there by myself," he said, glaring back. "And save the big-bad-dyke crap for the assholes outside."

Kieran held a hand up. "All right, all right," he said softly. He met Tommie's eyes. "But I think he's right. We need to put some faith in Sammy's SOS."

"Everyone?" Tommie called out.

"We agree," Allison called out from the back of the van.

"Right." Tommie shifted into park and turned off the engine.

"And there's Powell." Kieran pointed out the window. "Come to gloat."

The teens watched helplessly as Dr. Powell strutted confidently to the front of his heavily-armed guards. He waved his own pistol at the van.

"You will not escape me!" he shouted at his wayward students. "Come out and leave your weapons behind!"

"Yeah, right!" Gail stuffed her pistol into her rear waistband and pulled her shirt tail down over it."

"Gail?" Tommie raised an eyebrow at her.

"Kiss my ass, castrato boy," she said, pulling the passenger door open. "If they want it, let 'em try and take it!" She stepped down onto the gravel drive.

"Shit!" Tommie jumped out the other side.

Kieran pulled the handle and rolled the passenger door to the side. "Come on, people," he said. He took Magnus' hand and they exchanged a smile. "Stay alert. Any opportunity is better than none."

Tommie rounded the van to help Allison and Daniel get Sammy onto his feet. "You okay, little man?" he asked, easing Sammy onto the gravel drive.

"I'm okay," Sammy said, still gripping the compression bandage about his arm.

"I've got him." Daniel dropped down beside Sammy. "You and Allison need to be together," he said, slipping an arm about Sammy's waist. "If that's okay with you?" he added shyly, looking down at Sammy.

Sammy's pallor acquired a blush of color. "It'll be okay," he said to Tommie, not taking his eyes off

Daniel's. "I'm in good hands."

Allison took Tommie's hand in hers. "Can you handle your new empty-nest syndrome?" she asked, snuggling against his shoulder.

"I'll be just fine," he said softly, pulling her to him. "As long as we're together."

"Jesus on a donkey!" Gail groaned. "I'm going into battle with the fucking Teletubbies!"

"Love conquers all, Gail," Kieran said lightly. He looked up at Magnus. "This time we face the music together." He took both Magnus' hands into his. "Are we clear on that?"

"Very clear, ma'am," Magnus said with a nod.

"Great." Conner sidled up to Gail. "That just leaves us two."

"What?" Gail backed up.

"Say something sweet to me," Conner said, batting his eyelashes at her.

"Suck my dick!" Gail said sharply.

Conner turned to the other teens and said, "He loves me," and posed elegantly.

"Okay, crew," Tommie said, joining in the nervous laughter. He turned to face Powell and his goons. "Let's get this over with."

The young tribe gathered about Tommy and Allison. One by one, they linked arms except for Sammy who still gripped the bandage on his arm. Daniel and Kieran linked arms about Sammy's shoulder. Slowly the group began to make their way down the remaining distance toward their captors.

"Gail?" Tommie said softly, aware that the girl was lagging behind the group. "Gail!"

"Shut up!" Gail responded. "Keep moving."

"Gail!"

"I said keep moving!"

"Don't do anything stupid," Tommie warned.

"You don't worry about it," she replied softly, moving up behind him. "But," she said loud enough that all her friends could hear. "When I say *duck*, you had all better hit the dirt . . . fast!"

"Damn it, Gail!" Tommie heard her chuckling behind him and resisted the urge to turn and grab her. He exchanged a glance with Allison, but she merely smiled. He looked at each of the others but no one tried to object. "Shit!" he said, laughing at himself, and tightened his hold on Allison.

"That's close enough," Dr. Powell ordered when the teens were within fifteen or twenty feet. He waved his pistol in front of them. "Did you little fools really think you could just drive out of here?" He paused his aim directly on Tommie. "It's over." The edge of his mouth crept upward. "You will all regret your interference with my work."

"What about you?" Tommie shouted, ignoring the pistol pointed directly at him. "What kind of fool are you . . . thinking that you can get away with this?" He looked back at the flames billowing up from the side of the Institute. "You think this isn't going to be noticed?"

Powell's face contracted into a half-smile, half-sneeze. He waved his pistol at the dissipating flames. "As you can see, our fire control systems are gaining the upper hand. But . . ." He fixed his emotionless eyes on Tommie. "Accidents happen. Especially when kids are playing around where they're not supposed to be. That's about right, isn't it?" His laugh was hollow. "Kids mixing explosive chemicals. No doubt trying to fashion some sort of a bomb to cause more mischief. What an explosion . . . and what a tragedy." Powell scanned the group with the eyes of a predator. "Killed by your own bomb."

"You're an idiot!" Kieran shouted back. "You can't cover this up! All the light is now shining down on your dark little world. You *will* be found out."

"Ridiculous!" Powell responded. "There is no evidence of anything to be found except for the stupidity of a group of delinquents!"

"Well, not exactly." Sammy's voice piped up. All attention turned to him. Somehow he looked older. He still gripped his injured arm, but his face was without fear. "I have everything," he said evenly, staring Dr. Powell in the eyes. "Everything . . . your databases, your reports, archives, research proposals . . . everything!"

"Again, ridiculous!" Powell looked at him, not believing.

"I have uploaded it all to various high-security network storage facilities. You will never be able to penetrate those systems like I did. The data is out there . . . terabytes of it . . . in files so large they cannot help but be noticed. People will look at them . . . FBI, intelligence services, foreign governments." Sammy straightened, somehow taller. "You are so fucked!" he shouted.

Dr. Powell's face blanched. "You're lying," he said, shaking with rage. "You imbecilic child! You haven't got the skill or . . ."

"Oh, he's got the skill," Tommie interrupted, throwing an arm around Sammy proudly.

"He's been downloading your data for days," Kieran said, stepping to the front. "How do you think we figured all this out?" He laughed. "You are done for!"

"Fools!" Dr. Powell faced the teens. His half-smile chiseled in granite. "No one will believe it. It will all disappear as a fabrication of vindictive teenage runaways. There will be nothing to tie me to it. Nothing!"

"That's where you're wrong," Sammy piped up again. "That was before I cracked your surveillance encryption."

"Impossible," Dr. Powell stuttered.

"Difficult," Sammy said, "but not impossible. I jumped that little hurdle just before you threw us in the basement. For the past two days your own servers have been uploading video to my specially constructed net cloud by the shit-load!" He turned and nodded to the small camera housed on the light pole behind them. "It's still uploading."

All eyes went to the camera.

"Smile, Dr. Powell," Sammy said, chuckling. "You're on candid camera!" The rest of the teens were quickly caught up in Sammy's laughter.

Dr. Powell's fury escalated. A feral growl built in his chest until he exploded. "No one will give a damn that I have rid the world of your viral, perverted, cancerous, worthless lives!" He raised his pistol and aimed it at Sammy. "I will send you to hell myself!"

"No!" Tommy pulled Sammy down to the ground with him.

The crack of a pistol firing echoed off the stone walls. For a brief second, time stopped. Everyone stood frozen except for Tommy and Sammy, sprawled on the ground.

"Tommy!" Allison's scream broke through the group paralysis.

Tommy's head popped up. If not for the look on his face, his friends would have completely missed the sight of Dr. Powell toppling over, blood pouring from the large black hole in his forehead. Suddenly, the blare of sirens rose above the confused shouts of the guards.

"Get down!" Gail shouted at her friends. The teens all fell, flattening themselves onto the gravel drive. The gates in front of them crashed inward and open as a heavy, armored van broke through, followed by a host of vehicles with strobing red lights and blaring sirens.

Dr. Powel's guards scattered across the Institute's grounds, pursued by law enforcement vehicles, loud speakers calling out for their surrender. An extended wheelbase, black Bentley limousine stopped inside the gates. The back door flew open and a statuesque Amazon with long, black hair held back in a ponytail charged out, pistol drawn. She shouted orders to the uniformed men and the men in dark suits who flowed out of the other vehicles.

"Shit and hallelujah!" Gail jumped to her feet and shoved her pistol back into her waistband. "The Calvary has arrived—and it is woman!"

"Tommy!" Allison was on top of Tommie and Sammy in an instant. "Are you both okay?"

"We're good," Tommie said, pulling a dusty Sammy up from the ground with him. "Here," he said to Daniel who had been on the ground next to them. He shoved Sammy into Daniel's waiting arms. "You take care of this. I've got my own to worry about." With that he embraced Allison and kissed her hard.

"Who the hell are these people?" Kieran asked, pulling up from the gravel with a little help from Magnus.

"Who cares," Magnus responded, brushing the sand off of Kieran's back. "We're saved."

"Don't worry about me," Conner called out from the clouds of dust kicked up by the incoming emergency vehicles. "I'm okay, too." He stood up shakily. "If anyone cares."

"Of course we care," Kieran replied. He wagged a finger at Conner. "Now do something about your hair."

"Bitch!"

"Slut!"

"And proud of it!" Conner screamed above the din to the laughter of the other teens.

"Hey!" Gail bore down on the tall Amazon. "Who are you? What's up?"

The woman was standing over Dr. Powell's body. She looked up at Gail with a twinkle in her eye. "Good shot, young lady."

"I ain't no lady," Gail replied. She looked down at the corpse on the ground, her eyes wide. "You sure he's dead."

"Oh, he's dead alright." The woman's accent was thick and Germanic. "But next time aim for the heart. It's a surer, easier target than the head."

"I was aiming for the heart," Gail said with a shrug.

The woman laughed easily, stepping over the corpse. "I'm Gilda Strom," she said, holding out a hand. "Interpol."

Gail shook the woman's hand firmly. "Gail Doran . . . formerly of the Institute."

"Are you shittin' me?" Tommy pulled Allison along with him, followed by the other teens. He gave Gail's shoulder a shove. "You shot the asshole?"

Gail's hands went to her hips. "I told you I was gonna shoot someone. Turns out he was first in line."

"Girl!" Tommie bore down on her. "I am so gonna kiss your face!"

Gail's hand went to the pistol handle on her

waistband. "You park it right there, Tweety Bird! You're second in line."

"I think she means it this time, Tommie," Allison said behind him.

"Speaking of kisses." Sammy looked up at Daniel.

"What?" Daniel blushed. "Are you demanding immediate payment?"

"I don't want to have to charge you interest or anything."

Daniel shrugged. He leaned over and kissed Sammy lightly on the cheek.

Before he could straighten, Sammy grabbed his shirt. "I don't think so, jock-boy," Sammy said, pulling the taller boy's face back to his. He planted a kiss directly on the swimmer's lips.

Daniel straightened, laughing. "Wow!"

Sammy looked up at his assembled friends. "I deserve that."

"Yes you do," Tommie replied proudly.

"Now that that's over with." Kieran turned back to the tall Amazon. "How did you know?" he asked. "How did you find out?" He gripped Magnus' hand.

The woman looked over the group of teens. "Which one of you is Magnus?"

All eyes focused on Magnus.

"What?" He stuttered. "I'm Magnus, but I didn't . . ."

The woman held up her hand. "Your email."

"What?" Magnus asked, not understanding.

"The email you sent," Gilda replied. "It all began with your email."

"But . . ."

"What email?" Kieran shook Magnus' arm. "What's she talking about?"

"I don't know." Magnus shrugged to the group. "The only email I sent was to your mother."

"My mother?" Kieran's voice cracked.

"When we were at your beach house. I used your dad's computer."

Kieran turned to the woman. "What's my mother got to do with this?"

Gilda turned back to the Bentley. "Rachel," she called out. "It's okay. Come on out."

The back door of the limo opened again and a pair of slender, milky-white legs stretched out onto the drive below. They supported a lithe, elegant woman who climbed out of the limo. Cautiously, her eyes scanned the group of teens as if searching.

Gail looked back at Tommy. "Who is she?"

Tommy shrugged.

"She looks like a model," Allison whispered to Tommie. "I love her Audrey Hepburn hair?"

"She's hot!" Gail said, staring.

Magnus' eyes fixated on the woman. He wasn't sure what was captivating him so, her dark hair, her regal nose, or . . ."

"Oh my God," he said, grabbing Kieran's shoulders and spun him around. He looked into Kieran's flashing, violet eyes and then back to the woman and back again to Kieran.

"What is it?" Allison asked.

"I think . . ." Magnus nodded to the raven-haired woman by the limo. "I think that's Kieran's mom."

"No way!" Tommie stared at the woman. "But . . ."

"She's hot!" Gail repeated, unable to take her eyes off the woman.

"Shut up, Gail," Kieran muttered between his teeth.

"I'm not kidding," Gail said, ignoring him. "She's hot!"

"I said shut up, Gail!" Kieran's voice rose. He pushed through the group and walked slowly towards the limo.

Magnus started to follow, but the tall Amazon stopped him gently. "Let him do this alone," she said softly.

Magnus obeyed. "Is that really Kieran's mother?"

Gilda nodded.

"Hello, mother." Kieran stopped a couple of yards from the car. "Thank you for rescuing us." His voice would have been void of emotion except for the tension it conveyed.

"Hello, my little shaifeleh," the woman said with a nervous smile.

"Not so little or innocent, mother."

"Yes, you're right, sweetheart. Not so little anymore." Kieran's mother brushed a wrinkle from her silk skirt. She looked at her glistening, black patent shoes, as if unsure what to say.

"Well," Kieran said, turning away suddenly. "Have a nice flight back to . . . wherever."

"Kieran!" Magnus couldn't believe his ears.

"Rachel!" Gilda fumed at Kieran's mother. "You promised."

"Wait, Kieran." Rachel's hand went to her mouth. "Please wait."

Kieran looked at Magnus who, like an impatient school teacher, signaled him to go back.

Kieran sighed. "What is it, mother?" he said, turning back to face her again.

Rachel's violet eyes stared longingly into Kieran's own. "I know you think I abandoned you," she began.

"Think?" Kieran's voice was harsh. "Why don't we just let the facts speak for themselves?"

"That's not fair," Rachel said. "There were circumstances you weren't aware of. Problems with your father that made my staying on impossible."

"Impossible?"

"Impossible." Instinctively, Rachel took a step closer to Kieran.

He stood his ground, arms folded across his chest.

"Kieran." Rachel's eyes misted over. "Your father had information about me that he threatened to use if I divorced him. He could have taken you away from me completely."

"Seems to me that happened anyway," Kieran responded unmoved.

"No." A small smile illuminated Rachel's face. "Not completely. I think you've had yearly invitations to visit me in Lyon." She closed her eyes. "But you refused."

"What was I supposed to do?" Kieran glared at the ground. "Vacation where I wasn't wanted in the first place?"

"That's not true, Kieran," Rachel protested.

"But the other must be true."

Rachel's eyes widened. "What do you mean?"

"You poisoned grandfather. That's what your ... husband was holding over your head?"

Rachel's jaw dropped in shock. Kieran uncrossed his arms, sure now of his take on matters.

"You see?" Gilda shook her head at Rachel. "You see what your little secret has created. Your son thinks you're a murderess."

Rachel's head dropped. A flood of shame enveloped her, intensified by the triumphant smirk her own son aimed at her. She took a deep breath. It was time to tell the truth. "Kieran." She met her son's accusing gaze. "I did not poison your grandfather. He died of a stroke. He had already had three before he died."

"Oh, mother, really," Kieran said, rolling his eyes. "Everyone on the East coast knows that you . . ."

"They don't know any such thing," Rachel countered. "There was an autopsy. The cause of your grandfather's death was well-documented."

"But . . ."

"Rumors," Rachel continued. "Society gossip. That's all."

"What else was everyone to think when you off and skipped the country even before the damn funeral?"

"Yes, I left," Rachel responded, tears rolled down her cheeks. "Once my father was dead, I was free. My marriage to your father was a sham to cover up my pregnancy."

"What?" Kieran stepped back. "Now you're saying I'm a bastard!"

"No!" Rachel held up a hand to him. "No! At least my bartered marriage to your father ensured your legitimacy. It's just . . ." She shrugged helplessly. "Aaron isn't your biological father."

Kieran swayed precariously.

Magnus rushed over and embraced him from behind to keep him from falling. "Steady, Kieran," he whispered in the boy's ear.

"Your grandfather forced the marriage on me. He made sure I was alone and without any means of support but him."

"I . . ." Kieran broke free of Magnus. "I don't care about that."

"After you were born, your grandfather died suddenly. I tried to break off with your father . . . flee the country . . . take you with us."

Gilda had slipped up beside Rachel and put an arm around her.

"But your . . . father needed you to protect his income," Rachel said, her voice shaking. "His agents stole you from us in Copenhagen and spirited you back to the U.S. As your birth certificate father, he was able to pull the strings to keep you. It was a different time," Rachel said through tears. "They wouldn't let people like us back in the country then . . . especially after having . . . as your father claimed, kidnapped you."

Kieran's head was spinning. "But who is my father?" He almost screamed.

"An anonymous sperm donor," Rachel said, straightening. "Who cares who it was . . . you were ours!"

"Hot damn!" Gail clapped her hands. "Hot, hot, hot damn!"

"Butt out, Gail," Kieran said, glaring back at her.

"Dude!" Gail rushed over and shook Kieran by the arm. "Are you deaf?"

"What are . . ."

"Gilda's your mom's partner. Your mom's a dyke!" Gail said, jubilant. She eyed Kieran's mom. "A hot dyke!"

Kieran shoved her hard, toppling her onto the ground. "Stop talking about my mother like that." He leapt on top of Gail, pounding at her head with his fists.

"Whoa, boy!" Tommie jumped in to help Magnus pull the furious boy off of Gail.

"You punch like a girl," Gail yelled as Kieran was hauled off of her. She laughed in spite of herself. "This is too good!"

Magnus enveloped Kieran in his arms and held on tightly. "Calm down, baby," he said to his struggling boyfriend. "Calm down and listen."

Kieran settled against Magnus' chest, panting heavily. Magnus lifted the boy's face to his. "I've got you. It's okay." He fully embraced Kieran again. "You need to absorb all of this." He was beginning to understand it himself. "It's not all about you. Your mother and you . . . both of you have been victimized by your . . . father, or whatever he is . . . in different ways. Your mom's not the bad guy here."

Kieran's arms wrapped about Magnus' waist. He squeezed tightly.

Gail pulled herself up from the gravel drive, brushing the small pebbles from her clothing. "So," she beamed at Rachel. "Kieran, why don't you introduce me to your hot mama!"

"Goddamn it!" Kieran glared at her. "If you say that about my mother one more time . . ."

"Chill, baby." Magnus pulled Kieran's face back to him. "Let's be honest. Your mother *is* hot!" He recognized the violet in Rachel's eyes. "I can see where you get your looks from."

"The apple didn't fall far from the tree," Tommie agreed.

Kieran took a deep breath and released his hold on Magnus. Magnus continued to hold on.

"I'm okay," Kieran said, putting a hand on Magnus' arm. "I promise not to kill anyone." He glared again at Gail. "Unless . . ."

"It's cool," Gail said, holding up her hands in surrender. "It's cool."

Kieran looked from Gilda to his mother. "So," he

managed.

Gilda laughed. "So," she echoed.

Kieran looked at Rachel. "Why now?"

Rachel smiled at him. "Have you forgotten what day this is?"

"What?" Kieran's brow furrowed.

"What day is it?"

Kieran looked back at Magnus with a shrug.

"November 29th," Sammy piped up.

"Nov . . ." Kieran's eyes widened. "Oh, my God. I forgot!"

"Forgot what?" Magnus asked.

"Holy Shit!" Tommie threw his hands up. "It's your goddamn eighteenth birthday, girl!"

Kieran rolled his eyes at himself.

Magnus shook his head at Kieran. "I can't believe I didn't know this," he said, embarrassed.

"Happy birthday, Kieran," Allison shouted happily.

"I knew you had to be older than me," Conner said cattily.

Kieran waved them off and turned back to his mother. "What's my birthday got to do with all this?"

"First . . ." Rachel reached out to him. "Can I wish my little boy a happy birthday?"

Kieran allowed her to embrace him. "Mother," he said finally. "What's going on?"

Rachel stepped back, tears contradicting her broad smile. "Your grandfather left me a substantial trust fund."

"Yeah," Kieran said. "And you've been holding that over father's head all these years, giving him money to live on and . . ."

"Wrong, honey," Rachel responded. "He's been living off the interest from your trust fund."

"My trust . . ."

"Your grandfather left the bulk of his fortune to you. On your eighteenth birthday . . . today . . . it comes under your full control.

"My . . ." Kieran lost the ability to speak.

"How big a trust?" Tommie asked, hands clasped under his chin as if in prayer.

"A lot," Gilda said with a chuckle.

"What's a lot?" Tommie persisted.

Gilda looked at Rachel.

"Oh, I don't know exactly," Rachel said, shrugging. "It's certainly grown over the years . . . probably somewhere in excess of seven or eight hundred million."

"Seven or eight . . ." Tommie drew in a as much air as his lungs could hold before expelling it all noisily. He fell to his knees and embraced his friend's legs, and beamed up at Kieran. "I love you, Kieran!"

"Oh, get off!" Kieran jerked Tommie back to his feet and shoved him in Allison's direction. "Please keep him over there!" He turned back to his mother. "What about father?" He asked. "I mean, Aaron?"

Gilda grinned at him. "Pretty much at your mercy, I should think."

Kieran considered this. He looked back at his friends. "It's good to be eighteen."

Allison clapped her hands. "I'm just glad the rest of us will have a chance to find out."

Kieran reached out to Magnus. "Well, tall, blonde and beautiful, come and meet my mother."

Magnus took Kieran's hand and stepped up to Rachel. "It's nice to meet you," he said, shyly. "Thank you for answering my email."

Rachel smiled at him. "Hello, Magnus." She extended

her own hand. "I suppose I should ask you what your intentions are toward my son."

"Mother!" Kieran's voice rose an octave.

Magnus took her hand. "Well," he said with a shrug. Her question raised a serious problem in his mind. "I guess I don't have so much intention as regret."

"What?" Kieran felt a twinge in the pit of his stomach. "What do you mean?"

Magnus looked at him and then to his other friends. "The school's done for. We all have to think about returning to our former lives." His eyes moistened as he returned his gaze to Kieran's striking eyes. "I guess it's . . . well . . . like your said . . . everything that has a beginning . . . all good things come to an end."

Kieran's jaw dropped.

"Back home?" Sammy's voice shook. "I can't go back home. I don't have . . ."

"You're not going anywhere," Tommie said, holding up a hand. "None of us are going anywhere."

"Oh, my God!" Kieran's face was stricken. "I forgot. It never occurred to me." He threw himself into Magnus' arms. "We'll have to find other schools. It's . . ."

"No!" Tommie's baritone thundered. "Ain't no way." He thumped Kieran on the forehead. "Look, Daddy Warbucks, you've got money . . . lots of money, and a gi-normous town house in the Big Apple . . . room for everyone. They've got world-class schools . . ." He slapped himself on the forehead. "Oh my God! Julliard!"

Kieran laughed. "Tommie, I'm only eighteen. The rest of you are still minors. There's no way we can all shack up in New York together."

"He's right, Tommie," Magnus said, holding on to Kieran as if for the last time. "There's no way this would work—"

"Bull shit!" Tommie threw his hands out. "You people don't get it." He put a hand on Kieran's shoulder. "Kieran, your mom could stand in as our guardian. Hell she doesn't even have to live close by. Money talks!"

Kieran lifted his head from Magnus' chest. "But . . ." He tried to find something realistic about the idea.

"Girl," Tommie continued, "in your income bracket, you need a good tax write off. You could set up a trust fund to take care of all us wayward gay teens."

"You're not gay!"

"Okay, gay-ish teens . . . whatever. Just to get us through high school. I mean . . . Christ . . . a non-profit, matching grants, a couple hundred thou . . ."

"Are you serious?" Kieran couldn't believe his ears.

"Well?" Tommie shrugged. "It's either that, or we all say goodbye."

Kieran looked at his friends, then to his mother. "Mother?"

"It's doable if that's what you want."

"But . . ." Kieran shook his head. "I don't know anything about . . . how do I . . ."

"Sweetheart," Rachel said with a wave. "I can help you with all of that. Anyway, that's why God made lawyers, accountants, CPA's, and money managers."

Kieran grinned at her. "Thank you, mother."

"Happy birthday, darling."

"What about me?" Sammy leaned his head against Daniel. "And what about Daniel?"

"What do you mean, baby?" Allison asked.

"Daniel and I are only fifteen. You'll all be through with high school by the end of this year."

The others waited for him to tear-up but it didn't

happen.

Kieran turned again to Rachel. "Mother, he's right. The two of them will need a real guardian. There's no way I'll let him go back home. No way!"

"Me either," said Daniel, shaking his head sadly. "My Dad's already told me I'm not welcome back home."

"Well," Rachel said thinking. "That's a little harder."

"Not really." Gilda put an arm about Rachel's shoulders. "If their parents can be bought off."

Sammy's face brightened. "You mean offer them money to let us stay."

"No," Gilda said smiling down at Rachel. "Giving them money to give you up ... relinquish all parental rights."

Rachel returned her smile. "We could be their guardians?"

"Exactly," Gilda responded. "So, boys ..." She turned to Sammy and Daniel. "What do you say?"

Sammy hugged Daniel. "We have two mommies!"

"Then that settles it," Tommie said triumphant. "We stay together."

"So!" Kieran turned on Magnus. "Trying to get away from me once again."

"What?" Magnus stuttered. "No, I . . ."

"You're not going anywhere, mister!" Kieran shoved Magnus toward his mother. "Now, tell my mother what your intentions are. Just remember, that you'll be in indentured servitude the rest of your life just to pay my dowry!"

Magnus stood facing Kieran's mom. "Well ..." He blinked. "I guess I should first confess ..." He smiled broadly. "I'm not Jewish."

"What?" Kieran feigned shock. He pulled Magnus

away from Rachel. "Mother," he said dramatically. "I swear! I had no idea."

Rachel chuckled. "It's okay, dear." She took Gilda's hand. "Neither is she."

Kieran waved at the other teens. "We're a family again!"

All the couples applauded and embraced, leaving Conner and Gail to watch.

"Well, boyfriend," Conner said to her. "Don't feel bad. You'll find your own dream-dyke one day."

"Speak for yourself, baby-shit-for-hair," Gail replied, starting for Kieran's mom. "I already have and she's *hot*!"

Kieran let out a yell and started for Gail. Thinking fast, Magnus pulled the boy's lips to his own. After a moment, Kieran stopped struggling. Their lips parted, almost imperceptibly.

"Tell me you love me," Kieran whispered against Magnus' lips.

Magnus' electric blue eyes bore deep into Kieran's own violet ones. "I love you, Kieran."

They kissed again.

"How much?" Kieran whispered hoarsely.

Magnus encircled Kieran with his muscular arms, holding him in a protective embrace. He smiled down at his love. "Does seven or eight hundred million sound about right?"

"Bitch!" Kieran screamed, but Magnus silenced him with another kiss.

Laughter born of real hope surrounded them.

www.ingramcontent.com/pod-product-compliance
Lightning Source LLC
Chambersburg PA
CBHW030025180626
46810CB00001B/219